S0-BSX-842

"What kind of husband *would* you like, Katie?"

A slow smile stretched across Tom's face, sparking a glimmer in his eyes.

Katie stood tall and crossed her arms.

"I don't want a husband at all."

"Why not?" Tom scanned the length of her, then back again, as though assessing her.

Had he somehow found her lacking?

The momentary insecurity took Katie aback, and she chided herself. His opinion didn't matter in the least.

"I don't think there's much chance you'll need to worry about that."

Heat rose to her cheeks. "What do you mean?"

Tom's lighthearted smile faded. "You might be able to recite poetry or quote ancient philosophers, but I doubt you know enough to come in out of the rain. A man would have to be plain loco to consider asking for your hand. You'd argue even if obedience would save your own hide."

Katie's hands went to her hips. "And I suppose you think a woman would find you appealing?"

"You do...."

JUDY DUARTE

always knew there was a book inside her, but since English was her least favorite subject in school, she never considered herself a writer. An avid reader who enjoys a happy ending, Judy couldn't shake the dream of creating a book of her own.

Her dream became a reality in March 2002, when Silhouette Special Edition released her first book, *Cowboy Courage*. Since then she has published more than twenty novels. Her stories have touched the hearts of readers around the world. And in July 2005 Judy won a prestigious Readers' Choice Award for *The Rich Man's Son*.

Judy makes her home near the beach in Southern California. When she's not cooped up in her writing cave, she's spending time with her somewhat enormous but delightfully close family.

Lone Wolf's Lady

JUDY DUARTE

HARLEQUIN® LOVE INSPIRED® HISTORICAL

If you purchased this book without a cover you should be aware
that this book is stolen property. It was reported as "unsold and
destroyed" to the publisher, and neither the author nor the
publisher has received any payment for this "stripped book."

Recycling programs
for this product may
not exist in your area.

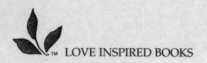

LOVE INSPIRED BOOKS

ISBN-13: 978-0-373-82996-5

LONE WOLF'S LADY

Copyright © 2014 by Judy Duarte

All rights reserved. Except for use in any review, the reproduction
or utilization of this work in whole or in part in any form by any
electronic, mechanical or other means, now known or hereafter
invented, including xerography, photocopying and recording, or in
any information storage or retrieval system, is forbidden without
the written permission of the editorial office, Love Inspired Books,
233 Broadway, New York, NY 10279 U.S.A.

This is a work of fiction. Names, characters, places and incidents are
either the product of the author's imagination or are used fictitiously, and
any resemblance to actual persons, living or dead, business establishments,
events or locales is entirely coincidental.

This edition published by arrangement with Love Inspired Books.

® and TM are trademarks of Love Inspired Books, used under license.
Trademarks indicated with ® are registered in the United States Patent
and Trademark Office, the Canadian Trade Marks Office and in other
countries.

www.Harlequin.com

Printed in U.S.A.

Get rid of all bitterness, rage and anger, brawling and slander, along with every form of malice. Be kind and compassionate to one another, forgiving each other, just as in Christ God forgave you.
—*Ephesians* 4:31–32

To my editor, Susan Litman, for going above and beyond. Thank you for believing in me and this book.

Chapter One

Summer, 1884
Pleasant Valley, Texas

"Caroline Graves is dead. And your job is done."

Tom "Lone Wolf" McCain turned in his saddle, the leather creaking with his movement as he faced Trapper Jack, his crotchety old traveling companion. "She left a six-year-old daughter behind."

"And the kid's being raised by a woman who's known her since she was born." Trapper Jack lifted his battered hat and mopped his weathered brow with the dusty red flannel sleeve of the shirt he'd worn for the past several days. "What are you going to do? Uproot her?"

"If I have to." As Tom met the man's glare, he had to admit that when push came to shove, he wasn't sure what he'd do. But he owed it to Caroline to see to it that her daughter was safe and well cared for.

If only Harrison Graves had hired Tom to find his granddaughter six months earlier, Caroline might have been alive when he'd followed her trail to Taylorsville. Then Tom would have had a chance to talk to her. He might have convinced her to go back where she belonged, to her grandfather's ranch in Stillwater.

"You ought to just tell the old man that Caroline died," Trapper added, as he surveyed the typical Texas town that lay nestled in the valley below. "And let that be the end of it."

"Harrison Graves is looking for an heir."

Trapper spit a wad of tobacco to the side. "Seems to me that Graves isn't too fond of *illegitimate* heirs."

Tom knew that better than anyone. And he'd given that some thought, too. After all, when Harrison had learned that his granddaughter was with child, he'd sent her to Mexico to have her baby, instructing her to leave it there. And he'd never mentioned anything to Tom about searching for the baby Caroline was supposed to have left behind in a Mexican orphanage—he'd only wanted his granddaughter back.

So how would the dying cattleman feel when Tom returned with Caroline's illegitimate child in tow? Would that appease him? Would he rewrite his will, leaving everything to the little girl? Or would he insist that Tom leave her where he'd found her?

Maybe Trapper was right. Maybe Caroline's daughter was better off not going back to Stillwater.

But was she better off being raised by a fallen woman?

From what Tom had gathered in Mexico, Caroline had run off with a former prostitute from Pleasant Valley. For the next few years, she'd managed to keep her friend on the straight and narrow—or so it seemed. But after Caroline had died, the woman had returned to the only other life she'd known, taking the child with her.

That might be true, but something didn't sit right. In fact, a lot of things just didn't add up.

"He could have hired any number of bounty hunters to search for his runaway granddaughter," Trapper said. "Why'd it have to be you?"

Tom wasn't sure why Harrison had summoned him, other than his reputation for being good at finding people who didn't want to be found.

"That old man doesn't deserve the time of day from you," Trapper added. "Not after all he did to make your life miserable. I still can't believe you'd even consider working for him."

"I'm not doing this for Harrison Graves." Nor was he doing it for the money. Yet when the wealthy cattleman had handed him the twenty-dollar gold piece, Tom had pocketed the coin rather than explain why he would have agreed to search for Caroline on principle alone.

Trapper chuffed. "I still think you're making a big mistake, kid. And I'm not about to sit around and watch you make a fool of yourself. I'm going back to Hannah's place. We've been away too long as it is."

"No one asked you to come along in the first place, Trapper. In fact, if you recall, I tried to talk you out of it, but you insisted."

"That's only because someone's got to look out for you, because no matter how much book learnin' you've had, you ain't got a thimbleful of common sense."

Tom sighed and squinted into the afternoon sun. He owed a lot to Trapper. That was a fact. But sometimes the old man forced gratitude to the breaking point.

Trapper grumbled under his breath, then said, "You can't blame me for worryin' about you. I've been lookin' after you ever since you was knee-high to a timber wolf."

If truth be told, Tom had no idea where he'd be today if the old man hadn't stumbled upon him about twenty miles outside of Stillwater when he'd been sick, starving and scared.

No, Tom owed his life to the man who hadn't been afraid to take in an orphaned ten-year-old with mixed blood and treat him like the son he'd never had.

"Suit yourself," Trapper said, turning his horse around.

Tom urged his mount forward, onto the road that ran down the hill, through the middle of town and continued along the boardwalk-lined main street, with its typical lineup of businesses—a good-size mercantile, a bank, a small laundry and a saloon.

His plan was to speak to the sheriff first. So he scanned both sides of the street, looking for the jail. He spotted it up ahead, next to the newspaper office, where, just outside the door, an attractive young woman with auburn hair pulled into a topknot studied the open periodical in her hand, her brow furrowed.

She was a pretty one, he noted. And curious, too. Otherwise, she would have waited to take the newspaper home to read it. He wondered what bit of news had caught her eye and held her interest.

Across the street, a group of boys snagged Tom's attention as they gathered around a small girl, taunting her. Most people didn't give much thought to childish squabbles, thinking that kids usually worked things out without adult interference. But Tom wasn't so sure about that. Probably because, more often than not, he'd found himself on the wrong end of a fistfight meant to "teach that half-breed a lesson" when he'd been in school.

And something about this one didn't seem right—or fair.

He pulled back on the reins and slowed his mount,

just as a tall, towheaded kid shoved the little blonde girl into the dusty street.

Before he could turn his horse in the direction of the bullies, the woman on the boardwalk called out, "Silas Codwell! You ought to be ashamed of yourself." Then she tucked the periodical she'd been reading under her arm and marched across the street in a huff.

The other boys froze, both startled and admonished by her arrival, but the ringleader, who was nearly twice the size of the girl, merely crossed his arms and shifted his weight to one hip.

The petite woman glared at the kid she'd called Silas as though she wanted to throttle him, and Tom knew just how she felt. He'd like to put a little fear of God into that one himself.

So he nudged his horse in the direction of the scuffle, ready to step in if the bully gave the redhead any trouble.

As if unfazed by Silas and his bluster, the lady bent to help the tiny heap of blue calico to her feet. "Are you all right, honey?"

The little girl, her bottom lip bloody and quivering, her light blue hair ribbons drooping from where they'd once adorned two blond braids, nodded.

Then the redhead turned to Silas, her eyes narrowed, her finger raised. "You're nearly thirteen years old. Shoving a small girl into the street is brutal and inexcusable. Apologize this instant."

The other boys began to edge away from her, but Silas only shrugged. "I don't know why you're so all fired—"

The redhead grabbed his ear and twisted until he cried out, "Ow! You aren't our teacher anymore. You'd better let go of me or my father will—"

Clearly undeterred by his threat, the redhead twisted

harder until the boy screeched out "I'm…sorry" in a long, drawn-out whine.

The lady, with her cheeks flushed and her eyes sparked with ire, released the boy's ear, just as Tom's shadow eclipsed them both.

Only then did Silas appear the least bit remorseful.

"You owe the lady and the child a real apology," Tom said. "I saw what you did. There was no excuse for it, boy."

Silas opened his mouth, as if he had something to say in his defense. Then, after his gaze locked on Tom's, his stance relaxed and he relented. "I'm sorry, Miss O'Malley. It won't happen again."

The lady, apparently the schoolmarm at one time, stood as tall as her petite stature would allow. "See that it doesn't."

Silas nodded, then, after a quick glance at Tom, took off to join his friends.

Tom's gaze turned to Miss O'Malley, whose rolled newspaper had fallen to the ground.

She glanced at it, but before reaching to pick it up, she said, "Thank you, Mr.…?"

"McCain."

She nodded, then released a pent-up sigh. "You'd never know it, but Silas's father is the minister."

"No, ma'am. You're right. I would have expected his father to be the town drunkard. Or maybe to hear that he'd been locked up in jail for the past ten years."

She clucked her tongue. "Silas has a mean, spiteful side to him that his parents refuse to see. I taught school here in Pleasant Valley up until last summer and watched that boy bully the other children many a time." She bit down on her bottom lip, as if she might be wondering if she'd shared too much with a stranger.

Her hands rested on the little girl's shoulders in a loving, protective manner.

Satisfied that the child was in good hands, Tom doffed his hat. "Good day, Miss O'Malley."

Then he urged the gelding across the street and on to the sheriff's office, where he planned to ask a couple of questions and get directions to a place known as the Gardener's House.

He might look like an uneducated half-breed, but he knew better than to ask a lady where he could find the town brothel.

Katie O'Malley held on to Sarah Jane's shoulders as she watched the dark-haired stranger ride away.

The man was frightfully handsome, with eyes the color of fine bourbon, high cheekbones and a square-cut chin. His copper-colored skin suggested he might have a mixed-Indian heritage. And for the first time in her life, she found herself more than a little awestruck by a man's appearance, especially one who spent his days in a saddle.

Mr. McCain wasn't the type of man she usually had reason to talk to—or the type she should find the least bit attractive. Yet she did.

She supposed that was because he'd come to her rescue, even though she hadn't needed him to. She did, however, appreciate the gallant way he'd made the gesture.

He'd studied her in a curious way, which had caused her pause. Then he'd simply said, "Good day," turned his mount and headed down the street.

She wondered what business he had in town. Unable to quell her curiosity, she watched him go until he stopped at the sheriff's office, where he left his big bay gelding tied out in front.

When he was finally out of sight, Katie returned her attention to the disheveled little girl.

"What are you doing in town all by yourself?" Katie asked.

"Blossom gave me a penny, and I wanted to buy a peppermint stick. I was going to wait for someone to take me to the mercantile, but then Sweet Heather told me to go outside and stay out of the way."

"Where's Daisy?"

"She wasn't feeling good, so she went to take a nap. But she's probably in the kitchen now. It's her turn to cook dinner."

Katie pulled a lace-edged handkerchief from her reticule and placed it on the little girl's small, bloodied lip, gently dabbing at the wound. She'd championed many causes in the past, but none had touched her heart as deeply as Sarah Jane Potts.

It was time once again to talk to Daisy and insist that the woman either agree to leave with Katie for Wyoming next week or that she allow Sarah Jane to go without her.

After adjusting the ribbons in the little girl's hair, Katie took her by the hand. "Come on, honey. I'll walk you home."

While they made their way to the brothel at the far edge of town, they talked about important things, like why dogs chased cats and why staring into the sun made a person sneeze.

It hadn't taken many chance visits with Sarah Jane for Katie to realize that she was an absolute delight, and the more time she spent with the charming child, the more she longed to rescue her.

As they stepped off the boardwalk and ventured to the outskirts of town, past several lots that were overgrown with weeds and littered with debris, they made their way to the green-and-white three-story structure that served as a brothel. People referred to it as the Gardener's House, a name that seemed fitting because of its park-like grounds, manicured lawn and rows of marigolds leading to a wraparound porch.

If one didn't know better, one would think that it was a respectable home owned by a wealthy family. But Katie knew better.

Her steps slowed as they neared the ornate wrought-iron gate, and her hold on the child's hand tightened. She took a quick scan of her surroundings, hoping to avoid being seen by a witness prone to gossip. As it was, her welcome in Pleasant Valley had worn thin, thanks in large part to the newspaper articles she wrote in favor of women's rights. And she'd been hard-pressed to find many upstanding citizens willing to write the letters of recommendation she needed to provide the school board in Granville, a growing town in the Wyoming Territory desperate for a schoolteacher.

Sarah Jane tugged at Katie's hand. "Come on. Daisy made a swing for me in the backyard. I want you to see it."

The child led Katie around to the rear of the house and pointed to an elm tree where two lengths of rope and a wooden slat hung from a sturdy branch.

"See?" Sarah Jane said. "Want to watch me swing?"

"Not yet. I'd like to talk to Daisy first."

The sooner she could speak to the fallen dove and get back to a more respectable part of town, the better.

"Let's see if she's in the kitchen," Sarah Jane said.

As they climbed the steps to the rear entrance, Katie's heart began to pound.

Fortunately, after Sarah Jane opened the door and entered the kitchen, they found Daisy seated at the big oak table, snapping green beans.

Daisy, a dark-haired woman with a fair complexion, first glanced at Katie, her big green eyes leery.

When she spotted Sarah Jane's swollen lip, she gasped and scooted back her chair. Then she got to her feet and crossed the kitchen. As she reached the girl, she dropped to her knees. "What in the world happened, sweetie?"

"That big boy named Silas said mean things to me again. And this time he hurt me, but Katie made him stop."

Daisy tensed, then brushed a wisp of hair from the child's face. "Boys can be mean."

They certainly could. While growing up, Katie had suffered a few taunts of her own. She knew what it felt like to be different from the other children, to be singled out in the classroom for not paying attention because she'd had her nose in a book when she was supposed to be drawing a map of Missouri. Or to be teased on the schoolyard because she'd never had a mother to teach her how to properly braid her curly red hair.

But those jeers, while hurtful and humiliating at times, were nothing in comparison to the ones Sarah Jane stood to face if she continued to live in Brighton Valley.

Daisy's gaze lifted and met Katie's. "Thank you for seeing her home."

But her *home* is a *brothel,* Katie wanted to shout. She bit her tongue, instead, unwilling to offend the woman before she could convince her to see reason.

She couldn't hold back her thoughts, though. Couldn't Daisy see the damage she was doing to the little girl by having her live here?

Katie's first impulse was to argue her case, which was a good one. But it wouldn't do her a bit of good to speak her mind if she wanted to convince Daisy to sign over guardianship to her or to leave the brothel behind and move to Granville.

"I don't think Sarah Jane should go outside without an adult present," Katie said, minding her tone and choosing her words carefully.

"She isn't allowed to go out alone." Daisy cupped the child's face. "You know better than that."

"I'm a big girl now." Sarah Jane stood tall, while a swollen, cut lip and traces of blood and dirt on her cheek mocked her self-confidence. "I'm *six.* Remember? I had my birthday when we lived at the other house with Mama."

"You know the rules." Daisy got back on her feet, then made her way to the sink, reached for a cloth and dipped it into a bowl of water. "Come here, sweetie. Let me wash your face."

Katie watched the woman's maternal motions, which demonstrated that she certainly cared about the child. Still, why had they moved into the brothel the very first day they'd arrived in town? Surely Daisy realized that no good could ever come of a decision like that.

"Wyoming is a beautiful territory," Katie said, preparing to state her case one more time. "I'd love to take you and Sarah Jane with me. You could make a new start in a territory where women are treated with dignity and respect, where they're considered equals. In fact, they even have the right to vote."

They'd had this conversation before, with Daisy clearly struggling with the decision.

"A move to a new community is sorely tempting," Daisy said.

"Think of the future Sarah Jane will have if she continues to live in a place like this."

"I have." Daisy bit down on her bottom lip. Then she placed a gentle, loving hand on the child's head. "Sarah Jane, why don't you go into our room and look in the closet. I hid a surprise for you there. It's next to your mama's carpetbag."

When Sarah Jane dashed off to do as she was told, Daisy returned to her seat at the table and pushed the bowl of green beans aside. "Sarah Jane's mother was like a sister to me. I'd be dead if it wasn't for her. And I love Sarah Jane as if she were my own. After the funeral, when she and I left Taylorsville, we didn't have a penny to our names. Please believe me when I say that I don't plan to work here very long. I just need to earn enough money to repay a debt. Then we can make a new start in a town far away from here, where people won't know me."

Now that she knew what had been causing Daisy to hesitate, Katie was finally able to formulate a convincing plan, thanks to the inheritance she'd invested wisely. "If you'll leave with me, I'll help you pay that debt. And I promise that you'll find that new life you're looking for in the Wyoming Territory."

"That sounds promising, Miss O'Malley. But why would you do this for me? You don't even know me.

Pardon me for asking, but what are you? Some kind of church do-gooder, bent on saving my soul? You have no idea how many people have tried that, including Sarah Jane's mother, but I'm afraid my soul is already lost."

A smile tugged at Katie's lips.

Daisy cocked her heard, clearly perplexed. "What's so funny?"

"There are a few church do-gooders in town who think *I'm* the lost soul."

"You?" Daisy's eyes widened, and she all but laughed.

"Actually, some of the townsfolk don't like me speaking my mind about a lot of things, especially women's equality. In fact, I've even had a few run-ins with the minister, who went so far as to complain to the Pleasant Valley school board, which resulted in my being replaced as the schoolteacher last fall."

"They replaced you because you believe women should be allowed to vote?"

"Well, the good reverend also complained that I couldn't control the children, although that wasn't true. It was only his son who gave me trouble. And if I'd had the least bit of paternal support—" Katie bit back the rest of her angry retort and clucked her tongue. "Anyway, needless to say, it's been nearly impossible for me to attend services on Sundays with a joyful heart. So I wouldn't call myself a church do-gooder."

Daisy arched a brow, fresh suspicion etched across her face, which was far prettier today without all the powder and paint she usually wore.

"It's not that I don't read my Bible or believe in God, it's just that I…" Katie blew out a sigh, not sure how to explain herself—or why she even felt the need to. "You see, I've always been a champion of the down-

trodden. And when I take up a cause, I'm rather outspoken about it."

"I see. So Sarah Jane and I have become one of your
causes."

Katie wished she'd chosen different words. "I
wouldn't put it that way. It's just that Sarah Jane is a
bright, beautiful child. She deserves a better future.
And, Daisy, so do *you*. You must be a smart, resource-
ful woman to have come so far on your own. But neither of you will get that if you stay in Pleasant Valley,
even if you move out of the Gardener's House and try
to make it on your own. So I'm offering you both a way
out. That is, if you'll take a step of faith and go with me
when I leave for Wyoming next week."

Had Katie said too much, pushed too hard? She hoped
not, but the words had come straight from her heart.

Daisy seemed to ponder her options for a moment,
then said, "The debt is sixty dollars. I've already managed to save twenty-three. If you're willing to pay off the
balance for me, as well as provide traveling expenses,
I'll go with you to Wyoming. Then, as soon as I'm able
to find work, I'll begin to repay you."

"You have yourself a deal." Katie reached out her
arm, and the two women shook hands.

Daisy glanced around the kitchen and smiled. "I'm
actually a pretty good cook. Maybe I can find work at
a restaurant in Wyoming."

Before Katie could respond, a knock sounded at the
back door, and her heart lurched, then railed against
her chest wall as if trying to break free. The last thing
she needed was to be seen by one of Daisy's "callers."

Katie didn't usually put much stock in what others
thought of her, but she had reason to be cautious now.

Thanks to Reverend Codwell and a few other more conservative citizens of Pleasant Valley, she was running out of people to approach for those letters she needed for the school board, and she couldn't show up in Granville empty-handed. So the instinct to escape was strong.

But unless she wanted to run through the brothel and go out the front, the only other possibility was the kitchen exit, which was now blocked.

Daisy crossed the room and swung open the door, revealing Mr. McCain, the handsome, dark-haired cowboy Katie and Sarah Jane had met on the street. His dark-eyed gaze snaked around her, nearly squeezing her heart right out of her.

Surely he didn't think she belonged here, did he?

About the time she feared that he did, he turned and gazed at the fallen woman. "I'm looking for Daisy Potts."

Chapter Two

"I'm Daisy. What can I do for you?"

After Tom had talked to Sheriff Droeger and had his suspicions confirmed, he'd learned that a child named Sarah Jane and a woman now going by the name of Daisy Potts had moved into the Gardener's House a few months ago. Because the sheriff said Daisy did most of the cooking and cleaning at the brothel, Tom had decided to bypass the front door and use the rear entrance.

He hadn't been surprised when Daisy answered his knock, but the red-haired schoolmarm standing in the kitchen like she owned the place knocked him completely off stride.

Of course, Miss O'Malley appeared to be more than a little surprised by his arrival, too.

"I'm afraid I need to leave now," she told Daisy. "But I'll be back on Saturday morning. We can talk about our trip to Wyoming then."

Tom had no idea what the two women planned to do in the Wyoming territory, but they wouldn't be taking Sarah Jane with them until he was convinced that she wasn't Caroline's daughter.

If he had reason to believe the girl was Caroline's child, she was going with him to Stillwater, where she belonged.

Of course, that was assuming that Harrison Graves had really softened and would actually claim an illegitimate child as his heir. And, to be honest, Tom had his doubts.

Miss O'Malley glanced his way one more time, her eyes as blue as the Texas sky.

She was a pretty one; that was a fact. And judging by the starched cotton blouse she wore buttoned to her chin, she didn't belong in the same room with one of the women who worked at the Gardener's House and, according to the sheriff, went by flower names.

She watched him doe-eyed, like a fawn sighting a man from across a thicket, curious yet ready to bolt at the slightest movement. Then she seemed to rally her courage.

"Good day," she said, as stiff and proper as the schoolmarm she'd once been.

He gave her a slight nod as she pushed past him, then watched as she let herself out.

When the door snapped shut behind her, he returned his gaze to Daisy.

The fallen woman, who was attractive in her own right, appeared to be in her early twenties and about the same age as the schoolmarm. "How can I help you?" she asked again.

"I was sent by Harrison Graves to find his granddaughter, Caroline. And my search led me here."

Daisy stiffened. "I don't know what you're talking about."

"I've been to Casa de Los Angelitos," Tom said,

"where you and Caroline met. And I followed her trail to several different towns in Texas, ending up in Taylorsville, where you both lived for the past year. You went by the name of Erin Kelly back then and worked as a cook at the restaurant until the owner went out of business. Caroline was a clerk at the hotel."

Daisy drew back but didn't deny it. Finally, she said, "If you're looking for Caroline, she's not here. She died a few months back."

"I know. And she's survived by a daughter, a girl who'd be about six years old now."

Before he decided how much to divulge of what he already knew, the child who'd been bullied on the town street entered the kitchen, carrying a handmade rag doll, and approached Daisy.

Tom hadn't noticed a resemblance to Caroline before, although he hadn't thought to even look for one. But he studied her carefully now.

Her blond hair was a bit darker than her mother's, more the color of sunflowers than fresh-churned butter. Yet there were other similarities—green eyes, a turned-up nose.

The fairness of her skin, too, which had made young Caroline appear to be angelic to a boy with mixed blood.

Had she also inherited her mother's kind heart, the inner beauty that had allowed Caroline to befriend the boy known as Tom Lone Wolf when so many others in Stillwater had turned their backs on him?

Daisy reached for Sarah Jane and drew her close. "I'm afraid I'm not able to talk to you now, so you'll have to leave."

Tom wasn't about to get into specifics in front of the child. Nor did he want to tip his hand about a possible inheritance at this point, especially with a woman who clearly could be purchased.

"I brought the child a gift," he said. "May I give it to her?"

Sarah Jane looked up at Daisy, her eyes wide, seeking approval. Finally, it came with a nod.

Tom reached inside his vest pocket and pulled a pair of beaded moccasins, as well as a small medicine bag he'd made for her when he'd learned Caroline had not only borne a daughter but kept her.

"When I was a boy," he said, "I knew a little girl who looked a lot like you. Her name was Caroline Graves. And one day, she did something very brave. As a reward for her bravery, my mother made her a pair of moccasins just like these."

"Thank you," Sarah Jane said, as she reached for the soft deerskin gifts. "That was my mama's name."

"I thought that it might be."

The girl studied the handmade shoes and the medicine bag, then gazed at Tom. "What did she do that was brave?"

"She saw a grown man being mean to an Indian boy, and she told him to get off her ranch and to never come back."

Sarah Jane's eyes grew wide. "What did the man do to her?"

"He was afraid that she'd tell her grandfather, Harrison Graves, who was a very powerful man. So he left the boy alone."

Daisy glanced down at the child, then at a bowl of green beans that sat on the kitchen table and back to Tom. "Thank you for your gifts, Mr. McCain. And for sharing the story. But I meant what I said. Now isn't a good time to talk."

"It won't take long. I just want to ask you a few questions and get some honest answers." Tom reached into his pocket and pulled out the twenty-dollar gold piece Harrison had given him. "Would this be enough to tempt you to find the time?"

Daisy's eyes, while wary, studied the coin for only a moment. "Come back Thursday morning. Most of the girls sleep in. If you come around eight, I'll be in the kitchen. And I'll have a pot of coffee on the stove."

"Fair enough."

Again his gaze settled on little Sarah Jane. Would Harrison see a resemblance to her mother? If so, would he take that into consideration?

Would he be pleased to learn that Tom had found Caroline's daughter? Or would he cast out the illegitimate child, just as he'd done to Caroline when he'd learned she was pregnant without a husband in sight?

Time would tell, he supposed, but first things first. In two days, he'd have to convince Daisy to let Sarah Jane go with him back to the Lazy G.

And if Daisy didn't agree?

He'd take her anyway. Caroline's daughter didn't belong in a place like this. And Tom wasn't about to leave her here.

On Friday morning, Katie hurried down the boardwalk to the newspaper office, her skirts swishing with each brisk step she took. She intended to pick up her copy of the *Pleasant Valley Journal* fresh off the press, just as she always did.

As she opened the front door, a bell tinkled to let the clerk know she'd arrived.

The bespectacled young man glanced up from his desk. When he spotted Katie, he smiled. "Here to read the latest rebuttal to your last article, Miss O'Malley?"

"Yes, Harold." Katie slipped off her gloves and tucked them into her reticule. "What does Reverend Codwell have to say this time?"

"He doesn't mention any new arguments, if that's what you mean." Harold adjusted his eyeglasses, pushed his swivel chair away from the desk and got to his feet.

While he went for her copy, Katie scanned the small office, breathing in the scent of ink and admiring the intricate machinery that worked the printing press. She'd actually considered the idea of becoming a reporter or even an editor herself. Edward Townsend, Harold's boss, had once offered her a job, but he'd told her she'd have to temper some of her outspoken comments if she wanted to work for him.

Katie, of course, had refused to do that.

Noticing the publisher wasn't around, she asked about him. "Where's Edward?"

"He went to visit…" Harold flushed a brilliant shade of scarlet, then adjusted his shirt collar. "Um…I'm not sure where he is."

Katie placed her hands on the countertop and leaned forward. "Harold Decker, you're holding something back. Why is that? What don't you want to tell me?"

"I'm sorry, Miss O'Malley. I shouldn't have mentioned it. It just isn't proper."

Katie arched a brow. "Where is this improper visit taking place?"

Harold ran a hand over his slicked-down hair, then

looked at Katie as though he wanted her either to ask someone else or to forget the question completely, but she wasn't about to do that.

She crossed her arms like a parent scolding an errant child. *"Harold?"*

"Oh, for goodness' sake. Edward went to see…one of the women from…um…the Gardener's House. She was assaulted and nearly killed yesterday."

Katie's hands unfolded and slipped to her sides. "What happened?"

Harold's ruddy cheeks grew a deeper shade of red with each tick of the clock. "Why don't you ask Edward when he gets back? I don't feel right talking to you about it."

"You might as well tell me. There will be an article in the paper, and we both know that Reverend Codwell will be proclaiming it from the pulpit. You heard him bring up Miss Potts and Sarah Jane last week, which caused a rash of public outrage against the woman and the child."

"You're right, I suppose." He ambled toward the counter and sighed. "And I certainly hope that didn't have anything to do with the assault."

"Why would it?"

"Because Daisy was the one who was attacked."

The unexpected news slammed into Katie like a hammer on a blacksmith's anvil. "Oh, no. At the brothel?"

"No, while she was coming to town to do some shopping at the mercantile."

"Who attacked her?"

"No one knows. The little girl was the only witness, but she's not talking. Doc Hennessy says the child is in shock."

"Dear Lord," Katie whispered out loud, as she

launched into a silent prayer. *Please look after Sarah Jane until I can get to her.*

"Don't worry," Harold added. "There's a group of concerned citizens who plan to take the child away from there and put her in an orphanage. Anything would be better than being where she is right now."

A thousand thoughts swirled in Katie's head, the foremost being the need to protect little Sarah Jane. She eyed Harold carefully. "What time do you expect Edward to return?"

"I'm not sure. After checking on Daisy, he was going over to the saloon to take up a collection for her. She's a nice woman." Harold stiffened. "I mean, she's nice for a…" He cleared his throat, then chuffed. "Oh, never mind."

Katie ignored the man's discomfort. Her only concern was for Sarah Jane. Daisy had already agreed to go to Wyoming. After all, she couldn't very well change her mind about leaving now.

Either way, Sarah Jane needed a champion, someone who would take her far away from this unforgiving town, someone who wouldn't allow her to be placed in an orphanage.

And Katie was just the one to do it.

As she turned on her heel and strode for the door, Harold called out, "Miss O'Malley, you forgot your newspaper."

"I'll get it later." Katie slammed the door behind her, nearly jarring the little bell off its perch.

She wasn't sure what the townspeople would say when she announced that she would be the one adopting Sarah Jane, particularly if the Reverend Codwell stepped in to raise a fuss, but she was taking Sarah Jane and Daisy to Wyoming.

And she was prepared to fight anyone who stood in her way.

Tom nursed a cup of coffee while he sat in the red-and-gold parlor of the Gardener's House, waiting for a chance to see Daisy again. The doctor was with her now, and as soon as he was finished with his exam, Tom planned to take her and Sarah Jane to a place they'd be safe.

The attack had been brutal. And there'd been no reason for it. Daisy had been on her way to the mercantile. Sarah Jane had been with her. At some point, she'd screamed. Blossom, one of the other women at the brothel, had heard her and come running. She'd fired a shot at the man, and he'd fled before anyone could get a good look at him.

Daisy, who'd been battered senseless, had no recollection of the assault. When Sarah Jane was asked if she could describe the man who'd attacked them, she'd shaken her head no. One day later, and she still hadn't uttered a single word.

The doctor said the little girl, who bore bruises along one of her arms, had been traumatized. Poor little thing. Tom had no idea what her life had been like so far, but losing her mother so young…and now this.

He reached into his pocket and pulled out his gold watch. What was taking the doctor so long? He was hoping to get out of town as soon as Daisy was able to travel. Unfortunately, Daisy couldn't mount a horse in her condition, even if she'd wanted to. And since Tom couldn't rid himself of the suspicion that the attacker had intended to kill Daisy for some reason and might want to follow them so he could finish what he'd started, it would be difficult to hide their wagon tracks.

Something else niggled at him, too. Something that could be a coincidence. But why had the two women moved so many times since meeting in Mexico? Had they been running from someone?

Too bad Trapper Jack had already gone home. Tom could have used the man's help today, even if he would have had to listen to his infernal jabbering and advice.

To make matters worse, Tom also had to look after Sarah Jane. And as much as he wanted to do right by Caroline's daughter, he didn't know squat about kids—especially little girls. And Daisy wasn't going to be much help since she couldn't even see to her own needs right now.

The doctor didn't think her skull had been fractured by the blows to her head, but she'd suffered a serious concussion.

If that weren't enough, that safe place he had in mind was a three-day ride from here.

Needless to say, Tom was growing too antsy to sit any longer. So he stuffed his father's gold watch back into his pocket and got to his feet. He might as well do something useful, like head to the livery and get that wagon. But before he could cross the room, a sharp rap sounded at the door.

Sweet Heather, a plump blonde wearing a black, low-cut gown, sashayed toward the entry. "I'm comin', sugar."

As she swung open the door and a familiar redhead strode into the parlor with a determined step, her smile drooped to a frown and her hand fisted against her hip.

This ought to be interesting, Tom thought, as he studied the lady who was clearly out of place.

Afternoon sunlight peered through the front window and glistened upon her red hair, highlighting shades of fire and autumn. Expressive blue eyes blazed in a passionate array of emotions—worry, concern, nervous indignation, he guessed.

In spite of the modest apparel, he had to admit that she intrigued him far more than any of the women who lived and worked at the Gardener's House.

As she scanned the parlor, the room grew still and intense with silent fury, like the air before a Texas twister.

"You again?" Sweet Heather asked. "What do you want this time?"

The redhead swept past her. "I just heard what happened. I came to see Sarah Jane and to talk to Daisy."

Sweet Heather crossed her arms under her ample bust. "I told you before. You aren't welcome here, so you'd better skedaddle."

"I'm not leaving until I see them."

Sweet Heather laughed heartily, her bosom bouncing like a bowl of calf's-foot jelly. "Then I guess you'll be here for a long, long time."

"I can wait." The redhead surveyed the room. When her gaze moved to Tom and recognition sparked, her breath caught.

Tom had to admit she had guts. Most decent women would rather drop dead than walk into a place like this.

"I told you to *go*," Sweet Heather bellowed, her face reddening, her mouth set in grim determination. "We lost two customers the last time you came here."

Sweet Heather looked like a ruckus ready to happen, and if the lady knew what was best for her she'd leave now.

Miss O'Malley didn't flinch. Instead, she strode deeper into the parlor, her head still held high. "Then I'll wait for someone to tell me where to find Sarah Jane."

Sweet Heather closed the gap between them. "You'll get out even if I have to pick you up and throw you out myself."

About that time, the women who'd gathered at the top of the stairs began to file down the steps.

Realizing things could get out of hand, Tom made his way to the lady. "Miss O'Malley, I think you'd better leave. Sweet Heather would actually favor a fight."

Miss O'Malley stood a bit taller, if that was possible. "I appreciate your concern, Mr. McCain, but I'm not going to leave until I'm ready to do so. And that's not going to happen unless someone tells me where I can find Sarah Jane."

Tom scanned the length of her. He could throw her over his shoulder and force her to leave, but it really wasn't any of his business.

How involved did he want to get?

He figured he might as well head to the livery stable.

As he made his way to the door, Sweet Heather called out to him. "Where are you going, handsome?"

Tom stopped long enough to turn and say, "I'll be back."

But that didn't seem to appease Sweet Heather, because she grabbed a vase and threw it at Miss O'Malley, who ducked just in the nick of time.

As the glass shattered on the floor, Sweet Heather looked as smug as a fat cat with its paw pressed down on a mouse's tail. "The next thing I break will be your teeth."

Tom sighed heavily. He sensed a real fight coming, and, in spite of his better judgment, he sauntered toward the redhead, lifted her feet off the floor and threw her across his shoulder like a sack of grain.

He'd been prepared for the weight of her—but not the delicate scent of lilac on her clothes and hair.

"Put me down this instant," she cried, her words coming out in raspy shrieks. She kicked her feet and pounded her fists on his back like an ornery cougar kit that had been caught and placed in an empty feed sack.

As feisty as the former schoolmarm was, she might actually hold her own in a tussle with Sweet Heather.

He wrapped one arm around her knees and tried to still her flailing legs as he carried her outside and down the porch steps to the lawn in front of the brothel.

"I said, put me down!" she shrieked.

"Stop fighting me and I will."

She took a deep breath, then groaned in exasperation before ceasing her struggle. He took in one last whiff of lilac, then lowered her to the ground. As he did so, she slid down the front of him, leaving them both standing in awkward silence.

Their eyes locked, and for one brief moment, something passed between them, something that stirred the senses. But Tom didn't have time to lose his focus.

He cleared his throat. "I'm sorry, ma'am, but your presence was creating more trouble than either of us need. Now get out of here before the sheriff is called and your reputation is in shreds."

"I don't give a fig about my reputation right now. I'm

going back in there, even if I have to climb in a window or slip down the chimney."

If that were the case, Tom would either have to let her go—or wrestle her himself. And right now, tangling with her any more than he already had didn't seem to be a wise option. Still, maybe he could ease her mind and send her on her way.

"Don't worry about Sarah Jane," he said. "I'm taking her someplace safe."

"That's not necessary. I already have plans to take her and Daisy to Wyoming just as soon as Daisy has recovered enough to travel. They'll both be able to make a fresh start there. Daisy will find respectable work, and Sarah Jane will have…well, rest assured that I'll provide her with opportunities she'd never have otherwise."

Tom lifted his hat, then readjusted it on his head. "First off, I don't think it's in either of their best interests to remain in town long enough for Daisy to recover fully. And, secondly, while I appreciate your concern for the child, I have reason to believe that she has family in Stillwater."

That gave Miss O'Malley pause. "You have *reason* to believe? You're not sure?"

Actually, he knew that she had a great-grandfather. But he wasn't convinced the dying old man would welcome her with open arms. "Let's just say that I'm sure enough."

The schoolmarm seemed to think on that, and as she did, she worried her lip. All the while, the sun continued to shine on her hair, dancing upon the glossy strands.

The autumn color was remarkable. Tom wondered what it looked like when she removed the pins, brushed out the tresses and let them hang long.

When she finally glanced up, her expressive eyes, the shade of bluebonnets, caught his. "But if she has a family, where have they been all her life? Why is she living in a place like this?"

"I'm still trying to figure out how that might have come about." He'd tried to talk to Daisy earlier, but her throat had been badly bruised by the near strangling. The doctor had given her something for pain and to help her rest, and she'd dozed off before he could get anything out of her.

"What if that family Sarah Jane supposedly has doesn't want her?" Miss O'Malley asked.

He'd thought of that possibility more than he dared to admit. "I don't know. I'll think of something."

Apparently, that wasn't enough to appease her, because she crossed her arms and lifted her chin in defiance. "I won't let you take Sarah Jane anywhere."

Tom snorted at her hollow challenge. "I wouldn't recommend fighting with me, Miss O'Malley."

She studied him a moment, as if calculating the odds, then softened her stance. "Daisy is Sarah Jane's guardian. And the two of us have reached an agreement. We're taking Sarah Jane to Wyoming."

"Daisy also goes by the name of Erin Kelly," he said. "Did you know that?"

A twitch at the corner of a single blue eye suggested that she didn't, yet she brushed off his comment. "I'm not surprised. I didn't think her name was actually Daisy Potts."

"There's a lot you don't know."

She stiffened. "I'm sure that's true. Nevertheless, Daisy—or whatever name she'd prefer to go by—has agreed to go with me to Wyoming. And I plan to leave town just as soon as Dr. Hennessy says she can travel."

"I'm afraid her plans changed when she was attacked and nearly killed."

"It seems to me that would be all the more reason for her to want a new life. And I can help her attain that dream—in Wyoming."

"And just whose dream is that, Miss O'Malley? Yours or Daisy's?"

She seemed to ponder that a moment, as if he'd finally tossed something her way that she hadn't expected. Then she seemed to shrug it off. "Does it matter? Some people become so downtrodden that they forget how to dream."

The fool woman had an answer for everything.

"At this point," he said, "the only thing that matters is getting Erin and Sarah Jane out of town before that man comes back and tries to finish what he started."

Her lips parted, and the color in her cheeks drained. "Do you think the man will come back and try to kill her?"

"Come now. You're a bright woman. Think about it. The man attacked a woman and child in broad daylight. He certainly wasn't a drunken, unhappy customer. And when another woman interrupted the attack, he ran off before she could get a good look at him. But as far as the attacker knows, there are still two witnesses."

She bit down on her bottom lip again as she considered what he was suggesting, so he continued to make himself clear. "From what I've been told, Erin has no memory of the attack—at least, not now. And Sarah Jane hasn't uttered a word since that morning. The doctor thinks she's traumatized by what she saw, and who knows if or when she'll speak again. But the attacker doesn't know that."

Tom didn't see any point in telling Miss O'Malley that he'd been following Caroline's trail for the past three weeks, from Casa de Los Angelitos in Mexico, where Sarah Jane was born, to the town of Taylorsville, where Caroline had died after a fall down a flight of stairs.

And that was another thing that just didn't sit right with him. Caroline had been a healthy and vivacious twenty-four-year-old. How had she managed to take a fatal tumble like that? And why had Erin left right after the funeral?

Something about that just didn't make sense. The women had put down roots several different times in the past six years. And then all of a sudden, they would up and move again.

Had one or the other been running from something? Or from someone?

If so, Tom didn't like the idea of Sarah Jane being caught up in the backlash of whatever the adults in her life had been involved in—or running from.

He hoped he was wrong, but the only one who could answer his questions was Erin, and she was in no condition to talk yet.

"How do you plan to travel with a child and an injured woman?" Miss O'Malley asked.

That wasn't going to be easy. And Tom didn't expect to do much sleeping on the three-day ride to Hannah's house, where he intended to leave Daisy to heal.

"I can see that you haven't thought that through," Miss O'Malley said, her tone and stance a little too smug for her bustle.

"Actually," Tom said, "I've done a lot of thinking."

More than she would ever know—and not just while he'd been on the trail looking for Caroline.

"Perhaps we should compromise," she said.

"About what? The way I see it, Miss O'Malley, you don't have a dog in this fight."

As though his words had fallen on deaf ears, she continued to speak her mind. "Erin and Sarah Jane need to get out of town fast, correct?"

"That's the way I see it." What was her point?

"And Sarah Jane might or might not have a family who might—or might not—want her. Is that a safe assumption?"

"I suppose so." Where was she going with this?

"If she has no family—or if they don't want her—she'll need another home."

He didn't dispute that.

"And if they want her, we'll need to determine whether they deserve her. And if they don't, then we'll still need to find her another home."

We? Who included Miss O'Malley in any of this?

"So you see, it's all very simple." Miss O'Malley crossed her arms and smiled. "I'll go with you. And if Sarah Jane needs a home for any reason, I'll be prepared to take her and Erin with me to Wyoming as planned."

She couldn't be suggesting that he travel for three days with her, an outspoken, headstrong schoolmarm. He'd be a fool to even consider such a notion. A woman like Miss O'Malley, no matter how pretty she was, would make the trip as unbearable as a throbbing ingrown toenail.

"Miss O'Malley, thank you for the kind offer, but I'm afraid that won't work."

"Why not?"

"To be honest, I'd run naked through a briar patch before I'd travel with you any longer than necessary."

Up went that pretty little chin again. "Traveling with you wouldn't be a picnic, Mr. McCain."

"It certainly won't. I'm not packing silver tea service or linen napkins."

"How dare you accuse me of being prissy. I've made it a point to not be cast in that mold."

"The mold of a lady?" He asked, awaiting a slap— or a sharp retort.

Instead, she uncrossed her arms and tossed him a pretty smile. "I don't really care what others think of me, Mr. McCain—you included. But that's beside the point right now. You're going to need help traveling with an injured woman and a traumatized child. And it looks as though I'm the only one willing to go with you. So the way I see it, you don't have much choice."

Trouble was, as much as he hated to admit it, she was right.

Chapter Three

MᴄCain glared at Katie as though she'd gone daft, then he shook his head. "Be ready in an hour—and not one minute more. We'll leave from here."

Before she could object to the unreasonable time limit, the man left her standing in front of the brothel and strode away as though it wouldn't take much to change his mind or to alter his travel plans.

While she should feel somewhat victorious, she had to admit that she felt as unbalanced as a blindfolded child in a sack race.

How in creation was she ever going to pack for a trip like that in so little time?

Well, she couldn't very well stew about it a moment longer, so she hurried home as quickly as her skirts would allow. She did, however, stop briefly to let Ian Connor know that she'd be leaving town.

Ian, who'd been a dear friend and a colleague of her late father, had suffered an attack of apoplexy last year that left the right side of his body so weak that he'd had to retire from his law practice. He now lived with his widowed sister in a white clapboard house just down the lane from Katie.

As she'd expected, Ian greeted her with a warm smile. "Katie, my dear, it's always good to see you. Please come in."

"I'm afraid I don't have time to come inside. I just wanted to let you know I'll be leaving and will be away for a week or so."

Ian stroked his right arm and furrowed his brow. "Where are you going?"

"I'm taking Daisy Potts and Sarah Jane out of town."

Ian stiffened. "You're *what?*"

"I take it you heard about the attack. Poor Miss Potts was assaulted and nearly killed. I'm going to escort her and the child out of town."

"Yes, I heard about the attack—and her injuries. But why in the world are you getting involved in that?"

"You know me."

"Yes, I'm afraid I do." Ian blew out a weary sigh. "May I remind you that you're an unmarried woman, Katie? Traveling the country with a small child and a battered prostitute is dangerous and…well, it's uncalled-for. Think of your reputation."

"I'll have an escort—Mr. Tom McCain. So I'll be perfectly safe."

Ian clicked his tongue and shook his head. "Why are they leaving? Wouldn't it be best if Miss Potts stayed here in town until she recovered?"

Katie didn't dare mention the danger Daisy and Sarah Jane might be in, so she chose another reason for their hasty departure. "The town hasn't been kind to the child, and there's been talk of sending her to live in an orphanage."

The dear old man who, along with his sister, had become as close as family members to her, especially since her da's passing, blew out a weary sigh. "Sending that poor child away isn't necessarily a bad idea, Katie. People around here aren't likely to ever forget what her mother did for a living."

"I don't know much about her real mother, God rest her soul. Sarah Jane once mentioned that she used to work at a hotel."

"That's probably what the child considers the Gardener's House to be."

"You may be right, but a little girl shouldn't be punished for her mother's mistakes."

"I agree. However, that's the way of it, Katie. When are you going to learn there are some things you can't change or fix? I'd think that after getting arrested last November for creating a public disturbance at the town hall meeting you'd be smart enough to figure that out."

"First of all, I'm not the only woman in this community who spent time in jail for speaking her mind." Katie leaned against the doorjamb. "And secondly, I have given up. At least, here in Pleasant Valley."

"What do you mean by that?" Ian asked.

"I'm going to leave as soon as I return from escorting Miss Potts."

His face paled. "Where do you think you're going?"

She understood his concern. And the last thing she wanted to do was to hurt him or to cause him any undue worry. "I'm going to Wyoming. The school board in Granville is looking for a teacher."

"I thought you didn't like teaching and that you gave it up for good."

"Well, I've had a change of heart. Since I can't get

through to the adults in this community, I've decided to use another tactic. I'll begin by training the children when they're still able to see reason."

Ian blew out a weary sigh. "I told your father that I would be happy to oversee your trust fund, but he didn't take me up on the offer, giving you full control. If he'd known that you'd become so independent, he might have listened to me."

"Da always admired my independence."

"He wouldn't have in this instance."

Katie watched the emotions play across Ian's face, and she knew she was in for a battle. But try as he might, he wouldn't be able to change her plans.

"I can't allow you to go to Wyoming. Your father would roll over in the grave if I let you traipse across the country unescorted."

"I won't be alone, Ian. If things go as planned, I'll be traveling with Miss Potts and Sarah Jane."

"You're going to travel with a prostitute?" His voice rose an octave, and his face grew rosy and bright. "Have you lost your mind completely?" Ian slapped his good hand upon his hip. "Katie, listen to reason for once in your life. Women of virtue don't go to the Wyoming Territory, especially with soiled doves. They stay home and wait for a man to court them."

It was the same argument he'd used each time she showed her stubborn streak, so she wasn't surprised. Still, her answer was always the same. "That's not going to happen. Getting married would strip me of what few rights a woman has in this world."

"Well, it's probably just as well that you remain a spinster. You'd drive your first husband crazy and the second to drink."

"You may be right," Katie said with a chuckle. "But if I should suffer a blow to the head causing me to reconsider marriage, I'll look for a man as fair-minded as you or Da."

"Humph. Don't try to flatter me."

Katie stepped forward and wrapped the old man in a warm embrace. "I love you, Ian. You know that, don't you?"

The tension in his stance eased, and he hugged her back. "I love you, too, Katie. You've been the daughter I never had."

Ian would be as angry as a hornet in a bowl of honey if he knew all the details of her trip, of the possible danger, of her determination to adopt Sarah Jane in the end, but he'd settle down in a day or so. He always did when he realized her mind was made up. And it was.

Katie was going to take Sarah Jane to Wyoming, and nobody was going to stop her.

Needless to say, Katie had packed her clothing and toiletries into a valise as quickly as possible, then she'd hurried to the livery stable and rented a gentle roan mare. After mounting and adjusting her skirts, she rode to the Gardener's House to meet Mr. McCain.

Since she preferred not to butt heads with Sweet Heather again, she decided to wait outside. So she dismounted and tied her mare next to McCain's big bay gelding and the snorting team of horses harnessed to a buckboard.

Someone had already packed the wagon and lined the bed with several quilts. They'd also rigged a small canvas tarp over the top to provide the injured woman with a bit of shade. Katie wondered if one of the fallen women had thought of it—or if McCain had.

Before she could consider the thoughtful gesture, the brothel's front door swung open, and McCain stepped onto the porch with Daisy—or rather, Erin—in his arms. The injured woman wore a light blue dress—a plain and simple style with long sleeves and a delicate bow tied at the neckline. With her dark hair swept up into a modest topknot, she appeared to be as proper as any of the other ladies in town.

Katie thought it made a clever disguise, if one could call it that.

As McCain carried Erin down the porch steps, Katie caught a glimpse of the black eye and the nasty bruise that marred one side of her face, mocking the ladylike clothing. As they crossed the yard, Katie had a better view of her injuries and winced at the brutality of the attack.

She'd been so taken by the sight of the battered woman that she just now noticed Sarah Jane trailing behind. The child, her head downcast, wore a yellow calico dress and a small pair of moccasins on her feet.

Katie made her way to the little girl, then dropped to her knees and hugged her close. But instead of returning the embrace, Sarah Jane's arms hung loosely at her sides.

"Oh, honey," Katie said, hoping to infuse a little warmth and joy back into her. "I'm so glad to see you."

Katie's heart ached at the thought of what the child had witnessed, what she'd been through.

"Come on," McCain said. "We don't have time for idle chitchat. Let's get them in the wagon."

Katie didn't intend to dawdle. For goodness' sake, she wanted to get the child—and herself!—as far away from the brothel as they could. But she couldn't help being concerned about the girl and ignored the man long enough to satisfy her curiosity.

"Are you all right, honey?" Katie asked.

Sarah Jane nodded.

"Who hurt you?"

The child's gaze dropped to the small, beaded moccasins she wore.

Katie placed her fingertip under Sarah Jane's chin and lifted her face. "It's all right. I'm here now, and I'll protect you. You can tell me what happened."

"She can't talk," McCain said.

Katie knew she'd been traumatized, but she'd thought, well, hoped that her arrival, her presence and voice, might soothe the frightened girl, might comfort her.

Footsteps sounded behind her, and Katie turned to see a tall blonde carrying a large basket in the crook of her arm. A stocky brunette followed behind toting a white ceramic chamber pot.

"I've packed some vittles for you to take," the blonde said. "It'll be suppertime before you know it. And since Doc don't want Daisy to walk or move around very much, we thought it might be best if you took this pot along, too. That way she won't have to climb in and out of the wagon."

Katie knew Daisy had been injured, but she hadn't realized how laid up she'd be on the trip. But that didn't matter. Katie was prepared to take care of her, as well as Sarah Jane.

She'd nursed her da for several weeks before he passed, so she was used to tending the sick. And while being on the trail would be different from being at home, she was prepared to do whatever needed to be done.

According to McCain, the trip would take several days. Katie wondered what they would eat after they'd finished the food in the basket. She hated to think that they'd have to scavenge the countryside for berries, seeds and wild game. Surely someone had thought to pack more supplies. But if they hadn't? Well, she'd think of something. She always did.

Katie stood, shook the dust from her skirts and reached for Sarah Jane's hand. "Come on, honey. We're going on a grand adventure."

McCain, who'd helped the injured woman settle into the bed of the wagon, glanced her way and frowned.

Didn't he realize that Katie simply had been trying to reassure the child? She certainly wasn't looking forward to spending the next few days sleeping outdoors and eating whatever they managed to find, especially under his watch. Would she ever see his gaze untouched by judgment? A small part of her couldn't help wishing so.

"By the way," Katie said to McCain, deciding she deserved more information than he'd given her. "Do we have any pans for cooking? Or maybe a coffeepot?"

His scowl confirmed that he might have agreed to take her along, but he certainly wasn't the least bit happy about it. When he finally spoke, his words came out short and snappish. "This isn't a picnic, Miss O'Malley."

Under other circumstances, Katie might have let loose with an angry retort, but she bit her tongue, knowing it wouldn't do her any good to irritate him further, at least until they were too far along for him to change his mind and send her home.

"Tom," the blonde said, "I've got one more box to go on that wagon, and I'll need some help lifting it."

"There's not much room, Rose."

"It's not big, just a wee bit heavy."

McCain started toward the house, then paused when he reached Katie. "Help Sarah Jane into the wagon."

If Katie weren't so eager to get the child away from the brothel and this town, she'd remind him that she didn't take orders, and that a "please" and a little respect would go a long way. But she let it go this time and helped Sarah Jane settle into the back of the wagon, next to where Erin lay.

Once the child was seated, Katie leaned against the side of the buckboard, reached into the bed and placed her hand on the prostitute's arm. "Mr. McCain told me that your name is Erin, which is what I'll be calling you from now on."

Erin, her eyes a bit dazed, merely nodded.

"I'm sorry things aren't working out the way either of us intended," Katie added, "but don't worry. Once you're feeling better, we'll leave for Wyoming."

Erin merely closed her eyes and sighed.

Boot steps sounded on the porch, and Katie looked over her shoulder to see McCain approach the wagon carrying a small wooden crate. After he placed it under the wagon seat, he reached into his pocket and pulled out a gold watch.

He lifted the lid and glanced at the time. Then he circled the wagon and approached Katie. "I'll help you up."

"You don't need to," she told him. "I'm not as helpless or as troublesome as you think. I can do it myself."

In spite of what she'd told him, he slipped behind her and offered his assistance, gripping her elbow and reaching for her waist.

His hands were strong, his touch warm, his movements deft. Yet it was the scent of him, a manly combination of leather and soap that caused her breath to catch.

Hoping he hadn't noticed, she climbed up, settled onto the seat and adjusted her skirts.

She was just about to reach for the reins when McCain tied his horse to the back of the wagon, beside hers.

"What are you doing?" she asked. "I can drive a buckboard."

"We're all going to ride in the wagon. From a distance, maybe we'll look like a family."

Katie nearly snorted at the thought of her and McCain as husband and wife, but she kept her reaction to herself.

It was all part of the masquerade, part of the plan to get Sarah Jane to safety.

Yet as McCain climbed into the seat beside her, like a husband would do, her heart gave a funny little flutter.

"Everybody ready?" he asked the passengers in back.

"Are you sure we have everything we need?" Katie asked, hoping he'd thought of the things she might have included had he given her enough time to plan.

"It doesn't matter. We're going to make do with what we have. We're burning daylight as it is."

She wanted to object, but she had to admit that McCain was right.

The sooner they left Pleasant Valley, the better.

Traveling with two women and a child wasn't going to be easy, and Tom doubted he'd get much sleep over the next few days. If he'd had the luxury of waiting until tomorrow morning, he would have planned to set out before daylight.

The fewer people who saw them leaving, the less chance there was that the attacker would catch wind of it and follow them. Hopefully, the man had fled to parts unknown, but Tom wasn't taking any chances. According to Sheriff Droeger, they hadn't uncovered a motive for the assault—no robbery, at least, not that anyone knew. So was it personal? Had the man gone after Erin for some other reason? If so, that would give him reason to come back and finish the job.

Tom had purchased the wagon at the livery, and, fortunately, the old man who ran the place had been more interested in pocketing the cash than in asking questions.

So now here they were, about twenty miles outside of Pleasant Valley. Tom would have pushed harder so they could have traveled farther, but Dr. Hennessy had warned him not to jostle Erin too much. Of course, the doctor had also given her something to make her sleep, so she'd rested easily all afternoon.

They'd finally reached a good place to set up camp. Tom remembered this spot when he and Trapper had ridden through a few days earlier. With a creek nearby, its water clear and fresh, and the scattering of trees to hide them from the road, it was a good place to spend the night.

But he still wanted to scout the area and assure himself that the women and the child would be safe, even though he planned to watch over them while they slept.

So, after unhitching the horses, leading them to water and waiting for them to drink, he returned to the campsite and tethered them to a tree.

"I'm going to have a look around," he told Miss O'Malley. "Do you think you can handle things here?"

"Yes, of course. Should Sarah Jane and I gather some dried twigs for a fire?"

"Wait until I come back." He didn't want them to

wander too far or build a fire until he was sure they weren't being followed.

Fifteen minutes later, after taking care to hide their wagon tracks, he'd circled back to the campsite. All the while, he'd watched and listened for any sign that they weren't alone while keeping his right hand close to his holster.

When he'd convinced himself that they were safe, he headed back to camp. Not far from where they'd left the horses and wagon, while he was still near the stream, twigs snapped and skirts rustled.

Tom turned to the sound and spotted Miss O'Malley and Sarah Jane heading back to camp. They each carried a canteen, so he figured they'd been getting water. The woman also held a black valise.

He glanced at the setting sun. It would be dark soon. He was just about to call out, letting them know that he was nearby, but he stopped short when he saw Miss O'Malley drop to her knees and tend Sarah Jane with gentle hands and a soft voice.

Fascinated, he watched the attractive redhead gently run a silver-handled comb through the child's tangled locks.

"You have the prettiest hair," she told the girl. "Just like captured sunbeams."

Sarah Jane raised her eyebrows with a look of such obvious hope that Tom's heart melted. The poor kid had been through far more than was fair—the recent death of her mother, the assault of the woman who'd been caring for her.

Miss O'Malley reached for a white ribbon and handed it to Sarah Jane. "Hold this, honey." Deftly forming a long braid, she took the satin strip and tied a bow to hold her work together. "There you go."

Then the woman removed a small bottle from her bag, twisted the lid open and placed a dab of the contents behind each of her ears. All the while, the child watched with rapt attention.

And so did Tom.

"It's lilac water," Miss O'Malley said. "It's my favorite scent. Would you like some?"

When Sarah Jane nodded, the woman smiled and applied a bit behind the girl's ears, too, her movements slow and gentle.

It was nice to see a softer side to her. Apparently there was more to her than met the eye, although what met his eye was rather appealing. In fact, the sight was almost mesmerizing.

But Tom couldn't very well continue to gaze at her like an awestruck kid with a crush on the schoolmarm. What if she caught him doing it?

The last thing in the world he needed to do was to let down his guard with a woman as outspoken as Katie O'Malley, no matter how pretty she was, no matter how softhearted she might appear to be.

He'd seen the feisty side of her. And right now, he had enough trouble on his hands.

For a moment, his resolve waffled. If circumstances were different, if he were just passing through, he might have said or done something stupid. But he had a job to do, a child to protect. And there was another issue he couldn't ignore.

Katie O'Malley was also white.

And Tom McCain wasn't.

That might not make a difference to people like Hannah and Trapper Jack, but there were others who'd object. Others who'd made it more than clear that Tom wasn't to step foot on their ranch.

Tom had been about nine years old when he'd gone to the Lazy G to deliver a pair of moccasins his mother had made for Caroline. The girl hadn't been home because she'd gone into town with the housekeeper, but Randolph Haney, Harrison's friend and solicitor, had been there.

He'd responded to Tom's request to speak to Caroline with a shove that had knocked him to the ground.

"She doesn't need anything from the filthy likes of you. Get out of here. And don't ever come back." Then, for good measure, Haney had kicked him while he was down, splitting his head open with the toe of his boot.

Tom still bore a scar from the attack, a reminder to keep his distance from the Lazy G, which he'd made a point of doing. But nearly a year later, at the urging of his mother, he'd gone back with her one cold, rainy afternoon.

Haney had answered the door that day, too. His mother had begged him to let her talk to Harrison. Haney had left them outside and gone into the house. A few minutes later, when he returned, he'd pulled his gun and ordered her off the property.

And take your whelp with you.

It had been a hard lesson, a painful one—because Tom's mother had died several days later.

That was why Trapper had objected to Tom taking the job to find Caroline in the first place. But there were some things a boy didn't forget, some promises meant to be kept.

So after taking Sarah Jane back to the Lazy G, assuming Tom was convinced that she'd be treated as a rightful heir, he'd leave Stillwater for good. He had no need for Randolph Haney or Harrison Graves.

He didn't need Miss O'Malley, either—except for the next few days. After that, when he got to Hannah's place, he'd ask Trapper to escort the troublesome redhead back to Pleasant Valley. Then he'd be done with her for once and for all.

Yet he continued to watch her until she glanced up and spotted him. As their eyes met, their gazes locked.

He knew how she felt about women's equality. But how did she feel about equality for all people, even those with darker skin?

He supposed it really didn't matter.

Either way, he couldn't let her think that he was fawning over her. So he'd better put some distance between them. They might have to share a seat on the same wagon, but there were other ways to create distance. One way would be to let her know who was boss.

"It's time to eat," he said. "There are some supplies in the wooden box under the seat of the wagon, but Rose packed a basket of food for us to eat this evening. That's probably going to be the easiest and best-tasting meal we'll have for the next few days. So when you're finished with whatever you're doing here, you can start setting it out."

Miss O'Malley pondered his request for a moment, then she straightened, crossed her arms and tossed him a pretty smile. "I'll be a while yet. So if you're hungry, then maybe you ought to do it yourself."

It's not as if Tom had never set up camp before or fixed supper for himself and Trapper. But he wasn't about to let the schoolmarm order him around as though he were one of her students, and she may as well get that straight.

Of course, he wasn't about to have a showdown in front of the child.

"Sarah Jane," he said, reaching into his shirt pocket and withdrawing a small paper bag. "Go see about Erin and, if she's awake, offer her one of these. You can have some, too."

Without the least bit of reluctance, Sarah Jane pulled free of the woman's grip on her shoulders and approached Tom with an outstretched hand.

When she reached him, he handed her the bag. She peeked inside before heading back to the campsite.

"What did you give her?" the schoolmarm asked.

"Lemon drops."

When Sarah Jane was out of earshot, Tom crossed his own arms. "It seems that neither of us likes taking orders, but let's get one thing straight. I'll be making all the decisions on this trip. You'll do what I say—and when I say it."

"I don't mind yielding to you because of your experience and know-how, but I'm not going to take orders blindly, just because you're a man and I'm a woman."

"Like I said, you'll do as I say. And you won't question my reasons or motives. That means you'll handle the meals."

"Apparently you didn't hear me." The petite redhead stood firm. "I'll return to camp when I'm good and ready. And if you have a job for me to do, you'll ask me to do it, rather than tell me. You'll also use words like 'please' and 'thank you.'"

"Listen here, Miss O'Malley. You're not in charge. *I am*. And you're lucky I don't throw you on the back of that nag you call a horse, turn it around and slap its rump to send you back to town in a dead run."

"Are you trying to intimidate me?" she asked, her voice coming out a bit wobbly.

"Do you scare easily?" he asked.

"No, I don't."

He flashed a taunting smile. "I suppose you're too smart to be afraid."

"I'm bright," she admitted, "and better educated than most—male or female."

"That might be true, but driving a wagon and crossing rugged territory takes more knowledge than you can find in a book. It takes common sense, instinct and courage—things you can't learn in school."

"What I lack in experience, I make up for in determination."

"A determined fool won't last a day on the trail."

She clenched her fists at her side. "I'm no fool, and I have far more courage than you think."

While he'd like to believe her, especially when he wasn't sure what they might face down the road, he couldn't help thinking of her as a young, trigger-happy cowboy out to prove himself. But he doubted arguing with her would get either of them anywhere.

"I guess that's left to be seen," Tom said. "Now let's get out of here."

"All right."

Yet neither of them made a move.

"What are you waiting for?" she asked.

"For you to go first."

When she didn't move, he said, "Listen, Miss O'Malley, I can be your ally or your enemy. It's your choice."

"I choose my friends wisely, Mr. McCain." She flashed an insincere smile then headed up the incline toward the wagon, passing him as she went and leaving a scent of lilac lingering in the air.

Tom raked a hand through his hair. He was going to need help with Erin and Sarah Jane over the next couple of days. And right now, the only human he had to rely on was a troublesome redhead who, given time, could surely provoke a gentle and pious preacher to spit and cuss.

Over the years, Tom had learned to trust God to see him through every difficult situation he had to face. The first time he'd called out to his father's God—he'd been a ten-year-old half-breed, cold, hungry and alone in a hostile white world.

Not ten minutes later, Trapper Jack had come along to change all that and to take him to live with Hannah McCain. She'd not only loved and cared for him, she'd shared her faith, and before long, Tom had become a believer himself.

Last night, Tom had prayed for guidance and help in protecting Sarah Jane and finding her a loving home. He knew God would answer that prayer. He surely did.

Trouble was, he feared that this time, instead of blessing him with a woman like Hannah, God had seen fit to punish him with Katie O'Malley.

Chapter Four

The next morning, as dawn broke over the eastern hills, Katie woke up stiff and sore. She'd no more than grimaced and tried to stretch out on the quilt-lined wagon bottom when she heard the sound and caught a whiff of coffee percolating on an open flame.

Apparently Mr. McCain had realized he shouldn't order her to cook all their meals. If so, why hadn't he backed down the day before? It would have saved them both some unnecessary trouble and anger.

Maybe he'd decided it was time for a truce. After all, they were stuck with each other for the next couple of days. Bickering wasn't going to do them any good. And it certainly wouldn't help Sarah Jane feel safe.

After biting back a groan, Katie rolled to her side and carefully climbed from the wagon, trying not to disturb the other woman and the child, both of whom still slept soundly. Then she made her way to the small campfire, where McCain sat upon a large rock, studying the flickering flame.

He hadn't shaved, and in the morning light, he appeared more rugged, more manly and even more handsome—dangerously so.

She lowered her sleep-hoarsened voice. "Good morning."

He glanced up for a moment, then gave her a cursory nod. "'Morning."

She bit down on her lower lip, unsure of how to broach an apology, then swallowed her pride and pressed on. "I'm sorry for being disagreeable yesterday. I'm afraid we both started off on the wrong foot, and I'd like to make amends. We have a common goal, and I think being at odds isn't going to help matters."

He seemed to ponder her words, then said, "You're right."

She let out the breath she'd been holding. "I think it's best if you call me Katie from now on. Miss O'Malley is too formal for this type of trip. Besides, if we're supposed to be traveling as—" she didn't dare say husband and wife "—as a family, then it's more believable, don't you think?"

Silence swirled around them like the steam from the coffee in his tin cup.

Finally she asked, "May I call you by your given name, as well?"

He reached into the wooden box that rested next to him and pulled out a second tin cup. "My name's Tom."

Another step in the right direction.

"I may not be one to take orders," she added. "But you'll find that I'm not afraid of hard work."

He filled the second cup with coffee. "I saw you tending Sarah Jane and Erin."

She waited for him to continue, for him to utter some kind of compliment or recognition of all she'd done to assist Erin yesterday and through the night by wiping the dust and perspiration from her brow, feeding her and changing the chamber pot.

When no other words followed, she supposed that was all he was going to grant her. She'd just have to be happy with that.

He handed the coffee to her, and she took the tin cup from him, being careful not to burn herself.

"Where do you plan to take Sarah Jane and Erin?" she asked.

"To stay with a woman named Hannah."

"Who is she?"

"A friend." A slow smile broke across his face, reaching his eyes and softening his expression. "She's a good woman, the finest one you'll ever meet. Sarah Jane and Erin will be safe there—and well cared for."

Katie's heart tumbled in her chest, although she wasn't sure why. Surprised by Tom's obvious respect and affection for the woman, she supposed. And curiosity, too.

Was he courting Hannah? Or was she merely a friend, as he'd said?

Katie took a sip of the hot, bitter coffee and bit back a grimace, wishing she had some cream and sugar to temper the taste. Yet she knew better than to voice a complaint. Instead, she relished the warmth it provided in the crisp morning hour as dawn broke over their campsite and accepted it as the first sign of their truce.

"How will Hannah feel about you bringing a couple of women with you and asking her to keep us until you return?" Katie asked.

"She's used to me bringing home strays."

Katie didn't like being referred to as a stray, and that's

certainly what Tom had implied. She hadn't led the same kind of life that Erin had, although smudged in dirt and covered in trail dust, they all seemed to be the same— except for the bumps and bruises Erin still bore.

Katie had half a notion to give Tom a piece of her mind for implying otherwise, but she wasn't about to hurt Erin's feelings, should she be awake and listening. Nor did she want their fragile truce to suffer a setback. So she kept her thoughts to herself.

Still, she didn't want to be a burden to a woman she'd never met, although she wouldn't mind a bit if Hannah got angry at Tom for bringing her a wagonload of trouble.

By the third day, the wind and sun had chapped and burned Katie's lips and cheeks. Sitting on the hard wooden slats had given her a backache and a crick in her neck, but she hadn't uttered a single complaint. The journey hadn't been easy on any of them, especially Erin, even though she'd managed to sleep through most of it, thanks to the medication Dr. Hennessy had told them to give her.

An hour ago, they'd stopped long enough to eat hard-tack, stale bread and apples for the noon meal, then they'd started out once again.

"How much farther until we reach Hannah's place?" Katie asked Tom.

"Late this afternoon or early evening."

Katie could hardly wait to be out of the wagon for good. She wondered if Tom was as eager to get there as she was. Most likely. He clearly cared about Hannah and undoubtedly missed her.

Again, she found herself curious about their relationship.

"I suppose Hannah will be happy to see you," she said.

As Tom flicked the reins along the backside of the team, the wagon swayed, causing his arm to brush against hers again, a warm touch she'd grown used to, an intimacy she'd actually found rather nice and comforting.

"Hannah will welcome me with open arms," he said.

Katie suspected as much and, if truth be told, she couldn't help feeling a bit apprehensive at meeting Tom's lady friend.

As the day wore on, her apprehension and discomfort grew steadily.

By the time the sun had lowered in the west, perspiration had dampened her collar and the fabric under her arms. Dust powdered her skin in spite of the long sleeves she wore, and the sun had no doubt burned her nose and cheeks.

She must be a sight. Yet, in spite of her reluctance to meet the woman herself, Katie looked forward to arriving at Hannah's house if it meant that she could stretch her legs and, hopefully, soak in a warm, soapy tub.

"How are our passengers faring?" Tom asked.

Katie glanced over her shoulder and spotted the child holding a rag doll while watching over a drowsy Erin, who'd had another dose of medication after they'd had their midday meal.

Sarah Jane turned, smiled softly and gave a little wave. What a sweet child. She seemed to like Tom, which was a bit surprising. Katie would think she'd find him intimidating. Of course, a six-year-old was easily swayed by lemon drops, handcrafted moccasins and the easy smiles that lit his eyes.

"They're both doing just fine," Katie said, as she scanned her surroundings.

It would be dark soon, which meant they were drawing near the end of their journey.

Up ahead, just beyond a small orchard chock-full of peaches to tempt hungry travelers, a white clapboard house sat surrounded by a whitewashed picket fence. Bright red geraniums blossomed in a planter beneath a single window in the front.

The two-story structure was clearly a home to someone, and it warmed Katie's heart to gaze upon it. She could easily imagine a loving wife, handsome husband and happy children living there. The vision was so clear, so strong, that she could almost feel it deep in her soul.

If she were to ever reconsider her decision never to marry, which she wouldn't do, she could imagine living in a home like that.

"That's a lovely little house and yard," she said. "Do you know who lives there?"

"Yes, I do. Hannah."

The woman's name rolled off his tongue simply, yet affectionately, and Katie's heart sank. She had to admit that she didn't like the idea of Hannah living in that particular house, although she couldn't say why.

Tom turned the team onto the property. When they reached the barn, he pulled the horses to a stop and surveyed the grounds, where a hen and several half-grown chicks pecked at a small patch of grass.

Four big pots of green plants and two flower boxes filled with pansies marked a walkway and graced the steps of a lovely little porch, where a roughly handcrafted bench and rocking chair beckoned anyone in need of peace and quiet. Yet in spite of the warm and colorful welcome of the house and yard, Katie felt uneasy about the type of reception they might receive.

Tom secured the reins and climbed down. Then he circled the wagon and reached up to help Katie. At one time she'd struggled with his assistance, but after traveling together the past few days, she found his help not only easier to accept but even comforting.

She took his arm and, as she lifted her foot to step over the side, he swung her to the ground, just as he'd done each day of their journey. But today, for some reason, her heart beat a little faster, her breath caught a little deeper.

As he released his hold on her, her legs wobbled a bit, and she reached for his forearm to steady herself, gripping the corded muscle, feeling his strength.

"Are you all right?" he asked.

"I will be."

"Good." He nodded toward the house. "If Hannah doesn't answer the door, take Sarah Jane inside. I'll get Erin out of the wagon and put her in the spare room. If you're hungry, you'll find cookies in a blue tin box in the kitchen."

Katie balked at his suggestion to just make herself at home. "I could never enter someone's house uninvited. If Hannah doesn't answer, Sarah Jane and I will wait on the porch."

"Suit yourself. Hannah usually keeps that tin full. I think Sarah Jane would like something sweet to eat."

The girl nodded and grinned, regaining a wee bit of the spark she'd had before the assault. She seemed to be healing—inside, as well as out. In fact, the bruising along her right arm had begun to yellow and fade.

Of course, the child who'd once been clean and dressed to perfection now had dirty hands and a black smudge across her nose.

"She needs a bath first," Katie said.

Tom chuckled, and his brown eyes sparked. "So do you."

He was teasing, of course, and probably didn't mean anything by it, but...

Katie ran her hands along the skirt of her soiled and wrinkled dress. She'd planned on bathing and changing into clean clothes, but to have Tom point it out left her uneasy and unbalanced.

As Tom untied the two horses from the back of the wagon and led them to the barn, she couldn't help but watch him go. He was an intriguing man and a formidable opponent. Yet she had to admit that she'd felt safe riding with him and knowing that he'd been watching over them.

As Tom entered the barn with the two saddle horses, Katie felt a tug at her skirts and glanced down at Sarah Jane, who pointed to the small outhouse in back.

"Good idea," Katie said with a smile. "And then we'll find the well and wash up outside. We don't want Hannah to think we're ragamuffins."

Again Katie worried about the impression her appearance might make, a concern she'd rarely had in the past.

What was the matter with her? She didn't care what others thought of her.

You're a lady, she reminded herself. Not a ragamuffin, a stray or a soiled dove. She was every bit as good and kindhearted as Hannah, no matter what she looked like on the outside.

Besides, Katie had no need of a life like Hannah's. She was going to Granville, where she would have a small but cozy home behind the school. She would be a fine teacher, an upstanding and respected woman in the community. A happy spinster. Life would be just as she'd always wanted.

So why did her tummy feel so fluttery?

Maybe she'd eaten something that hadn't sat very well.

After using the outhouse, she found the well and drew a bucket of water. Then she dampened her handkerchief and washed Sarah Jane's face and hands. When she finished cleaning the girl, she washed herself the best she could, then she led Sarah Jane back to the front porch and took a seat.

Katie chose the wooden bench, knowing Sarah Jane would prefer the rocker.

Moments later, Tom sauntered out of the house, where he must have taken Erin, and stepped onto the porch. Before Katie could question him, he headed for the buckboard, which he'd left near the barn. As he began to unhitch the team, a dog howled in the distance, catching his attention.

Katie turned to the sound and spotted a black buggy approaching the yard with a beast of a dog trotting beside it.

The driver, a stout, gray-haired woman, called out, "Lord be praised. You're home, Tom!"

Katie watched as the dog, which looked more like a wolf, barked and then raced toward the man.

Oh, dear. Should she grab Sarah Jane and run inside

for safety? Perhaps she didn't need to do anything yet. The house was still a good distance from the barn. And the creature didn't seem to notice anything other than Tom. So she and Sarah Jane were probably safe enough for now.

Tom laughed, the smooth, easy timbre calming her nerves. Then he started toward the road, bracing himself as the black wolf-dog leaped into his arms and gave him a slobbery lick across the face.

"Hey," he said to the creature. "How are you doing, boy? Is Hannah feeding you enough?"

The gray-haired woman pulled the buggy into the yard and halted the horse. "That dog eats better than you do, young man. It's good to have you home. I hope you'll be here longer than the last time you came."

"I can only stay for dinner. I need a good night's sleep, then I'm leaving in the morning." Tom set the wolf-dog down and ruffled its black woolly head before he strode to help Hannah down from the buggy. "Where's Trapper? He told me he was going to meet me here."

"He stopped by a couple days ago. I asked him to go with me when I called on the widow Johnson this afternoon. I took her some chicken stew and peach cobbler for her supper tonight, and he stayed at her place to do a few chores. But he should be back soon. He knew you'd be coming home any day."

"Good. I need to talk to him."

Hannah glanced at the buckboard, which the quilts still lined and the canvas tarp still shaded. "What's that? And where's your horse?"

"Caballo is in the barn. And that? Well, I suppose you could say that I brought you a surprise."

"Not another wolf puppy, I hope." She shook her gray head, chuckling.

"I think you'll like this one a lot better." He continued to talk to her, but he lowered his voice to the point it was impossible to hear from where Katie and Sarah Jane sat.

Hannah nodded, then spoke, too, her voice also a whisper.

When Tom pointed toward the porch, Katie got to her feet. While she was no longer concerned about meeting the woman she'd once thought Tom might be courting, she still wondered what kind of reception she would receive.

However, if Hannah held any ill feelings about Tom bringing three houseguests, she masked them with a warm smile on a rosy face.

Katie turned to the rocker, where Sarah Jane watched the homecoming. "Come on, honey. Tom has someone he wants us to meet."

The child's big blue eyes implored Katie to participate in the introductions without her.

"You can play on the rocker later." Katie held out a hand. "I promise."

Sarah Jane sighed, then stopped the swaying motion with little moccasin-clad feet and reached her small hand into Katie's.

As they approached Hannah and Tom, the big dog studied them intently. Too intently, Katie realized. She paused in midstep, determined to avoid a quick movement that might provoke the creature to pounce upon them with teeth bared. Katie waited, ready to jump in front of Sarah Jane as a shield, if need be.

"He won't hurt you." Tom stooped to one knee and

held out his hand to Sarah Jane. "Come here, sweetheart. I have a friend I want you to meet."

The child made her way to the man and dog, apparently not the least bit apprehensive.

"Sarah Jane, this is Lobo. He's part wolf, but don't let that scare you. I've had him since he was a puppy, and he's both loving and loyal." Tom placed a hand upon the animal's head. "Lobo, this is my friend. And now she's your friend, too."

The child warmed to the dog immediately. Judging by the way Hannah smiled warmly as she watched the little girl and the wolf-dog, Katie seemed to be the only one with any apprehension whatsoever.

"Sarah Jane," Tom said, "I also want to introduce you to a very special lady. Her name is Hannah McCain, and she used to be a schoolteacher."

Hannah *McCain?*

Was she his grandmother—or perhaps an aunt?

With a rather large nose, a wide mouth and a gap-toothed smile, Hannah wasn't much for looks. In fact, Katie doubted she'd been any more attractive in her youth, but her obvious pleasure at greeting Sarah Jane softened the harsh wrinkles etched on her face.

Hannah slowly lowered herself to her knees, grimacing as she went down, but she seemed to shake off any discomfort as she cupped Sarah Jane's face and smiled. "I have a cookie tin that never goes empty. And if you like storybooks, I have a shelf full of them. Reading is one of my favorite things to do."

Tom chuckled. "But watch out for the pianoforte in the parlor. Hannah thinks every child should learn to play as well as she does."

Books and a musical instrument? Hannah was certainly educated. But if Tom was calling her by her first name, then she wasn't his mother. Of course, there didn't appear to be a family resemblance, either.

Curiosity flared, and Katie was determined to learn more about Hannah McCain and how she and Tom had become so close.

The wolf-dog gave Sarah Jane's face a lick, which triggered one of the smiles Katie had been longing to see.

"Hannah," Tom said, "forgive me for skipping formalities, but now that Sarah Jane is at ease, I'd like to introduce you to Katie O'Malley."

The older woman returned to her feet and waddled to Katie, her pudgy hand outstretched. "How do you do, dear? It's nice to meet you."

Katie accepted the greeting. "I'm fine, thank you. Tom assured me that you wouldn't mind having us stay with you."

"I'm delighted to have you." Hannah turned to Tom. "Son, will you please put some water on to heat? These young ladies are going to need a bath. In the meantime, I'll get supper underway."

"I hate to be a bother," Katie said.

"It's no bother at all. Any friend of Tom's is a friend of mine."

Tom had said as much, but Katie suspected the kindly woman would have taken in anyone who'd needed a warm meal and a soft bed.

"We won't be staying with you very long," Katie told her. "Erin and I have plans to take Sarah Jane to Wyoming."

Tom's smile waned, and his expression grew stern. "I thought we had that settled."

"We *did* get that settled. You're going to Stillwater to check on a few details, and my plan to leave for Wyoming merely has been delayed until you get back."

Tom shot her a glance that suggested their truce might be short-lived, then he clucked his tongue and returned to the buckboard.

While the women went into the house, Tom unhitched the team and led them to the corral, where he could brush them down and give them some grain and water.

All the while, he grumbled under his breath. He'd lowered his guard when it came to dealing with Katie O'Malley, and now that they'd reached Hannah's house, she was back in rare form.

Where was Trapper when he needed another man to even things out?

He'd no more than wondered that question when Lobo's ears perked up and he barked.

A moment later, Tom heard it, too—the sound of a horse riding onto the property. As Lobo made a dash toward the road, Tom placed his right hand over the gun that rested in his holster.

He hadn't thought they'd been followed, but he couldn't be sure. A sense of uneasiness had dogged him from Pleasant Valley, and he hadn't been able to shake it.

Still, he was glad to spot Trapper riding up on his Appaloosa. He released the team of horses into the corral, then met his old friend in the yard.

As Trapper dismounted, he surveyed the buckboard and scrunched his face. "What's that contraption?"

Tom told him about the assault and why he'd brought Erin and Sarah Jane to Hannah.

Trapper, who'd gotten a shave and a haircut after his

return from Pleasant Valley, lifted his hat and mopped his brow. "Something just don't seem right."

"That's the conclusion I came to back in Pleasant Valley. We trailed Caroline from Casa de Los Angelitos in Mexico. And each time she'd settle down in a town and find a respectable job, she'd pack up and move a year or so later. But they stayed in Taylorsville nearly two years. So why didn't Erin stay put after Caroline died? Why would she take Sarah Jane to live at the Gardener's House? It doesn't make sense."

"You still think they was runnin' from someone or something?" Trapper asked.

"What else could it be? And you know how I felt about Caroline taking that tumble down the stairs."

"You had trouble believing it was an accident."

"The sheriff in Taylorsville hadn't found it suspicious, but something just didn't feel right about it to me."

"What did Erin have to say about that night?" Trapper asked.

"I hadn't gotten a chance to ask her before the attack. And those blows to her head really rattled her brains. Even if she wasn't so medicated and drowsy, her throat is so bruised that she doesn't have much of a voice now anyway. The doctor suggested we wait about a week for her brain and her throat to heal before we question her about anything."

"Maybe she'll tell you more then."

Maybe so, but Tom didn't have time to wait. He glanced down at his boots, then back at his friend, taking in the clean clothes, the haircut, the shave. "Well, now. Don't you look nice."

Trapper shrugged. "Did it for Hannah. Maybe one

of these days she'll agree to marry me. Then, whenever I'm passing through, I won't have to sleep in the barn."

Tom smiled. "Maybe she will if you ever get up the nerve to ask her."

The two were an odd match—the grizzled old trapper and the proper lady. But they were good friends who looked out for each other. Who knew what the future might bring?

"You going back to Stillwater?" Trapper asked.

"I'm leaving in the morning. I can't take Caroline back to the Lazy G now, but I can take word of her and the life she'd been living."

"You figure on takin' the little girl with you when you go?" Trapper asked.

"No, not until I'm sure of the welcome she'll receive."

"Good idea. I'll bet Hannah's thrilled to have another kid in the house. She loved being able to mother you. I'll bet she'll do the same thing with that little girl."

There was no doubt about that, assuming Katie O'Malley would let her.

Tom figured he might as well tell Trapper now, since he was going to find out soon enough. "By the way, Erin and Sarah Jane aren't the only women I brought home."

Trapper arched a woolly brow. "Who else came with you?"

"An outspoken ex-schoolmarm who'll likely be the death of me before this is all said and done."

"How'd *that* happen?"

"Don't ask." Tom scowled. "Come on. Help me with the team. Then we need to bring in the bathtub for Hannah and heat some water."

"I'll help you, but just hold on a minute. Does this ex-schoolmarm got a name?"

"Katie O'Malley. And while she may look like a lady, don't let that fool you. She's as stubborn as a mule. Hot tempered, too." Tom turned and lifted his finger at Trapper. "And no matter what you do, don't let her get it in her pretty head to try and take Sarah Jane anywhere. She's got some fool notion that the child is hers. And like it or not, Sarah Jane belongs to Graves."

Trapper crossed his arms and shifted his weight to one hip. "Belongs to him, huh? You make the poor kid sound like a stray pup. But don't worry. I ain't gonna let anyone take the little girl anywhere until you get back."

"Thank you. I'd appreciate that."

Trapper took a deep breath and sighed. "Kind of wish I wouldn't have gone in search of Caroline with you in the first place. I really missed Hannah this time."

Tom didn't doubt it. Hannah and Trapper provided each other with something they'd each wanted but never had—respectability for Trapper and a little romance for Hannah.

For years, Hannah had dreamed of being a wife and mother, but men hadn't found her the least bit attractive.

"Hannah might not be the prettiest woman in the world," Trapper added, "but she's the most loving one I've ever met. And each time I see her, I have a growing notion to settle down once and for all. You ought to try it sometime, kid. Find yourself a woman to love."

Tom scoffed. Yet for some reason, thoughts of feisty but pretty Katie O'Malley came to mind. When they did, he quickly brushed them aside. "I'm too much of a loner."

"That's what I thought before I met Hannah."

"Yeah, well, you and I aren't anything alike."

Trapper uncrossed his arms and wagged a finger at

him. "You could use a little of that kind of respectability yourself."

By respectability, Trapper meant love. And they'd had this talk before, back when Tom had though Sarah Jorgenson might make a good wife. But her father hadn't liked the idea of his fair-haired daughter being courted by a half-breed.

Tom remembered the man's claim to have his shotgun loaded and cocked if Tom should ever come calling.

"I don't need respectability—or matrimony," Tom told the old man.

"Humph." Trapper shoved his hands into his trousers' front pockets. "So when are you headin' out?"

"I didn't get much sleep over the last few days, so I'm going to turn in early—sharing the loft in the barn with you, I guess. I'll leave in the morning, but I spent nearly all my cash on supplies and a buckboard I'll never have any more use for. So I have to stop by Izzy Ballard's place on my way. He owes me some money, and I don't like the idea of riding into Stillwater with an empty pocket."

"That ain't as bad as ridin' into town with an empty gun."

True, but Tom wouldn't dwell on the danger. Instead he said, "Don't worry about me, Trapper. I wouldn't go to a church social unarmed."

Chapter Five

The inside of Hannah's house was no less inviting than the outside, especially with the scent of yeast and cinnamon filling the air.

In the parlor, a polished cherrywood bookcase holding a small library lined one wall and a stone fireplace adorned another.

Crocheted doilies that graced the backs of an overstuffed chair, a lovely brocade-upholstered settee and a colorful braided rug atop the hardwood floor added a cozy appeal, turning the little house into a home.

"I woke up this morning craving peach cobbler," Hannah said, "so I made two of them. I took one to Mary-Ellen Johnson, a widow who's been sickly, but there's one for our supper tonight. I also have a chicken stew on the stove."

"You have no idea how good that sounds," Katie said. "Our last meal was hardtack and beef jerky."

"Hopefully, we'll put those last few days of traveling behind you in good speed. Tom will have the bathwater ready before you know it. And since I need to put a few extra potatoes in the soup, we'll have time to bathe

Sarah Jane before supper. Then once we've all eaten our fill, you can have your turn in the tub."

A bath. Warm water, soap, lilac water…

Katie thought she might die of anticipation before her chance to bathe came.

"If you and Sarah Jane will wait a minute or two for me in the parlor," Hannah said, "I'll be right back."

Katie ushered the child to the settee and did as she was asked. Minutes later, Hannah returned and took a seat in front of an ornate, hand-carved pianoforte. Soon a medley of waltzes carried Katie's thoughts away to another time, another place.

Before long, Tom entered the room. He stood for a moment, waiting until the last song ended. Then he announced that the first bath was ready on the back porch.

Hannah graciously led Katie and a solemn Sarah Jane into the small enclosed area, where a metal tub full of water awaited.

"A warm bath will do us both good," Katie told the child. "After you're nice and clean, I'll braid your hair."

Hannah pulled a towel from a shelf. "Tom says Sarah Jane doesn't have any clean clothes, so I'll launder her dress tomorrow. In the meantime, I have a blouse she can wear. We can roll the sleeves and tie a satin ribbon at the waist. It won't be as pretty as the little dress I intend to cut out and stitch for her while she's here, but it will do for the time being."

"That's very kind of you." Katie lifted the soiled cotton dress over Sarah Jane's head and noticed a small leather bag hanging from around her neck. She lifted it. "What's this?"

Sarah Jane's only response was to hold the pouch close to her chest.

"You'll have to take that off while you bathe." Katie reached for the strap, but Sarah Jane shook her head and leaned back. Small fingers clutched the bag tightly.

"Well, I'll be." Hannah clicked her tongue and smiled. "A medicine bag, just like Tom's. He must have made it for her."

Had he made the moccasins, too?

He must have.

"What's a medicine bag?" Katie asked.

"A keepsake, I'd say. But powerful medicine, if you ask the Comanche, who are Tom's people."

There was a lot Katie didn't know about the man, and she found herself growing more and more curious about him and how he'd come to meet Hannah.

"What's inside the medicine bag?" she asked.

"Special things—healing plants, a magic feather, a bear claw. It's hard to say. Tom's had one for years. His mother made it for him. I don't have a clue what he keeps inside. It would be disrespectful to ask or to look."

Katie's curiosity about the contents of what Sarah Jane kept in her bag shifted to what Tom kept in his. She hadn't given him much thought before, other than his appearance, which she found most appealing. But she was going to make it a point to learn more about him.

As Katie helped Sarah Jane climb into the tub, the leather bag still in place, she said, "We'll try not to get it wet, honey."

Sarah Jane looked at the pouch. Pausing only slightly, she lifted the strap over her head and handed over the prized possession.

Katie placed it on the small table that held a cake of soap and a soft cloth for scrubbing. The little girl blessed her with a trusting grin.

"Katie," the older woman began, "you're welcome to stay with me as long as you like."

"Thank you." Katie immersed the washcloth into the warm water and reached for the soap. "I'd like to leave as soon as Tom returns."

She just prayed he wouldn't want to take Sarah Jane back to Stillwater with him. If he did, Katie fully intended to go, too, so she could meet these supposed relations. There was a reason her mother hadn't been close to them. What if they weren't good people? Or weren't kind to Sarah Jane?

What if they didn't want her?

Of course, if that were the case, and they were actually her relatives, perhaps they'd sign over guardianship to Katie. It would certainly make things simpler that way. She'd wait to see what Tom learned in Stillwater. And if he wanted to take Sarah Jane back, she'd insist upon going with them.

The women remained quiet for the rest of Sarah Jane's bath. By the time they helped her from the tub and dried her off, the aroma of chicken stew and biscuits filled the house.

"I'm sure you must be hungry," Hannah said. "I'll have food on the table in no time at all."

As they entered the parlor, Katie glanced out the open door, and her feet stilled as she spotted Tom standing near the barn with the wolf-dog.

"Maybe I'd better wait to call Tom to supper until he's finished talking to Lobo," Hannah said.

Katie turned to the elderly woman and cocked her head. "He's talking to the dog?"

"They have an unusual bond. Lobo won't be happy

about staying behind, but he'll look after Sarah Jane and me if Tom tells him to."

Katie scoffed. "If the dog doesn't tag after Tom, it's probably because he knows he has plenty to eat here."

Hannah touched Katie's arm. "You're wrong, dear. Tom and Lobo understand each other. Their loyalty is unbelievable."

Unbelievable was right. Katie had a pet once, a gray and yellow finch named Pretty Boy. The little bird chirped and sang to her every day. One afternoon, when she let it out of the cage to play, it flew away and never came back.

She glanced across the way at the man and beast. They certainly seemed to have a bond, an unusual friendship of sorts. They certainly had a closeness Tom and Katie didn't share.

They had reached a truce for the sake of Sarah Jane, but could they become friends? Could they form a relationship based upon mutual respect and trust?

They'd have to get to know each other first. And that meant setting their differences aside.

Katie was willing, but she wasn't so sure about Tom. He seemed too set in his ways to see reason. Of course, she was a bit stubborn, too. But she would try to talk to him as soon as she could get him alone.

But when an interesting old man entered the house, Katie feared that chance might never come.

"Miss Katie O'Malley," Hannah said by way of introduction, "this is our dear friend, Jack Cavendish."

The old man grinned, sporting yellowed teeth—one of them missing. "Pleased to meet you, Miss O'Malley. Tom told me about you, and while he said you were

pretty, I have to tell you, he didn't do you a bit of justice. No sirree."

Katie wasn't so sure Tom had said anything of the
sort, but she accepted the old man's compliment. "How
do you do, Mr. Cavendish."

"Call me Trapper—or just plain ol' Jack. No need
for us to be formal."

He smiled, his blue eyes glimmering like a child's
at Christmas, although she couldn't imagine what he
found so amusing.

Ten minutes later, after giving Erin her fill of chicken
stew, which was merely a few bites, they sat down to a
delicious meal, during which Trapper Jack chattered on
about one thing or another. When the dishes had been
washed, Katie excused herself to take her bath. It wasn't
until afterward that she thought she might have a chance
to catch Tom alone.

Since Hannah had taken Sarah Jane into the small
guest room to read a storybook, and Trapper had apparently gone into the barn, Katie used that opportunity to
search for Tom. She found him standing on the porch,
peering into the darkness, the wolf-dog resting on its
haunches beside him.

When she opened the screen door, he turned. For a
moment, as their gazes met, her breath caught.

What was it about the man that stirred her senses?

Unable to come up with an answer, she shook it off
and asked, "What time do you plan to leave tomorrow?
And when will you be back?"

"I'm leaving in the morning. If all goes well, I'll be
back in three days—more or less." Tom leaned back
against the porch railing and sighed before returning his

gaze to hers. "I just hope Harrison Graves is still alive when I get there."

Tom had mentioned that Sarah Jane was the old man's only heir. "If it's decided that she is his great-grand-daughter, who will care for her when he dies?"

"That's not my immediate concern."

A chill settled over Katie, leaving a trail of goose-flesh in its path. "Well, it certainly should be. What will become of her? Who will love her?"

"Harrison's housekeeper looked after Caroline when she was a girl, but let's take things one day at a time."

Patience had never been one of Katie's virtues. "But what if Sarah Jane isn't happy there? What if she isn't welcome? What if she isn't even the heir that dying cattleman is looking for?"

"Take it easy." Tom took a step forward and lifted his hand as if to...

As if to what? Reach for her cheek? Offer comfort?

She'd never know because he dropped his hand back to his side as quickly as he'd raised it and said, "Maybe he'll let you take her to Wyoming until she's of age. There are other, more immediate concerns. But keep in mind that I'm not taking Sarah Jane yet. I'm leaving her here, where she'll be safe."

"Safe? But what if the man who hurt Erin followed us here?"

"If I thought there was a good chance of that, I wouldn't leave. But just in case, Trapper will stay behind. And Hannah can handle a gun. Besides, you'll be here, too."

She lifted a brow. "Does that mean you trust me to look after her?"

"I'm not sure how successful you'd be, but you'd probably die trying." A smile tugged at his lips. "You're feisty, Katie. And I'd pity any man who tried to put you in your place."

Like Tom had once tried?

She returned his smile.

He studied her for a moment in the moonlight. It seemed that the truce they'd reached earlier might have grown a wee bit stronger.

"Just so you know," he said, "Hannah said that you, Erin and Sarah Jane are welcome to stay with her for as long as it takes."

"That's kind of her," Katie said. "But tell me something. I've been curious. How did you and Hannah meet?"

"Trapper brought me to stay with her when I was a kid. My mother had just died, and I didn't have anyone else in the world to look after me. Hannah took me in and raised me. And when I had trouble at school, she taught me at home."

"Did you struggle to learn?"

He stiffened. "I wasn't in need of tutoring, if that's what you mean. Apparently, some of the townspeople didn't like the idea of an Indian boy going to school with the white kids. They voiced their disapproval, and some of the boys thought they could take it out on me. I came home with several black eyes and split lips, but after a pretty serious beating, Hannah refused to send me back."

The children had singled him out, just like Silas and his friends had turned on Sarah Jane.

Katie's heart went out to the lonely boy Tom had once been, and she gained an even deeper respect for Hannah.

"I'm sorry you lost your mother," she said.

He gave a shrug. "It happens."

"I know. I lost my mother, too. When I was a baby. I suppose, in some ways, that's easier. But at least you have memories of yours. I don't have any."

Katie's father hadn't talked much about her, thinking it might be easier that way. So Katie had sometimes created memories in her mind of a woman who'd been too good to be true.

One day, when Katie had been about nine, the teacher had given the girls an assignment and asked them to write about their mothers. Katie had won a prize for having the best essay of all. She'd written about her imaginary mother, who wore yellow dresses, lilac water and a smile. A woman who baked cookies every day and kept a library of books that children would enjoy.

A kind, loving woman who could have been Hannah, only Katie had imagined her tall, slender and blonde.

Growing up without a mother had been very hard, which was why Katie was so determined to stand by Sarah Jane and provide her with a loving home. That's also why Katie wanted to know who'd be looking out for her, who'd be mothering her.

"Maybe I should go to Stillwater with you," she told Tom.

If truth be told, the words had surprised her as much as they surely surprised him, but if Sarah Jane had to live with strangers, Katie wanted to make sure they would treat her well.

"Don't be ridiculous."

"I'm serious." She placed her hand on his arm to convince him of her sincerity and felt the warmth of his skin under his shirtsleeve. Their gazes met again, and for a moment, the intimacy seemed to meld them together.

That is, until he drew back his arm and pulled away.

"You don't want anyone to see you travel alone with a man, especially a half-breed. It might ruin your chances of landing an upstanding husband."

If he thought she gave a hoot about what others thought of her, he was mistaken. In fact, after that unfortunate confrontation with Sweet Heather at the Gardener's House, he should know that about her by now.

She stood tall and crossed her arms. "I don't want an upstanding husband."

A slow smile stretched across his face, sparking a glimmer in his eyes. "What kind of husband *would* you like?"

"I don't want a husband at all."

"Why not?" He scanned the length of her, then let his gaze drift back to her face again as though assessing her. Had he somehow found her lacking?

The momentary insecurity took her aback, and she chided herself. His opinion didn't matter in the least.

"I don't intend to be some man's pretty little slave he refers to as a wife." She hadn't meant to say "pretty." It sounded so…well, so vain.

Katie never had placed much value on beauty or the lack of it. Her auburn hair always garnered a compliment or two, but not the freckles splattered across her nose. Nor her outspoken personality, for that matter.

"I don't think there's much chance you'll need to worry about that, Katie."

Heat rose to her cheeks. "What do you mean?"

His lighthearted smile faded, and a thought-provoking expression took its place. "You might be able to recite poetry or quote ancient philosophers, but I doubt you know enough to come in out of the rain. A man would have to be plain loco to consider asking for your hand. You'd be useless as a wife."

Katie stood tall. *Useless?* The word struck a hard blow. All her life she'd struggled to prove her worth, her value, her competence.

He took a step closer. "You'd argue even if obedience would save your own hide."

Katie's hands went to her hips. "And I suppose you think a woman would find *you* appealing?"

"*You* do."

The fact that he was right set her scampering to deny it, and she snorted, making a most unladylike noise. "When it rains lemon drops."

"Is that right?" His grin returned, blossoming into a full-blown smile. "Has anyone told you that the shade of your eyes darkens whenever you're not being completely honest?"

She let out another unladylike sound. "Are you insinuating that I'm lying?"

"Your eyes are usually the color of the summer sky. But when you're not being truthful, they turn a blue-gray."

If that were true, it wasn't dishonesty causing change. It was anger. And sheer disbelief. She shook her head. "It's too dark out here for you to even see the color of my eyes." Then she turned on her heel and returned to the house.

The sound of his low chuckle merely stirred the tempest within—and surely deepened the color of her eyes to a stormy gray.

The morning sun streamed through the crocheted curtains and cast a dappled light into Hannah's guest room, where Katie sat up amidst the rumpled sheets of the four-poster feather bed and rubbed her eyes. Sarah Jane had risen without waking her, and obviously so had Hannah, because the aroma of freshly ground coffee and fried bacon wafted through the air.

Her mouth watered, reminding her it was time to eat. She didn't need a clock on the bureau to tell her she'd slept later than usual, but that shouldn't be a surprise. After the past few days of eating dried beef and hardtack and sleeping in a wagon, it had been such a comfort to rest in a cozy, warm bed.

Rising quickly, she tidied up her room. Then, after combing her hair and dressing for the day, she headed for the kitchen, eager for a cup of coffee.

She'd written two letters last night, one to the Granville school board, explaining her situation and promising to arrive as soon as she could. The other had been to Ian Connor, letting him know she was safe and in good hands. She would ask Hannah to mail them for her, since she planned to leave the next day with Tom, although she expected him to fight her on it.

When she reached the kitchen, she found Hannah at the stove, frying bacon.

"Good morning," Katie said.

Hannah turned, and her smile made her almost look… Well, pretty wasn't the word, but there was something about her, a kindness, a warmth that Katie found appealing.

"Can I get you some coffee, dear?"

"Yes, please. That would be lovely."

Hannah poured a cup, then handed it to Katie. "Careful now. It's hot."

"Thank you."

"Cream and sugar is on the table."

Katie sweetened her coffee and added a drop of cream, then lifted the cup and blew across the rim to cool it. "I'm afraid I slept like a rock last night. How did Erin do?"

"She rested well. I offered her a little poached egg this morning. She ate nearly all of it. Then I gave her some medicine. She's sleeping again."

"That's good. Where's Sarah Jane?"

"Outside."

"Is she all right out there alone?"

"She's fine. Lobo is with her."

In spite of Hannah's attempts at reassurance, Katie scooted back her chair and carried her cup to the back door, where she peered outside to check on the child. She'd never been particularly fond of dogs, especially those that looked more like wolves.

It didn't take long for her to see that Hannah might be right, because Sarah Jane hooked her arm around the dog's woolly neck and cuddled against him.

About the time Katie was going to turn away, she spotted Trapper Jack coming out of the barn and heading for the house.

"Good mornin'," he said, his voice resonant and clear.

Katie greeted him, then stepped aside so he could enter the kitchen.

"I hope breakfast is ready," he said. "I'm hungry enough to eat a mule."

Hannah chuckled as she poured him a cup of coffee. "You're always hungry, old man. But now that you're here, I'll go outside and tell Sarah Jane that it's time to come inside for breakfast."

As the older woman made her way to the door, Katie took a sip of coffee, then asked Trapper, "Where's Tom?"

"He left a little bit ago."

"He *left?* Already?"

"Didn't get a chance to tell him goodbye, huh?"

"Well, no. But I'd actually hoped to go with him."

Trapper studied her for a moment, then stroked his chin. "Now that's a real shame that he left without you. As far as I'm concerned, it would have been best if you'd gone with him."

She wasn't used to men agreeing with her so readily. "Why do you say that? I mean, I have a good reason for going with him. I want to meet those people in Stillwater myself so that I can decide whether they're suitable to care for Sarah Jane."

"That's a good idea. Just 'cause folks have money don't mean that they're kind."

Katie blew out a sigh of relief, glad that Trapper understood her concern. "I couldn't agree more, and while that's been a real worry, it's too late for me to go now."

"I'm not so sure about that. Tom had a stop to make about three miles from here. The lonely old feller he went to see will probably talk his ear off, so we could catch up with him in no time at all."

"*We?* You mean you'd take me to meet him?"

Trapper stroked his chin again, as a slow grin stretched across his craggy face until it crinkled his eyes. "That fool kid would probably skin me alive for not stayin' put until he gets back, but how could he get mad at either of us when we're just lookin' out for that poor little girl?"

Katie figured Tom could get *plenty* mad at her, and if truth be told, a part of her was tempted to stay here and wait with Erin and Sarah Jane. But Tom said he'd be back in a couple of days, which meant that Stillwater was probably only a day's ride—more or less. And while Tom would be upset, he'd probably get over it. Particularly since they both had Sarah Jane's well-being in mind.

"So what do you say?" Trapper asked.

"Well, for one thing," Katie said, "on the ride here, he complained about the horse I borrowed from the livery. He said she wasn't a trail horse. I'm afraid I'd never be able to keep up with him."

"You can ride Hannah's sorrel mare. Gully Washer is a bit testy, but strong and sturdy." Trapper's eyes fairly glimmered. "I'll have Hannah pack you some vittles while I saddle the horse."

He made it sound so easy, but Katie knew better than that. Still, she loved a debate and a challenge. And she'd have several hours to change Tom's mind—if not his mood. "Okay. I'll pack a few things for the ride. I just wish I would have brought some bloomers with me. They'd make riding a horse a lot easier."

In a fit of anger, her da had burned her only pair. She would have ordered another—or perhaps several—but he'd died shortly thereafter, and she hadn't felt nearly so rebellious when she'd been grieving his loss.

Still, a pair of bloomers would certainly come in handy now.

Trapper scrunched his face and shook his head. "I never did see any point in women wearing those fool things. You might as well wear men's britches."

"I would if I had a pair that fit."

"Hmm. Now, that's an idea. Hannah packed up all the old clothes Tom outgrew and put them in the hayloft. I could find a pair that might fit you, but you'd probably look a sight."

"I don't care how I look. I mean to be comfortable and capable on the trail, and I want Tom to see me as an equal while we travel."

Trapper eyed her carefully, and a slow grin tickled his lips. "Those britches might be a bit snug, but I don't suppose they'd look too bad."

"As long as they fit and I can move around, I'll be happy."

The old man chuckled. "All righty. I'll get your traveling clothes while you pack. But be quick about it. If we don't catch Tom by the time he reaches the pass, it'll be too late."

Katie nodded and turned toward the house. Trapper had said to hurry, and she would. Still, she heard him chuckle and mutter, "The kid needs respectability more than he thinks."

She wondered what he meant by that, but it didn't matter. She was going to Stillwater with Tom McCain whether he liked it or not.

However, thirty minutes later, when Katie was packed and mounted on Hannah's sorrel mare, she was having second thoughts about leaving.

"You know, Trapper..." Katie paused, took a deep breath and slowly let it out. "I'm not so sure this is a good idea, after all."

"Why? This is the best idea I've ever had. Tom needs your help."

"He needs *my* help?"

Trapper nodded. "More than either of you know. Tom might be ornery at times and act as tough as nails, but inside, he's as soft as butter. And whether he's told you or not, he's downright worried about those folks in Stillwater, the ones that want the little girl."

Katie's senses reeled at the mention of Sarah Jane. "What's wrong with them?"

"Tom don't trust them to be good to her. But he's gonna make sure they ain't planning to make her sleep in the barn. And that they'll feed her at least once a day. Course, he ought to make sure they don't take too big of a stick to her when she don't get her chores done by nightfall."

Katie pointed her finger. "Believe me, Trapper. That child won't live with anyone who treats her as less than royalty."

"That's what I was hoping you'd say. Hannah's right attached to the little thing. She'll be glad to know you won't let those people be mean to her."

"Tom is in for a fight if he believes the only requirement of a good home is sleeping indoors and eating one meal a day. And I'll take a stick to anyone who even thinks to strike her." Katie clenched her firsts, her fingers tightening around the reins. "And if Tom disagrees, he'd better brace himself for a tangle with me."

"I figure there'll be a tussle between you. Course, I doubt Tom stands a chance." Trapper grinned from ear to ear. "And to tell you the truth, I'd like to see him get his comeuppance from a pretty little gal like you."

"If he tries to challenge me, he'll wish he hadn't."

"A tangle with you might be the best thing that ever happened to him. Might bring him some respectability."

Katie still didn't know what respectability had to do with anything, but she'd put a stop to any fool notion Tom McCain had of leaving Sarah Jane in an unsafe or unhappy situation, even if she had to fight him tooth and nail.

Chapter Six

"This is where we part ways."

"Here?" On a trail surrounded by trees and brush? Katie didn't like the idea of being stranded in what appeared to be the wilderness.

Trapper removed his hat and mopped his brow. "Tom hasn't gotten this far yet. And you're downwind from him. He won't catch on before you spot him. And by then, it will be too late for him to send you back."

She wondered if she should reach for her derringer, something she'd purchased to protect herself after her father had died. For the first mile she'd ridden along with it tucked in her pocket, but with each swaying step of the sorrel mare, she'd worried the small gun would go off, wounding her in the leg. So she'd removed the loaded firearm and placed it in her saddlebag, where it was still within reach.

"Ride due south," Trapper instructed. "Wait near that patch of cottonwood trees growing along the stream. Tom should go that way."

He *should* go that way? "What if he doesn't?"

Trapper turned in his saddle, the leather creaking

with his movement. He scanned the rolling horizon and pointed at a small wooden structure. "See that cabin over yonder?"

Katie craned her neck and spotted the rustic log structure perched upon a grassy hillside. "Yes, it looks like it has a newly patched roof."

"It does." Trapper chuckled. "I fell clean through the old one last spring, trying to help Tom fix a rotten spot that leaked like old fury whenever it rained."

"Why were you two fixing the roof?"

"My friend and neighbor, Izzy Ballard, lives there. The old cuss and I go way back, and he owes me. I near broke my neck when I fell through and landed inside. Izzy will get you back to Hannah's place if Tom has already passed through."

"Are you sure he won't mind?"

"Not if he's still alive."

"Izzy might be *dead?*" Katie shuddered at the thought of walking into the cabin and finding a body.

Trapper laughed again. "Izzy's too stubborn to roll over and die. He'll be right flattered to be asked to help a pretty woman in distress."

Katie didn't like the idea of being pretty or in distress. But she liked being stranded even less.

Before she could give it much thought, Trapper said goodbye and headed back the way they'd come, leaving her on her own.

She wasn't sure how long she waited to catch sight of Tom or his horse. She supposed it had only been a few minutes, but she'd gotten so caught up trying to follow the trail that she'd nearly missed seeing him ride down the hillside, away from Izzy's cabin.

When he lifted his hat, adjusting it, a stray beam of sunlight reflected off his coal-black hair, reminding her of an Indian brave, a warrior.

She meant to call out, to confront him with her plan, to insist he take her with him, but a second thought silenced her. In spite of what Trapper had said, she doubted Tom would be pleased to see her. And since they were only an hour's ride from Hannah's house, she realized he might send her back with Izzy. So she nudged her mount forward, keeping her eyes on the broad shoulders of the man she'd better keep up with.

The tight-fitting dungarees definitely made riding more comfortable, and Trapper had been right about Gully Washer. Hannah's sorrel mare certainly had more get-up-and-go than the old roan.

However, an hour later, Katie had nearly lost sight of Tom's gelding. She urged the mare along, worried she was too far from Izzy's cabin to find it again. She was just about to call out to Tom in spite of her reservations, knowing he'd hear her. But before she could do so, a rattle sounded from the brush, followed by the horse's whinny.

The mare reared. Katie grabbed for the pommel, but only caught a few strands of mane and fell to the ground with a thump.

As she struggled to catch her breath, her eyes locked on the largest snake she'd ever imagined let alone seen. A bloodcurdling scream seemed to come from someone else, as she froze in fear.

Gully Washer, on the other hand, had taken off like a rifle shot in the same direction as Tom, leaving her to stare at a coiled, black-and-brown diamondback that hissed and rattled in anger.

If Katie still carried the derringer in her pocket, she could have shot it, but the gun was stashed in the saddlebag strapped to the mare, so she had nothing to use in defense.

She ached in a hundred different spots, most notably her right ankle, which had taken the brunt of her fall on the hard dirt. But she didn't dare move. Instead, she sat quietly, waiting, hoping that the vile creature would just give up and go away when he realized she wasn't a threat to him. Either that, or that Tom would have heard her scream and come looking for a damsel in distress.

It seemed like ages, but it was probably only a matter of moments before the big, ugly snake finally slithered to the tall grass off to the side of the pathway. With her heart still pounding like a blacksmith's hammer, Katie reached for her right ankle, which throbbed something fierce.

Before she could even attempt to stand, a stranger's voice interrupted her efforts. "What do you know, Georgie. Look what we got us here. We done found us a woman."

Katie glanced over her shoulder, where two men atop their horses looked down at her. A short, stocky man did the talking. The other one appeared awestruck, his gaping smile revealing a mouthful of yellow teeth.

"Why, I ain't never had such luck before. She's a pretty one, even in britches." The stocky man spit a brown stream of spittle to the ground and wiped his mouth with the back of a beefy hand.

"Are we gonna keep her, Ned?" the one called Georgie asked.

Katie wondered if his wide-mouthed stare was due to his reaction at seeing her or if his lips just couldn't close over his mouthful of teeth.

"Sure, we'll keep her. You don't expect us to just walk away from a gift that fell out of the sky, do you?"

They both seemed to find that funny, but the idea sickened Katie. She had no weapon. And even if the horse hadn't run off, she would've been hard-pressed to snatch the gun out of the saddlebag without them taking notice.

She wished she had something to fight them with— a hatpin, a rock, a stick. All she had was her wits, and something told her those might not be enough.

Where was Tom?

Surely he'd heard her scream and was on his way.

Or had he gone after Hannah's horse?

The short, stocky man named Ned stepped closer, a wicked gleam in his eyes. His belly hung over the straining waistband of his dirty gray britches. He reeked of month-old sweat and something else she couldn't be sure of—rancid grease, she suspected. And she cringed at the thought of him touching her.

She fought the physical reaction and struggled to gather her wits. "I do believe I'm the lucky one, gentlemen. I fell off my horse, and it ran off. I don't suppose I could talk either of you into running after it for me, could I?"

The man called Georgie stood ramrod straight and beamed. "I'll get it for you, ma'am." Then he turned to his stocky friend. "You don't care, do ya, Ned?"

"Go on. We'll have to take turns having a go with her anyway. And I aim to be first."

Katie's stomach reeled, but she pointed in the opposite direction of where the fool horse had run. "It's a sorrel mare."

"Don't use her all up," Georgie told his friend, before spurring his mount and riding off.

Taking advantage of the man's departure, Katie batted her eyes and smiled. "I don't suppose I could talk you into doing another favor for me, as well."

Ned eased closer. "After I'm done, maybe."

"Of all the luck," Katie said with a sigh. "It seems I lost my bag of gold coins."

At that, Ned slowed to a stop. "Did you say *gold?*"

"Yes, I had it in my hand, counting out the coins when the horse reared and threw me. The bag flew out of my hand and fell into that tall brush over there, and I heard them scatter."

Katie reached for her booted foot, stroking it carefully. "I'd get the bag and collect them all myself, but it seems I've twisted my ankle."

Ned strode to the edge of the road nearest Katie, bent and began to brush the grass aside with both hands. A rattle sounded too late for him to jerk back.

"Aagh! I been snake bit!"

Katie used the diversion to hobble to her feet, her ankle aching. "That's a real shame," she said. "You could surely die from that nasty bite."

Ned screamed again, this time louder. Then he fired his gun in the air. "Georgie! Git on over here. I need your help!"

Katie prayed that Tom had heard the commotion, because she could certainly use some help, too.

"I'm gonna die," Ned said. "For sure and certain."

"You need to see a doctor," Katie said. "So I suggest you ride to the nearest town. And fast."

Moments later, horses approached, their hooves crunching along the twigs and leaves. Katie watched as Tom rode his gelding and led Hannah's sorrel mare by the reins.

He looked fierce on that big gelding, his gun drawn, his eyes blazing. Katie never thought she'd be so happy to see anyone in her life, especially a man as frightfully angry as he appeared to be.

Ned strode forward, his wounded hand clutched tightly to his chest. "Help me, mister. I don't want to die. You've got some injun in you, don't ya? You gotta know all kinds of secret brews and remedies."

Tom looked at Katie, his face never so stoic, so unreadable. "What happened here?"

"He intended to hurt me. And that snakebite serves him right."

"You tricked me!" Ned, his hand clutched tightly to his chest, glared at Katie. "There weren't no bag of gold in them bushes. You knew that snake was there, and you wanted me to get bit."

"I didn't know that snake was still in those bushes. Not for sure. It could have slithered off for all I knew."

Tom dismounted and pulled a knife from his belt.

"What are you going to do with *that?*" Ned asked, his eyes growing even wider.

Did he actually fear a scalping? From the look on his face, she suspected he might.

"I'll help this time," Tom said, "but don't ever come near this woman—or any other woman—again."

"I didn't know she was *yours,*" Ned said. "I thought she was free for the takin'."

"Free?" Tom snorted. "This woman is going to cost some man plenty."

Katie didn't know what he meant by that, but she was too relieved to see him to take any offense—and she wasn't at all ready to risk stirring things up any more than they already were.

Tom surveyed the area. "Where's his friend?"

"He went for Gully Washer, but I sent him in the wrong direction." Katie studied Tom, who wouldn't have fallen for her story about the bag of gold and who wouldn't have chased after a runaway horse without looking at the tracks first.

"Take off your shirt," Tom told Ned.

When the man complied, Tom ripped off a sleeve and used it to cinch the man's arm tight. Then taking his knife, he sliced into the darkening wound.

Ned cried out. "What are you doing? Don't cut my hand off."

Tom pulled him closer. "Suck the blood and spit it out. It'll help remove some of the poison."

Ned nodded, then did as he was told. Between spits and sputters, he looked up at Tom and asked, "Am I going to die?"

"Maybe. And maybe not. Either way, you'll probably get pretty sick. You'd better find a doctor fast."

When Georgie returned, Ned wasted no time in convincing him to hightail it back to town.

As Katie and Tom watched the two men ride off at breakneck speed, she returned her attention to the man who'd come to her rescue and had to admit that she was glad that he had. She might have outsmarted Ned and Georgie temporarily, but she wasn't sure how long she would have been able to keep them at bay.

But when she saw him slap his hands on his hips, she realized her moment of reckoning was at hand.

* * *

Tom studied the headstrong woman wearing one of his long-outgrown shirts. He would have recognized that blue-and-green-plaid material anywhere. Hannah had stitched it together one evening by candlelight, and he'd worn it with pride until it no longer had fit.

He assumed the pants and boots had once been his, too, and doubted that she'd found the old clothing on her own.

Trapper must have given them to her when he put her up to tagging along after him. Tom could see the old man's hand in all of this. He'd probably figured Tom would have to return her to Hannah's place and maybe give up his plan to go to Stillwater altogether. He never had liked the idea of Tom working for Harrison Graves. But it didn't matter. Tom's mind was set, and no one was going to change it.

"I suppose you want to know why I'm here," Katie said.

"For a start. I'd also like to know why you were riding Hannah's horse. You're lucky I spotted her running off—and that she came to me when I called. You were also lucky I heard that gunshot and Ned's holler."

"The poor horse was frightened by a rattlesnake and took off like a shot. Why did she go to you so easily?"

"I have a way with animals," he said.

"Apparently so." She tossed him an easy grin as if she could sweet-talk her way out of all the trouble she'd become. "I must say, Tom McCain, you're a sight for sore eyes—and an answer to a prayer. You came just in time." Her grin deepened into a pretty smile, as if that could make everything all right.

To be honest, it did help a little. When he'd realized

Ned and Georgie had planned to take advantage of her, he'd wanted to tear them limb from limb.

But that didn't mean Tom was no longer upset that Katie had followed him. Nor that he'd forgotten another time when a woman and a snake had gotten a man into trouble, taking all of mankind with them.

"What'd you do?" he asked. "Sweet-talk Trapper into helping you?"

"I really didn't have to." She brushed the dust from the denim jeans. "It was as much Trapper's idea as mine. He seemed to agree that I should accompany you to see Mr. Graves."

Tom didn't doubt that. And while he would have preferred to haul Katie back to Hannah's house, he couldn't afford to spend the additional time it would take to rid himself of her. So that meant that he was saddled with her for at least the next three days—long enough to go to the Lazy G Ranch, take care of business and then ride back to Hannah's.

Tom blew out a sigh. This wasn't the least bit funny, and once it was all said and done, he'd find a way to get back at Trapper for his shenanigans.

"Mount up," he told her. "We'll talk about it while we ride."

"I promise not to be any trouble."

Tom clicked his tongue. "You'd be a bushel of trouble if you were sound asleep."

She stood tall again and placed one hand on her hip. Her chin lifted, exposing an ivory-skinned neck, where her pulse fluttered.

When he faced her, close enough to breathe in her lilac scent, close enough to touch, he couldn't help but run his knuckles along her cheek. As he did, her breath caught, though she didn't draw back. She didn't smile, either. She just watched him with eyes as big and wide as the sky.

For a moment he forgot why he was here, why he was angry at her for tagging along, for slowing his pace.

But as reality set in, he slowly shook his head and said, "Let's go. I've wasted enough time already."

As she turned to take a step toward the mare, her right leg gave out. He reached out and caught her before she fell.

"What's wrong?"

"I twisted my ankle when I fell. If you'll just help me to my horse, I'll be fine."

He knew she wasn't the type of woman to ask for help, even if she were in a real fix. In fact, any other woman would have screamed and cried when the horse threw her. And then again when those ruffians found her.

Just thinking about what might have happened to her turned his stomach inside out. Ned and Georgie didn't seem to have a single brain between them, but that didn't mean they wouldn't have hurt her, given the chance.

Of course, Tom had to give her credit for outsmarting them, but what would have happened if that rattler hadn't been in those weeds?

And what if Tom hadn't recognized Hannah's mare? What if he hadn't heard all the commotion and come riding fast to see what was going on?

Katie might insist that she was fine, but he knew better than to believe her. So he scooped her into his arms, intent upon assessing her injury.

"You don't need to carry me. A shoulder to lean on would have been sufficient."

"It's easier this way."

He was surprised at how little effort it took to hold her—and amazed at the light scent of lilac that laced the smell of trail dust and leather.

In spite of the rugged denim she wore, she felt small in his arms—and soft. Yet he wouldn't underestimate her. He knew that he held a powerful pack of woman. And that it would take a special kind of man to tangle with a spitfire like her on a daily basis.

Tom might be stuck with her over the next couple of days, but once they returned from Stillwater and he sent her back to Pleasant Valley, he'd be through with her, and she'd be another man's problem.

He carried her to a good-size boulder and set her down on it. Then he reached for her right boot and gave it a gentle tug. She grimaced until it slipped off her foot.

Her ankle was bruised and swollen, although he didn't think that it was broken.

"Can you get that boot back on?" he asked.

"Yes."

After she'd done so, he lifted her into his arms again and carried her to Gully Washer.

It was easier that way, he told himself. It was nicer, too. He enjoyed the feel of her in his arms, the way she clung to him as if she needed him, as if they'd entered a dream world where their many differences no longer mattered.

But that world didn't exist.

After helping her mount, he said, "Let's go. We're burning daylight."

Then he climbed onto his gelding as if nothing had happened, as if he'd never held her in his arms.

As if he'd never imagined there could ever be anything more between them.

* * *

When Tom finally called a halt to eat the midday meal, it was already so late in the afternoon that Katie thought she'd ridden as far as she could go without collapsing from exhaustion and falling off her horse.

The dust alone made her clothing feel pounds heavier than when she'd started out this morning, and her stomach had growled and rumbled itself into a knot.

She licked her parched lips. What she wouldn't give for a cool glass of well water, a bowl of Hannah's chicken stew and a warm bath, but she'd die before admitting her discomfort. After all, she'd promised not to be any trouble, and she'd meant it.

Tom swung down from his mount and then surveyed the area he'd chosen for them to rest and eat. "There's a stream where you can wash up. I'll take care of the horses."

As much as she wanted to stretch her legs, she wasn't sure if she could dismount on her own.

Fortunately, Tom was by her side before she could try or ask for help. When he reached for her, she was tempted to object and claim she could do it on her own, but she feared she'd collapse into a heap if she didn't accept his assistance.

His arms were strong, his stance sturdy. So she leaned into him until he swung her from the horse. Yet he still held on to her.

"Can you stand on your own?" he asked.

"I'll try."

As he released her and took a step back, her right leg wobbled. Before she knew it, he wrapped his arms around her and drew her close. As her cheek rested against his shoulder, his scent, a swirl of musk, leather and soap, sent her senses reeling.

As if knowing that he'd somehow added to her unbalance, his eyes searched hers, holding her in some kind of silent dance—or maybe it was a duel. She couldn't be sure which.

"I'm fine," she said. "My ankle feels better now. It's just a little stiff and sore."

When he loosened his embrace and allowed her to stand on her own, a weakness settled over her. A weakness from the long, hard ride, no doubt.

But before she could gather her wits, a soft rattling sounded to the right of her. She stifled a scream, reached for him and held on tight. "Oh, no. It's another rattlesnake."

"It's cicadas."

"What's that?"

"A kind of locust."

"Are you sure it's not a rattlesnake?"

"I'd be in a real fix if I didn't know the difference between the two."

As she tried to take a step, her right ankle nearly gave out on her again, and she grimaced.

"Does it hurt that badly?" A hint of compassion softened his voice and warmed his gaze.

"No, not really."

"I don't believe you."

"All right, it does, but I'm not one to complain."

He lifted his brow as though challenging her honesty.

"I'm *not*."

"Maybe not about pain, but you don't keep your complaints or objections to yourself. Not as a rule."

"I suppose you have a point."

A slow smile slid across his face. "That being agreed upon, I'm going to take you down to the stream that runs along here. I'll find a safe spot where you can rest. I think soaking your ankle will help relieve the pain. But the path may be a bit crooked and steep."

Then, in a move that was becoming all too familiar, he lifted her into his arms and carried her along a tree-lined path to the water's edge.

Katie held on to his shoulder with one hand and felt the corded muscles that lay hidden beneath his cotton shirt. At one time, she might have struggled with her vulnerability, but here, in the dappled sunlight with Tom McCain, she didn't feel the least bit helpless.

Why was that?

After he set her down on the sandy shoreline, he held her steady until she could balance herself—perhaps holding on a bit longer than necessary.

"Are you going to be all right alone?" he asked.

She nodded, not at all sure that she would be. Then she scanned the grassy brush that surrounded the creek. "You…uh…don't suppose there are any snakes around here, do you?"

"I'm afraid this is where they live, Katie."

She'd hoped to hold her reaction, but she feared her face had paled and her expression had given her away.

Thankfully, he seemed to take pity on her, because he said, "Just so you know, snakes don't attack. They only try to protect themselves. If you stay in the clearing, you should be safe."

Katie wanted to question him further, to insist that he stay nearby, just in case she needed help. But in her heart of hearts, she knew it was more than fear of snakes that had her wanting him to stay close.

The man held a dark and rugged appeal she was at a loss to explain, and she liked having him near.

But she couldn't very well admit to any of that, so she let him go, watching as he walked away and feeling more and more exposed with each step he took.

Chapter Seven

Tom watered the horses downstream, then he retrieved Katie's valise and returned to the spot where he'd left her to soak her ankle. He hoped her bag held everything she'd want or need. It was certainly bulky enough.

When he'd realized she'd been following him, he'd wanted to lash out at her for her rebellious nature, for her insistence upon going to Stillwater to meet Harrison Graves. He'd also wanted to throttle Trapper for setting up the fool travel plan.

But when Tom realized that Katie had been in danger and that she'd been injured, he'd softened to the point that he'd felt an overwhelming urge to protect her with his life. And then he'd wanted to lash out at himself.

What had he been thinking?

It must have been the scent of lilacs, the feel of her in his arms, the way she gazed at him as if he'd been some kind of hero, at least in her eyes.

For a moment, he'd even liked the thought of it.

How could he be the least bit tempted by a woman who'd surely be the death of him if he'd so much as consider her as a...

As a what?

A woman to court, to marry?

No, that was plum crazy, and he scoffed at the very idea.

When he neared the stream, his breath caught at the sight of her sitting on a rock. Even wearing boy's clothing, there was no mistaking her for anything but a woman through and through.

She'd rolled up her pant legs, and her bare feet hung in the cool water.

If he'd had all the time in the world, he might have remained in the shadows, watching her from several paces back. But he was determined to make it to the Lazy G before dark. And even if he hadn't had anything pressing to do, he wouldn't waste his time daydreaming about things that would never be.

"I brought your bag," he said. "I thought you might need it."

"Thank you."

He made his way toward the stream. "Does the cold water help?"

"Yes, my ankle feels much better now." She bit down on her lower lip, as if wanting to add something more but pondering the wisdom of it. She finally said, "I'm sorry for slowing your pace. I know you're in a hurry. I really didn't mean for this to happen."

A sharp retort would have come easy, but for some reason, he shrugged off his irritation. "I suppose we'll have to make the best of it."

At that point, he should have excused himself and left her alone, but he didn't. Instead, he studied the way she wiggled her toes in the water, the way she leaned forward, the way the sun highlighted the gold strands in her auburn locks.

She was an intriguing woman—not at all like the others he knew. She was pretty, to be sure. And as feisty as all get-out. Rebellious to a fault. She was also bright.

He really had to give her credit for outsmarting those ruffians who'd tried to take advantage of her. Another woman might have fallen apart at the seams, but she'd kept her composure.

Still, while he admired her wit, it was her outspoken nature he objected to.

"You must be a real challenge to the men in your life," he said.

She looked up and smiled. "That's true. My father valued education and taught me to read when I was very young. Once I mastered that, he taught me to debate. And I must admit, it frustrated him at times, but he appreciated a well-thought-out argument."

"I imagine you had some interesting conversations at the dinner table."

"We certainly did." Her smile drifted away. "But not everyone was as understanding. My teachers didn't like to be challenged. And the other children at school often avoided me for that reason. And for other reasons, as well. My childhood, while it seemed typical to me, was much different from the other girls."

"In what way?" he asked.

"I grew up with an imaginary mother instead of a real one—and a library of books instead of a playroom of dolls and toys."

Her candor surprised him.

"Children can be cruel," she added, "especially when they perceive another child to be different, which is why

I didn't put up with that kind of behavior in my class-room when I was a teacher."

Katie didn't have to tell Tom about how mean kids could be. At least the taunts she'd suffered hadn't led to fistfights, black eyes and bloody noses.

It was odd that they could be such opposites yet share some similarities. Of course, Katie could have saved her-self a lot of trouble by keeping her mouth shut. And he couldn't do anything about the color of his skin or the Comanche blood that ran through his veins.

"Do you think you can walk?" he asked her.

"Yes, I'm sure I can." She removed her feet from the water, then reached into her valise and pulled out a hand-kerchief. After drying her feet, she put her boots back on, taking extra care with the right one.

He made his way to the rock where she sat, then reached for her hand and helped her stand. Before he could turn away, she swayed on her feet.

He grabbed her wrist and slipped an arm around her waist to hold her steady. "I thought you said you were all right."

"I was," she said. "I *am*."

As her gaze locked on his, the tint of her eyes took him aback, and as he watched, the hue deepened, dark-ened.

Her hand held his forearm, the warmth of her touch flaring from her fingertips. In spite of his better judg-ment and his resolve to keep his distance, he felt him-self weaken.

Her lips, the color of wild strawberries, parted as if begging for a kiss.

He looked at her expression for disapproval, for a sign that he was about to overstep his boundaries, but as their gazes continued to hold firm, he was caught up in something too big to ignore.

He'd be sorry for this later, but he'd always been partial to strawberries.

As Tom leaned forward, as his lips met hers, Katie's heart skipped a beat. She probably should resist kissing him, but she was too taken by surprise, too swept up in the wonder of it all.

It started out sweet and innocent, like the time Orson Billings kissed her behind the mercantile when she'd been fifteen years old. But while that kiss had been a bit awkward but nice, this one was…oh, so much more.

The kiss deepened and, as she slipped her arms around him, she marveled at the scent of him, at the feel of his embrace, at the taste of his sweet kiss. Before she knew it, her knees nearly gave out, and she leaned into him for support.

The world tilted, and the sun spun round and round.

What was she thinking? What was she doing, kissing Tom McCain as if there were no tomorrow?

And there most certainly would be a tomorrow—in *Wyoming!*

She placed her hands on his chest, allowing them to linger just long enough to feel the steady beat of his heart pounding in time with hers. Then she pushed back and turned her head, pulling her lips from his and ending that mind-numbing kiss.

"I'm sorry," she said. "I don't know why I let you do that."

"You *let* me do that?" He chuckled.

Her cheeks warmed, and she knew they must be as red as new apples.

"You were every bit as willing as I was," he said. "And you liked it."

That was true. But she didn't dare admit it, so she let out a most unladylike huff. "No, not really."

"Oh, no? There's a telltale flush on your cheeks and throat, and your eyes have deepened to a lovely shade of liar blue."

Katie quickly glanced away, unwilling to allow his dark eyes to challenge hers any longer. She really wasn't lying.

All right, so she was, but she certainly didn't want Tom to know it. She started to walk away—and would have if he hadn't chosen that moment to chuckle again.

Childhood taunts in the schoolyard and the memory of all the snide male comments and laughter while she'd spoken on the dais in Pleasant Valley in support of women's suffrage hadn't prepared her for the sound of this particular man's ridicule. Without a conscious thought, her Irish temper flared, and she swung out her hand and slapped his cheek.

The sound, the sting, the jolt of her thoughtless reaction shocked her as much as it had him, because she froze in midmovement the moment it happened, wishing she could somehow take it all back—the kiss, the slap…

His laughter ceased, and he caught her wrist in an ironclad grip. "Don't ever strike me again." His dark eyes narrowed, and for a moment she witnessed a wounded look, a glimpse of something he usually kept locked deep inside.

"Then don't laugh at me," she said, her voice more a whisper of defense than a threat.

Without another word, he dropped her wrist, turned and walked away.

She wasn't sure what had just happened, but she sensed that they'd inadvertently shared an intimacy of sorts, a peek through cracks in the walls they'd both built around their hearts, allowing them each a glimpse inside the other.

A glimpse at something that went far beyond an earth-spinning kiss, a chuckle and a slap.

For once Tom's lack of conversation hadn't bothered Katie a bit. In fact, she considered it truly a blessing. She relished the time she had to sort through her reeling senses. If truth be told, her thoughts and feelings were all atumble.

He'd pointed out her lie, and he'd been right. She *had* wanted him to kiss her. And she'd liked it—a lot. She just hadn't been prepared to deal with the repercussions of it.

She still wasn't about to talk about the kiss, but after four hours on the trail with nary a word out of him, she'd grown tired of the silence.

"It's a lovely day," she said.

He merely gave a cursory scan of the horizon.

So much for an attempt to draw him into a conversation.

"Are we nearing Stillwater yet?" she asked.

No response.

Nevertheless, she asked, "How much farther do we have to go?"

This time, when he didn't reply, she lowered her voice and answered for him, deciding to carry on a conversation by herself. "Not much farther, Katie. It's been a long trip, hasn't it?"

"It certainly has," she said, returning to her own voice. "I'm just so grateful you were such a fine traveling companion. I don't know when I've ever had a more pleasant journey."

"Well, Katie," she answered, mocking him, "I must admit that I hate traveling alone. Thank you for joining me."

She cast a sideways glance, pleased to see the stubborn man had coked his head and caught her eye.

"You're not going *loco* on me, are you?" he asked.

She hadn't realized how much she'd missed his voice, especially with such a pleasant tone. *"Loco?"*

"That's Spanish for crazy."

She smiled. It wasn't her idea of a conversation, but it was a start. "I don't believe so, but how would one know for sure?"

"You probably wouldn't."

What did he mean by that? If she were crazy she wouldn't be aware of it? Or there wouldn't be any telltale difference in her behavior whether she was crazy or not?

She could have made an issue of his comment, but didn't. After six hours without any conversation at all, she was glad to have him talking again. And even happier to have that kiss behind them.

"How much farther do we need to go?" she asked, hoping this time to receive an answer.

"We've been on the outskirts of the Lazy G for the past hour, ever since we rode through that pass."

"The *outskirt*s of the Lazy G?" Katie looked over her shoulder and scanned the sage-dotted landscape for a sign of habitation. "How large is the ranch?"

"Fifty thousand acres, more or less. The Lazy G was once a Spanish Land Grant."

"That's impressive. Mr. Graves must be very wealthy."

"He made most of his money growing fields of cotton

and raising longhorn cattle for hides and tallow. Just before the war, he began crossbreeding his herd. The last few years he's been running cattle drives and making a second fortune selling beef."

Katie could scarcely imagine the size of the ranch or the money it would take to control and run it. Her curiosity of Sarah Jane's family mounted. "Tell me about the people we'll meet."

She wondered if her question would anger him or if it would elicit more silence, but he responded as though they'd gone back to that truce they'd formed earlier.

"There's not much to tell. Harrison Graves is as rich as they come, at least around here. He has land, property, money and respect."

Katie had surmised that much. "But you said he was ill."

"Dying."

"What about his wife? What happened to her?"

"She passed away from a fever after giving birth to his only child, a son named Robert. Harrison was too busy running cattle and building a fortune to remarry."

Katie could hardly believe her ears. Tom was not only talking to her, he was actually relaying information. She'd have to remember that all it took to have him finally open up was a kiss, a slap and six hours of guilt-laden silence.

"You mentioned that Sarah Jane's mother was his only heir. I assume she was Robert's daughter, and that Robert passed away, too."

"He died in a stampede while on a cattle drive when Caroline was six."

"And Robert's wife?"

For a moment Tom seemed to withdraw from the

conversation. About the time Katie wondered if he'd ever speak again, he said, "Robert's wife, Juliana, was a blonde and frail woman from New England. I heard she couldn't take the heat or the separation from society as she knew it, so she returned to the East, taking baby Caroline with her. She caught a fever and died about two years later."

Now it began to make sense. "So Juliana took Caroline back East, and that's why Harrison was looking for her?"

"No." Tom stared straight ahead, his back ramrod straight. "Caroline was barely a year old when her mother left Texas, but Harrison went after the baby and brought her back."

"Juliana gave up her child?"

Tom turned in the saddle, and his dark eyes locked on hers. "You're the suffragist and the daughter of an attorney. You know how the law works. The child belonged to her father, and Juliana had no right to her. Harrison merely went after his granddaughter and brought her home to Texas."

"After Juliana died?"

"No, before she got sick."

A knot formed in Katie's stomach. Had Juliana really died of a fever? Or of a broken heart? And what about the baby? Had Harrison just taken her away from her mother?

No wonder there had been a family rift. The cattleman must not have a loving, paternal heart.

"I realize I've never met Harrison Graves," Katie said, "but I can tell you right now, I don't think I'm going to like him."

Tom shrugged. "You wouldn't be the only person who doesn't."

"So what happened to Caroline? When did she leave the ranch?"

"When she was sixteen, she and her grandfather had a falling-out, and she ran off."

"What did they argue about?" When Tom didn't answer, she prodded him. "You don't know?"

"For the most part, it's speculation on my part."

Katie waited for him to explain. When he didn't, she asked, "Where was she last seen?"

"When she was sixteen, a friend of the family took her to Casa de Los Angelitos in Mexico."

"I'm not familiar with that place. Is it a town or village?"

"It's a home for women who get themselves into trouble. Their families take them there before their neighbors realize they're pregnant. Then they leave the unwanted babies behind at a Mexican orphanage."

"Caroline was pregnant?"

"Harrison had hoped she would return home with her reputation still intact. He sent Jeremiah Haney, his solicitor's son, to pick her up when her confinement was up, but she was gone before he got there."

"And Sarah Jane? She was the baby?"

"Yes. Caroline refused to give up her daughter and return to the ranch."

"I can't blame her for that. So when Harrison Graves learned he was dying, he hired you to find Caroline?"

"Yes, but he never mentioned a thing about finding the baby."

Katie thought about that for a moment, realizing that was good news for her. If the man wasn't interested in an illegitimate heir, then maybe he'd be happy to sign over guardianship to her. If so, her plan to take Sarah Jane—and Erin, if she was willing to go with them—to Wyoming would come to pass.

They continued to ride, with Katie still trying to sort through all Tom had told her.

"So how does Erin fit into all of this?" Katie asked.

"She and Caroline met at Casa de Los Angelitos. And they both left together."

"Did Erin have a baby, too?"

"The nuns told me that Erin's child, a boy, was stillborn."

They rode in silence for a while, although Katie's thoughts remained on Caroline and the baby she'd refused to give up.

Had she remembered losing her mother at a young age? Is that what had compelled her to rebel against her grandfather and to face public scorn?

Or had her child been conceived in love?

"Do you know anything about Sarah Jane's father?" Katie asked.

"Just that he was one of Harrison's ranch hands."

"What happened to him? Where is he?"

"He quit working at the Lazy G before Harrison found out about the pregnancy, which was lucky for him. Otherwise, Harrison might have killed him. At first I thought Caroline had gone looking for him, but I learned that he died while working on another spread about fifty miles from here."

So Sarah Jane was all alone—other than for Katie. And Erin, of course.

"Do you think Harrison Graves would sign over guardianship to me?" Katie asked.

Instead of an answer, Tom lifted his arm and pointed. "Do you see that hacienda on the hill?"

"You mean that large house? It looks like a small town."

"Wait until you see it up close." Tom urged his mount on. "Come on. You're going to have your chance to meet Harrison Graves face-to-face. That is, if he's still alive."

As Tom and Katie rode up the dusty drive to the Lazy G, an old man wearing a white shirt, faded black pants and leather sandals knelt near an ornate iron gate, pruning flowers in one of several terra-cotta pots.

When he spotted riders, he shielded his eyes from the sun with a gnarly hand. It took a moment for recognition to dawn, but the old man got to his feet to greet Tom.

"Abel," Tom said. *"Cómo está?"*

"Bien, Lone Wolf. And you?"

Surprised that the groundskeeper had called him by his Indian name, Tom shook off the urge to glance at Katie so he could gauge her reaction.

Not that it mattered, he supposed.

"I'm fine, thank you. But Señor Graves. How's he doing? Is he still…?"

"Alive? Yes, but he's getting worse—weaker, sicker each day. And he's wearing a path in the floor, waiting for you to return." Abel glanced at Katie and smiled.

"This is Miss Katie O'Malley, Abel. She came along with me because she'd like to meet Mr. Graves."

Abel bowed graciously. *"Mucho gusto, señorita."*

"I see you're no longer working with the cattle," Tom said.

"Last winter, when I became too crippled to ride, Señor Graves let me work in the yard."

Tom hadn't expected the rigid cattleman, whose parents had been killed by renegades, to be so accommodating to an old employee, especially one who was of mixed blood—Comanche and Mexican.

"I'll go inside and tell Señor Graves that you're here," Abel said. "Then I'll see to your horses."

"Thank you." Tom dismounted, then went to help Katie down. He waited to see if her ankle would give out on her. It didn't, and he noted only a slight limp.

As Katie scanned the courtyard, Tom watched Abel shuffle away, his worn leather sandals sliding along as he walked. It must be difficult to get old, especially for a man who'd once been a legend. Tom had only been a little boy when his father had told him tales of Abel's valor and skillful horsemanship.

"It's beautiful," Katie said, breaking into Tom's thoughts.

He followed her gaze to the flower-adorned adobe walls, the tiled floor of the courtyard, the water fountain gracing the patio.

"I've never seen the like," she added. "It's rustic, yet charming."

The double door to the hacienda swung open, and Randolph Haney strode onto the patio, his countenance displaying obvious displeasure as he raked his eyes over Katie.

"She's not Caroline Graves, McCain. You're a fool to think you could pass her off as such."

Even if Tom and Haney hadn't had a history that dated back to the time Tom was only a boy, he wouldn't have liked the pompous solicitor. But before he could enlighten him, Katie moved forward as if she were wearing a ball gown instead of a flannel shirt and a pair of denim jeans. "My name is Kathryn O'Malley, and I've come to have a word with you, Mr. Graves."

The gray-haired lawyer, his stance as formal and overbearing as before, crossed his arms and frowned. "I'm not Mr. Graves."

"He's Randolph Haney," Tom said, "attorney-at-law."

Katie lifted her chin in that defiant way Tom found amusing at times and annoying at others. "How do you do, Mr. Haney. And as I said, I'd like a word with Mr. Graves, if that's possible."

"I'm afraid he's resting and not taking callers."

"I'll wait," she said. "I've come a great distance to speak to him, and since I heard that time was of the essence, I didn't dare waste an extra day to rent a carriage and hire a driver."

Haney softened only slightly. "Perhaps I can be of service."

"Perhaps. But it's ultimately Mr. Graves I must speak to."

He studied her a moment. "You do look a bit worn. Would you like a refreshment? Water perhaps?"

"That would be most kind. Thank you."

Tom crossed his arms and watched propriety take charge. Of course, he still doubted that Haney was any happier to see Katie than he was to see him.

"And you?" Haney turned to Tom. "Why are you here? Do you have any news?"

"My business is with Harrison, not you."

"He'll ask me to listen to anything you have to say."

Tom shrugged a single shoulder. "Maybe so, but that'll be his decision."

A rap-rap-rap sounded at one of the windows at the side of the house. All eyes turned to see Harrison Graves tapping a cane against the glass. He nodded to Abel, who stood at his side, and the gardener opened the window.

"Come inside," Harrison said.

Tom studied Haney out of the corner of his eye. The austere solicitor stepped back, hands to his side, lips tightening, and a muscle near his eye twitched as he allowed Tom and Katie to enter the house before him.

Katie's heart tightened as she stepped onto the Spanish-tiled entry of the hacienda and waited for Harrison Graves. Moments later, aided by a gold-handled cane, the white-haired gentleman entered the room.

She wasn't sure what she'd been expecting—someone sickly, of course, but powerful. And while both seemed to be true, the wealthy cattleman appeared to be broken, as well, although she couldn't say how.

Perhaps it was his rumpled appearance, and the fact that he'd hurried to meet them—or rather, Tom.

His thinning white hair stood on end, and in spite of having guests, he hadn't taken the time to comb it.

"Come with me," he said. Then he turned and headed down the hall, his pace slow and slightly unsteady. He led them into a sitting room, its walls white plaster, its ceiling open-beamed.

"Have you found Caroline?" he asked, his voice unable to mask a grandfather's hope.

"I think so." Tom nodded toward Mr. Haney. "But if you don't mind, I'd like to talk to you in private."

The gray-haired solicitor stepped forward. "That's not necessary, Harrison. Caroline was like a daughter to me. I'd like to hear what the bounty hunter has to say."

Was like a daughter? Katie stiffened. Did he already know she was dead?

"Mr. Graves," Tom said, "I won't discuss anything unless we're alone."

"Very well."

As Tom stepped behind the dying cattleman, Katie proceeded to follow, but Tom stopped abruptly and turned to her. "I said alone."

"But I—"

"You can discuss anything you'd like with Mr. Graves at another time. This conversation is private."

Katie watched as the two men, one old and dying, the other young and vibrant, walked across the Spanish-tiled floor and into the hall.

Moments later, they entered another room. When the door closed, she turned to the well-dressed lawyer, wondering if the exclusion bothered him more than it had her. A scowl on his face validated her suspicion.

With his lips pressed tightly together, the elderly gentleman made a sweeping assessment of her clothing, his cool gray eyes clearly finding her lacking.

"Why are you traveling with that breed?" he asked.

The jab of his question surprised her, irritated her. "I have something to discuss with Mr. Graves and needed an escort."

His narrowed eyes indicated his disapproval of both her quest and her appearance.

Undaunted in the least, Katie crossed her arms. "My father, God rest his soul, was an attorney in St. Louis before his passing, and I used to help him prepare for his trials. I'm well versed in the law, and while I might not appear to be much more than a backwards ragamuffin, I assure you that's not the case, Mr. Haney."

"You must have traveled a great distance."

She decided she'd given him enough information.

"So what do you think of Texas?" he asked, mellowing and offering her a bit of decorum.

But as far as she was concerned, it had come too late. He'd made assumptions based upon her appearance and her traveling companion.

"I'm afraid Texas—or rather Texans—aren't quite what I'd expected," she said.

Randolph glanced at the nail beds of his long, tapered fingers. "What did you expect?"

"That Texans had manners, and as far as some of the attorneys I've met, I've come to find that I was misinformed."

"Lemonade?" a woman asked from the doorway, her voice tinged with a Spanish accent, her arms holding a tray laden with glasses and a pitcher.

"Yes, please," Katie told the woman. "Thank you."

Then Katie turned to the attorney. "Manners are usually learned as a child, but perhaps, if you try very hard to observe those around you, you'll catch on."

"Touché, Miss O'Malley." Randolph Haney began to smile, then chuckled. "I apologize for being rude."

"Apology accepted," Katie said, although her heart hadn't quite meant it.

"Perhaps we Texans have more of a distrust of Indians than you're accustomed to. My brother lost his life in a massacre, and I've learned to be leery."

"Tom McCain has been a perfect gentleman," Katie said.

And while she'd had several occasions to be angry at the bounty hunter who'd seemed invincible on the trail, she felt the overwhelming urge to defend and protect him now.

Chapter Eight

Tom took a seat across the broad mahogany desk from Harrison Graves. The old man, who'd grown frailer in the past couple of months, grimaced as he settled into his cushioned chair.

"Did you find Caroline?" he asked.

"She's dead, sir."

Harrison's shoulders slumped, and the furrow in his craggy brow deepened. "Are you sure?"

"I'm afraid so."

"I had so much to…" He placed his bent elbows on the desk, then buried his face in his hands. "Oh, Lord. What'll I do now?"

Tom should have felt some sense of satisfaction at seeing the cattleman suffer. After all, if Harrison Graves had shown some compassion for a dying Comanche woman and her frightened son…

Yet the words Hannah had taught him, the scripture she'd shared with him over the years, came to mind instead. *And be ye kind one to another, tenderhearted, forgiving one another, even as God for Christ's sake hath forgiven you.*

"Are you all right?" Tom asked.

Harrison looked up, his eyes filled with tears. "I…I had so much to say to her. I wanted to tell her that I loved her, that I was sorry for being so stubborn. That I forgave her for the things she said to me when she left. I know she didn't mean them. She was just angry. And she had every right to be."

"I suppose you'll have to be content to tell God," Tom said. "It's His forgiveness that matters most."

"I have, although I must admit that I feel pretty unworthy of His forgiveness."

The man's humility took Tom aback.

"At one time, I was the master of my own universe. And now?" Harrison lifted a withered arm and slowly lowered it. "I'm broken and dying."

"In truth," Tom said, "we're all broken and dying."

Harrison seemed to ponder that a moment, then said, "The Reverend Mitchell has been coming out to the ranch lately. And he said as much. If he'd told me that five years ago, I would have run him off. Back then, I thought I was invincible, but you're right. I was broken and dying all along and just hadn't known it."

Tom studied the man a moment. Had he experienced a physical realization or a spiritual reckoning?

Either way, he supposed he deserved to know about Sarah Jane—if Jeremiah Haney, Randolph's son, hadn't told him already.

"Caroline had a daughter," Tom said, "but I suspect you know that."

Harrison stiffened, then raised his gray head. "I heard it was a boy. And that it died at birth."

If Sarah Jane hadn't favored her mother more than Erin, Tom might have questioned what he'd been told, too. He glanced at the large portrait that hung on the south wall of Harrison's study, at the lovely young blonde wearing a pale blue gown. Then he returned his gaze to Harrison.

"The child is a girl, and I've see her." Tom didn't mention her resemblance to Caroline as a child. Not when Harrison thought Tom's first and only introduction to Caroline had been the portrait he'd seen in this office just months ago.

"As much as I'd like to believe you," the cattleman said, "Jeremiah Haney, my solicitor's son, went to Casa de Los Angelitos to bring Caroline home six years ago. And the nuns told him Caroline's baby, a boy, had died at birth. They also told him that she'd left with another woman, a harlot who'd given birth to a girl. So you can understand my doubt."

Had one of the nuns been confused and given Haney's son details about Erin's baby, the one that had been still-born?

Tom didn't know Jeremiah, but he still sported a scar he'd received from the tip of the elder Haney's boot, a wound he'd received when his head had scarcely reached the top of the man's gold belt buckle.

"I'm not calling Jeremiah a liar," Tom said, "but you hired me to do a job, and I took my assignment seriously. While I was at Casa de Los Angelitos, I asked to see the baptismal records. And I assure you, Caroline Graves gave birth to a daughter who was born alive."

"Do you know where the child is now?" Harrison asked.

"Yes, I do."

"Then bring her back here. Let me see her for myself."

Tom couldn't bring Sarah Jane back. Not yet. He had to stall for time—time Harrison Graves might not have.

Should he explain why? Tell this grieving old man that someone had tried to murder the child's guardian? And that Tom also found her mother's untimely death a little suspicious?

He could, but he had nothing on which to base those suspicions, and something told him Harrison Graves wouldn't settle for a gut feeling.

Of course, bringing Sarah Jane to the Lazy G just might flush out the murderer—if Tom's suspicions had any merit. But that might also put her in jeopardy.

"If I bring the child here," Tom said, "and if you do see a resemblance to Caroline, what will happen then?"

"She'll become a very wealthy young lady. But I'll want proof that she's my great-granddaughter, and I'm not sure you can provide that."

Assuming Tom had both the time to get her here and that Harrison would accept her resemblance as proof, then what? After Harrison passed, who would take care of Sarah Jane?

If Tom could trust his gut—and he'd learned to do that years ago—Harrison Graves would undoubtedly leave custody of his great-granddaughter, as well as his holdings, to his old friend and solicitor. And while Sarah Jane deserved to inherit what should have gone to her mother, she didn't deserve to be raised by a man like Randolph Haney.

So how did Tom go about insuring that she receive all that was rightfully hers without falling prey to Haney's influence?

Harrison lowered his head again.

Years ago, Tom might have felt vindicated to see Harrison get what he deserved, to see him brought low by grief, as well as disease, but he didn't find any pleasure in knowing the old man would never receive Caroline's forgiveness—nor grant her his.

When Harrison looked up, his eyes red rimmed and filled with tears, he said, "I need some time to be alone. Will you ask Maria, my housekeeper, to come in? She can show you to a room. I'll talk more to you about this later."

"I'll do that. I've also brought along a woman who'd like to speak to you when you're feeling up to it."

"I'm afraid that will have to wait, as well. Other than having a moment with Maria, I don't want to talk to anyone else today. I just want to be left alone."

"I'll let Miss O'Malley know. And I'll send in Maria." Tom got to his feet. After softly closing the door to the man's study, he made his way down the hall and entered the sitting room, where he found an audience awaiting his return—the hopeful schoolmarm, the angry solicitor, the weary gardener and the worried housekeeper. They each watched him, waiting for him to speak.

Maria, who'd worked for Harrison as long as Tom could remember, had been the only woman in Caroline's life, as far as Tom knew. Her luminous brown eyes begged for news, but Tom wouldn't be the one to tell her. That was up to Harrison.

"Mr. Graves would like to see you," Tom told her.

When Tom shared the cattleman's request, Maria reached for a glass of lemonade and carried it down the hall.

Haney stood and grasped the lapels of his gray jacket with each hand. "So tell me. Did you find Caroline?"

Tom swiped a strand of hair from his brow, his thumb

grazing the narrow ridge of the scar he'd received from Haney's boot. "Mr. Graves will have to give you those details."

"I don't know why you're being so secretive. Harrison tells me everything."

"That's his choice, Mr. Haney. But I don't think he's going to tell you anything this afternoon. He asked to be left alone."

Katie stood. "When can I talk to him?"

"Later. Maybe tomorrow."

Maria returned to the sitting room, her face drawn, her eyes filled with tears. She managed a weak smile. "Señor Graves would like me to show you to a room, Señorita. I'll have one of the stable boys bring in a tub of warm water."

"Thank you," Katie said.

The housekeeper turned to Tom. "I'll be back to show you to your room, Mr. McCain."

"Don't worry about me," Tom said. "I'll bunk with Abel."

"All right, if that's what you'd rather do." Maria turned to Katie. "Please come with me."

Katie followed the housekeeper out of the sitting room and down a narrow hall.

"Señor Graves said that Señor McCain believes Caroline died," Maria said.

"From what I was told, she fell down a flight of stairs."

"She was very light on her feet," Maria said. "Her grandfather insisted that she be a lady, but she was more comfortable riding with the vaqueros. I always feared that she might have an accident while on horseback—like her father."

"I wish I could have met her," Katie said. "I'm sure I would have liked her."

"She was a wonderful young woman, so full of life. I can hardly believe she's gone. This house was never the same after she left." Maria's long braid swished along her back as she led the way down the hall. "Poor Señor Graves. All he thought about, all he prayed about, was for Caroline to return."

Katie continued to follow Maria until she stopped before a doorway.

Maria turned to Katie and attempted a smile. "This is Señorita Caroline's room. You may sleep here. The sheets are fresh. Señor Graves had wanted it ready for her."

"Perhaps he'd feel better if I slept elsewhere."

Maria opened the door anyway. "It is best that you stay in here. He should not spend so much time alone in her room. With a guest in here, he will have to stay away."

"If Mr. Graves feels the least bit uncomfortable with me staying in this room, I'd prefer to sleep elsewhere." She just hoped that "elsewhere" wouldn't be in the bunkhouse with Abel and Tom.

"I have worked for Señor Graves for more than thirty years," Maria said. "Believe me. He doesn't come in here to spend time with her memory. He comes to pay penance with his guilt. And he's already paid plenty. It's good that he has a reason to stay away."

Katie wasn't so sure about that, but when Maria stepped into the large airy room, she followed.

Caroline's bedroom had the same brown-tiled floor,

white plaster walls and rough-beamed ceiling as the rest
of the hacienda, but yards of lace and flounce made the
setting decidedly feminine.

"Señorita Caroline didn't spend much time indoors."
Maria gazed at the lace curtains. "But when she did, she
liked pretty things."

"It's lovely." As Katie took in her surroundings, a
small, wood-framed portrait on the wall near the window caught her eye. It was the painted image of a woman
holding an infant.

Katie stepped closer, drawn to the willowy beauty
who wore a faint smile.

"Who is this woman?" Katie asked.

"Señora Juliana." Maria smiled wistfully. "Caroline
was a pretty baby, no?"

"No," Katie said. "I mean, yes. She's precious, but
I wasn't talking about the baby. I was looking at the
mother. She's hauntingly beautiful."

"Her unhappiness shows."

It did at that. Katie tried to spot a family resemblance,
but couldn't say that she did. And the fair-haired baby,
plump and sweet, could have grown up to be any blonde
girl.

"I don't suppose you have a photograph of Caroline
when she was a little older?" Katie asked the matronly
woman.

"Yes, I do." Maria strode to the bureau where a brass-
framed photograph rested upon a crocheted doily. She
gazed wistfully upon the likeness prior to handing it
to Katie.

A girl slightly older than Sarah Jane stood beside a
potted fern and a wicker chair. Dressed in white lace,

she held a porcelain doll in one hand and a flower in the other.

Katie studied the picture, praying she wouldn't spot a resemblance to the child she loved.

And dying a little on the inside when she did.

After he'd made sure the horses had been properly cared for, Tom went in search of Abel and found him dipping water from the well. The old gardener had been around for years, once riding the range, herding the stubborn longhorn and, later, managing fields of hay and cotton.

The old man looked up and brushed a dribble of water from his tanned, weathered chin. "I'm glad you came back."

"I said that I would." Tom scanned the courtyard. Abel had done wonders as a gardener. Red blossoms climbed a wooden trellis against the adobe wall. Plants, lush and green, hung from wrought-iron baskets throughout the patio. Colorful shocks of flowers grew abundantly in large clay pots.

Age might have reduced the old man's abilities while riding herd, but not his determination to see a job well done.

Abel crossed his thin arms, his wise old eyes crinkling. "There are some who hoped you would not return."

"That doesn't surprise me. I've never been welcome here."

"Other men would have stayed away."

"I'm not other men."

"No, you're more of a man than most. Your father would have been proud."

Tom didn't appreciate Abel's mention of his father. Not here. Not now.

"You don't favor him in looks," Abel said, not letting the subject die. "You're darker, taller. You also carry distrust in your heart. Your father wasn't so hard."

"He didn't have to be."

"No, but you always had a stubborn streak, like a wild horse unwilling to be broken. I'll never forget the day you tried to fight Haney." Abel chuckled and stroked his chin. "The man didn't expect a child to challenge him."

"He hurt my mother. I'm not one to forget cruelty to a woman."

"I can understand your anger at Señor Haney, as well as your sense of duty to Señor Graves."

"I don't owe loyalty to anyone. At least, not to anyone in Stillwater."

"Then you have come back for the reward?"

"I'm not after the money."

"Then what do you want?"

Tom's connection to the Lazy G had been a deep, dark secret even before his parents had died, leaving him orphaned and a thorn in the backside of Texas society.

"Respect maybe?" Abel asked.

That went without saying, but it was even more than that. Tom owed it to Caroline. On those rare occasions when they'd been allowed to play together, they'd formed a bond, a friendship. And if things had been different...

Abel studied Tom as though he knew what he was thinking, what he was feeling. Maybe he did.

Of all the people on the Lazy G, Abel was probably the one person Tom could trust. But he wasn't going to talk about it. And his lack of response didn't go unnoticed—or unacknowledged. And so that line of questioning was dropped.

"Did you find Caroline?" Abel asked.

"She died about six months ago."

The old man frowned. "Are you sure?"

"Yeah. I'm sure." He pondered whether he should mention Sarah Jane but held his tongue. "Caroline fell down a flight of stairs and broke her neck. She's buried in a town called Taylorsville."

Abel grimaced. "Does Señor Graves know?"

"I just told him."

"How is he taking it?"

"I'm not sure." Tom still wasn't convinced that Harrison was truly sorry, although he appeared grief stricken. Or was it more guilt and fear of meeting his maker?

"Your father would be proud of you," Abel said again.

"That's not why I'm here. And I'd appreciate it if you'd keep those thoughts to yourself."

"I've kept my mouth closed for more than twenty-five years and won't let my tongue run away from me now." Abel's brown eyes glistened, and a slow smile eased the harsh lines on his tired face. "Who's the woman you brought with you?"

"Her name is Katie O'Malley."

"Is she yours?"

His? The sharp-tongued woman with fiery hair and expressive blue eyes? For a fleeting moment he had a vision of her standing at his side, felt her reach for his hand, thread her fingers through his. But he shook off the image and scoffed. "No, she's not my woman."

"That's too bad. *Ella esta muy bonita.*"

Tom snorted. "There's more to a woman than her

beauty. Katie O'Malley wouldn't be happy unless she had a man on his knees and at her beck and call."

Abel laughed. "I might be old now, but there was a time I would have liked waiting on a pretty lady hand and foot."

"Not me. Once she started ordering me around, I'd send her on her way as soon as I could be rid of her." And that's exactly what Tom intended to do, once he returned with her to Hannah's. In fact, he might even offer someone a good week's pay just to drive her back to Pleasant Valley.

"She looks like the kind of woman a man ought to keep for himself," Abel said.

"Then *you* keep her," Tom said.

When Abel laughed as if he'd been let in on a secret Tom had yet to learn, Tom shook his head and strode away from the house, eager to put some distance between him and Abel.

And eager to squelch any thought of Katie O'Malley as anything other than a pain in his backside.

As the ornamental clock on the mantel struck ten, which was well past Randolph Haney's usual bedtime, Jeremiah Haney sat in his father's study and stretched out his long legs.

He didn't know why this conference couldn't have waited until morning, but he'd come when his father had summoned him—as he always did.

When he'd arrived, he'd found his father pacing like a cornered bobcat. His suit, usually neat and pressed, appeared to have been slept in.

"I've never seen you like this," Jeremiah said. "What's wrong?"

Randolph, his eyes bloodshot, stopped his pacing long enough to ask, "What do you think McCain told Harrison?"

Jeremiah reached for a cigar from the silver case that sat upon his father's desk and chose his words carefully. "I don't know what that half-breed told him. Maybe he's just trying to get into the man's good graces."

"For financial gain?" Randolph shook his head. "Not likely. Even in his befuddled mental state, Harrison wouldn't give a wooden nickel to a man like McCain. There's too much Indian running in his veins."

Jeremiah scoffed. "Who knows what a dying man would do? Harrison once rode the range like a king. Now he sits and mourns a woman who doesn't want to be found."

"Perhaps you're right. Harrison did, after all, cast Caroline out without a backward glance. And you've gone in search of her time and again—to no avail. And she certainly hasn't made any attempts to contact him."

None that Harrison knew about, anyway. Jeremiah studied the Cuban cigar he held in his hand, then reached for a match and leaned back in the brown tufted leather chair. "As long as Harrison doesn't change his will, his waning emotional state shouldn't bother us in the least."

"You're right, son. I wrote the will, and I'm not about to let Harrison talk me into changing it. Besides, Caroline is the sole heir, and if she insists upon staying away, as executor I have full control."

Jeremiah bit off the tip of the cigar and struck the match. "For what it's worth, I may have picked up her trail on my last search in a place called Taylorsville. I don't know for sure, but I think she may have suffered an unfortunate accident right before I arrived."

"What do you mean, you might have picked up her trail?"

"I was just piecing together some rumors. And if it was her, she was going by another name." Jeremiah lit the cigar, drawing on the end until the first wisps of sweet tobacco entered his mouth and filled his lungs. "Why do *you* suspect she's dead?"

"Caroline was always headstrong and impulsive, so I wasn't surprised that she ran off. But disappearing like a trail of smoke in the wind?" Randolph crossed his arms, resting them against the red silk vest that covered his distended belly. "She would have come home by now."

"If she's dead, then the only one left to inherit is you," Jeremiah said. *And, in due time, me.*

Randolph stood and walked toward the oak filing cabinet that held a cut crystal decanter of his favorite brandy. "The half-breed worries me, though."

Jeremiah found McCain a bit worrisome, too, although he kept that concern to himself. "So what do you want to do about him?"

"Nothing, but I want to know what he told Harrison. Or at least, what Harrison's thoughts are." Randolph poured two glasses, then handed one to Jeremiah. "And Harrison refused to talk to me until tomorrow, which is highly unusual. And *that* bothers me."

Jeremiah swirled the liquid in his glass. He'd prefer to savor his cigar rather than have a drink, especially when his father had clearly imbibed more than a fair amount already.

"There's a woman traveling with him," Randolph said. "Maybe she'll talk. Her name is Katie O'Malley."

"Why are you telling me this?" Jeremiah asked.

"I'm going to introduce the two of you. I want you

to do whatever you must do in order to find out what that breed knows."

"That shouldn't be a problem. I've always been able to charm the ladies."

Randolph clucked his tongue. "Don't remind me. Your charm nearly caused your father-in-law to disinherit you two years ago."

"My wife doesn't see to my needs."

"She has a wealthy father. That should fulfill a few of your needs."

"It does." Jeremiah inhaled deeply, then blew a large smoke ring. He watched it curl and twist above his head.

His father didn't need to worry about him. He'd had a rather indiscriminate beginning, but he'd learned to be discreet. And careful.

"So how would you like me to proceed with Miss O'Malley?" Jeremiah asked.

"First of all, we need to find out whether Caroline is alive or dead. Then we need to learn whether there's a child that may hold any claim to the estate. Surely you've thought about that."

Oh, Jeremiah had thought about it, all right. "I'll tell you what. The Cattleman's Ball is tomorrow night. Make sure Miss O'Malley is invited. I'll sweep her off her feet and find out all we need to know."

"It's not necessary for you to charm the pantaloons off her," Randolph said. "Just get her to talk."

"I'll have her talking her pretty head off before you can blink an eye." Jeremiah chuckled.

And if her pantaloons slipped off in the meantime? Then so be it.

Chapter Nine

Moonlight filtered through the lace curtains and danced upon the crisp white sheets, but Katie found sleep elusive.

She kicked the covers aside and climbed from bed. The cool tile floor chilled her bare feet. Had she been a guest in anyone else's home, she might have slipped into the study to find a book to read, something to lull her active mind to rest. But she didn't feel completely welcome at the Lazy G, so wandering through the house at this late hour wouldn't be polite or acceptable.

Instead, she strode toward the window, placed a palm against the rough-grained frame and looked out into the starry Texas sky. There was something mournful yet vital about this land, and she thought about the many people who had fought and died to hold on to it.

Outside, a shadowy figure moved, sending her heart thumping and her pulse racing—until she recognized him. Tall, broad shouldered. That solitary stance.

Tom McCain.

Without a conscious thought, she decided to join him—just for a moment—so she could talk to him about

Mr. Graves. She wanted to get an idea about what the man's decision would be when she broached him about her desire to adopt Sarah Jane.

She slipped into a robe Maria had set out for her, a garment that had once belonged to Caroline, and left the room, tiptoeing softly down the hall. In her haste, she neglected to look for slippers, but she continued anyway. If she took time to search for something to cover her feet, he might not be there any longer.

She saw him clearly in the moonlight. Never had she seen a full moon so large, so silvery.

Nor had she seen a man who seemed so alone.

Without shoes, her footsteps hardly sounded. She wondered if she would surprise him, but she shouldn't have considered it. The man turned sharply, as if he'd had the hearing of a wolf—a lone wolf, like the name Abel had called him when they'd arrived.

The name seemed to suit him.

In spite of her efforts to be quiet, he turned before she'd gotten within ten feet of him.

"What are you doing out here?" he asked.

Why did he have to sound so gruff? So threatening?

"I couldn't sleep, and when I saw you outside, I thought you might like some company."

Now who was she trying to fool? He'd never given her reason to believe he'd enjoyed having her company before.

"You shouldn't be outdoors," he said. "It isn't safe."

"Even with you?"

"Especially with me."

She fingered the lace-trimmed lapel of her robe.

"See what I mean?" he nodded at her hand. "I scare you."

She released her lapel and dropped her hand to her side. Then she lifted her chin and stood as tall as she could in her bare feet. "You most certainly do not. You'd never hurt me."

"Wouldn't I? Don't be so sure." He stepped forward in a move that ought to give her a start, then cupped her cheek in a large callused hand with a tenderness that surprised her. "I could tarnish your reputation if anyone saw me touch you."

Her breath caught, but she didn't step back.

His hand moved slightly, his fingers reaching into her hair, combing the strands. She reached for his wrist to pull his hand away, or so she thought. Instead, she found herself holding his hand in place.

"Go into the house," he said.

"All right." Yet she didn't move away. Something beyond her control rooted her in place.

He smelled of leather and soap, and his breath, which blew softly against her skin, held a hint of peppermint. "Go into the house before I forget myself."

"And kiss me again?"

"Yes, but this time, I don't want to get a slap for my effort."

"I didn't slap you for kissing me," she said. "I slapped you for laughing at me afterward."

In the moonlight, she watched him search her face. Had he realized she was inviting him to kiss her again?

That's not why she'd come out here, but if truth be told, she wouldn't mind sharing another embrace, another kiss.

"I promise not to slap you this time," she said softly. Then she reached up, slipped her hands behind his neck and drew his mouth to hers.

His lips were soft, warm, and as they moved against hers, the kiss deepened. She leaned into him, her arms holding him tighter.

She didn't dare open her eyes, but if she did, she imagined the stars would be spinning overhead. Her heart certainly was.

Before her conscience had a chance to speak up, Tom pulled away, breaking the kiss and putting the starry night back to rights again.

"Go inside," he said, his voice a bit huskier than she'd remembered. *"Now."*

"But—"

"But nothing. Being alone with me, especially here, isn't good. And it isn't right. You need to go back into the house. You've had your last kiss from me."

Then he turned and walked away. As his boot steps faded into the night, she pressed her fingers against her lips.

At the very thought that he might never hold her again, that she might never feel his lips on hers, a nagging sense of loss shuddered through her.

What was wrong with her? She couldn't afford to let anyone have that much power over her. Shaking off the crazy effect, she turned and padded back to the house.

Once inside Caroline's bedroom, she slipped off her robe and tossed it over the upholstered chair near the window. She told herself to forget Tom, to be glad he'd walked away, that he'd tried to talk some sense into her.

He'd been right. Kissing him out in the open, where anyone could see, wasn't proper. And in her nightgown and bare feet, of all things. Why, her da would be rolling over in his grave if he could see her unladylike behavior.

Still, against better judgment, she drew back the cur-

tains and peered outside. Had Tom retired for the evening? Or had he remained outdoors, to commune with
the moon and stars?

She spotted him near the fountain, where he continued to stand alone—a haunting figure who called
to her heart.

Her heart?

No, that couldn't be. She knew herself too well. If she
ever weakened to the point of considering courtship or
marriage, she would choose another man, an intellectual, a moral equal. Someone who'd value a bright and
capable wife.

Marriage to a man like Tom McCain would be just
plain awful. She could envision them living in a sod
house on the prairie, where she'd have to sweep dirt
floors, wash laundry in a dirty creek, slop pigs and milk
a goat. Why, she'd have to work herself to an early grave,
no doubt.

Even if they were to have a home like Hannah's, she
could still see him issuing orders and placing demands
on her. Why, there'd never be a peaceful moment between the two. She'd have to fight for every ounce of
respect she could get.

As she climbed into Caroline's soft, goose-down bed,
she pulled the linen sheet to her chin and sighed. In
spite of her best intentions to forget the man and the effect he had on her, she couldn't seem to put that knee-
weakening, mind-spinning kiss out of her mind.

What kind of woman was she?

A brazen hussy, no doubt.

When he'd gazed into her eyes, she'd wanted him to
kiss her more than anything. So she'd gone so far as to
stroke his cheek, to bring his mouth to hers.

Could another man's kiss move her that much?

She certainly hoped so. Because if it couldn't, she'd be hard-pressed to ever forget Tom McCain.

And then where would she be?

Katie slept much better than she might have guessed she would in a strange bed, but she'd dreamed of Tom McCain all night long and woke with her arms wrapped around her pillow.

After freshening herself, she donned one of the dresses she'd packed, a light yellow-and-white floral print. Then she took a quick glance in the mirror to make sure she looked presentable, if not a bit wrinkled no matter how carefully she'd packed the frock in her valise.

As she made her way out of the bedroom, the aroma of fresh-brewed coffee drew her to the kitchen. She expected to find Maria bustling about, preparing breakfast. What she hadn't expected was to see Maria gone and Randolph Haney seated at the head of a long, rectangular table.

He stood and bowed his gray head in greeting. "Good day, Miss O'Malley."

"Good morning. You're here early. Or did you stay the night?"

Randolph laughed as though he found her witty. "No, but I do spend a lot of time here. Harrison is my friend, and I know he would be supportive of me in my last days."

The image of a vulture wearing a suit and tie came to mind as Katie scanned the kitchen. "Where's Maria?"

"She took breakfast to Harrison." Randolph got to his feet, strode toward Katie and took her hand with his. "I'd like to apologize for my rudeness yesterday. It was uncalled-for."

He was right, of course. And perhaps she'd been too hard on him, as well. She didn't appreciate his distrust of Tom merely because his mother had been an Indian, but she really couldn't fault the lawyer for trying to protect his old friend and client from being taken advantage of by strangers. Besides, it wouldn't do to upset the man who might ultimately have some say over where Sarah Jane might live.

"I accept your apology. We were all on edge yesterday, Mr. Haney."

He smiled broadly and pulled out a chair, the legs scraping across the tile floor. "Call me Randolph, and please sit down."

"Thank you." Katie withdrew her hand from his, then took a seat.

"I don't know how long you intend to stay, but the Cattleman's Ball is tonight. It's a yearly event—and more like a community dance than a formal cotillion—but I'd like you to go with my son and me. I think you'd enjoy it."

Katie wasn't sure that she would, but it wouldn't hurt to get to know the people in Stillwater. "I'll give it some thought, although I really don't have anything suitable to wear."

"My dear, a pretty woman like you would look lovely in a grain sack."

Katie tried not to roll her eyes. She wasn't susceptible to flattery and didn't appreciate his attempt. Still it was an olive branch, she supposed, so she accepted it and thanked him.

Moments later, Maria swept into the room, her colorful skirts skimming the floor. "*Buenos días,* Señorita O'Malley. Did you sleep well?"

"Yes, thank you." Katie couldn't help thinking of the man and the kiss she'd dreamed about and glanced out the large kitchen window.

"If you're looking for Señor McCain," Maria said, "he and Abel were up early this morning, but I don't think they left the yard."

"I wasn't looking for him," she lied.

Maria poured a cup of coffee, then handed it to Katie. "Can I fix you some breakfast?"

"Yes, please. That would be nice."

"I'd like fried eggs and ham," Randolph said. "And make sure the yolks are runny this time. You know I don't like them overcooked."

A shadow moved outside, and Katie craned her neck. As she suspected, Tom and Abel were in the yard.

"Excuse me," she said. "I'll be back in a few minutes."

"Where are you going?" Randolph asked.

"For a walk."

His forehead furrowed, but she reached for the brass doorknob and continued outside, her skirts rustling with each step. She'd intended to speak to Tom about Mr. Graves last night, but the conversation…well, needless to say, it had taken an unexpected turn and had ended before she'd had a chance to steer it back on course.

As she made her way to the place she'd seen Tom, memories of the kiss dogged her, but she shook them off. She had a perfectly good reason to come out here bright and early this morning. And fawning after Tom McCain wasn't it.

Baritone whispers stilled when she neared the fountain where Abel and Tom stood.

Tom wore denim jeans today and a white shirt unbuttoned at the collar. He didn't wear a hat, and the sun glistened on the black strands of his hair.

Both men turned at her approach.

"I'd like to speak to Mr. Graves as soon as possible," she said.

Tom crossed his arms. "What's your hurry?"

She sighed, then glanced at Abel, unsure of whether she should speak in front of the gardener.

"Abel knows how to hold his tongue," Tom said.

"All right then," Katie said. "I think Sarah Jane is his great-granddaughter. And when he sees her, he's going to believe it, too."

"I agree," Tom said.

"Does that mean you're going to bring her here?"

"Not until I'm sure she'll live to see her seventh birthday."

Katie's stomach clenched. "If you don't think she'll be safe, then you shouldn't bring her back here at all."

"That's still left to be seen."

"What are you waiting for?" she asked.

"There's a man I want to talk to."

"Who?"

Tom paused, as if he wasn't sure if he trusted her with the information. "Jeremiah Haney."

"Is he related to Randolph?"

"They're father and son."

"Then I'll look forward to meeting him."

Tom grasped her arm, his fingers tightening into her flesh, and his eyes narrowed. "Stay away from him. I don't want you getting involved in this."

Katie lifted her chin. "I'm already involved. In fact,

Randolph Haney has invited me to attend the Cattleman's Ball with him and Jeremiah tonight."

Tom's gaze locked on hers. "You're a stubborn woman, but you'd better not cross me on this."

"I told you before, obedience doesn't sit well with me."

"It had better when the order is mine."

Katie tried to twist and pull her arm free of his grip, but her efforts didn't succeed. When she stopped struggling, he finally released her.

"Don't try to bully me."

"Then don't cross me."

She folded her arms, facing off with him. "Or what will happen?"

"I'll haul you back to Hannah's—*pronto*. And I'm not opposed to binding your hands and feet and throwing you over my shoulder."

"That sounds rather savage," she said.

His expression hardened. "Consider it this warrior's attempt to be civilized."

Abel shuffled his feet as a slow grin formed on his wrinkled face. "Don't worry, *señorita*. He only jokes with you. Lone Wolf doesn't mean it."

Tom turned to the old man. "You might not think I'm serious, Abel, but if she doesn't watch her step, she'll be riding over the rump of a mare all the way back to Pleasant Valley."

Katie unfolded her arms and slapped her hands on her hips. "The only steps I intend to watch are the ones that lead me within an arm's reach of Mr. *Lone Wolf*."

Tom's dark eyes narrowed as he returned his attention to Katie, making her wonder if she might have gone a bit too far. She hadn't meant to mock his Indian roots, but she sometimes didn't temper her words when angered.

Nevertheless, she turned on her heel and marched off. But instead of heading for the kitchen, where Randolph Haney was sure to say something to catch her off guard, she rounded the house and went to the courtyard, using the main entrance instead.

As she headed for the hallway toward the bedroom she'd been assigned, Harrison Graves shuffled out of one of the rooms.

His surprise at running into her rivaled her own at seeing him.

Did she dare speak to him now?

She might have, had her tongue not suffered momentary paralysis.

"Good morning," he said, his gaze never leaving her eyes.

Unable to waste time with formalities, she took a deep breath, then pressed on. "Mr. Graves, we haven't been formally introduced, but I'm Katie O'Malley."

"Yesterday wasn't a good day."

"I don't suppose it was, but I've come a long way to speak to you. Would now be a good time to talk?"

"I suppose so. I'm not sure how many more days I can prolong anything. Let's go into my study."

Katie followed the elderly man down the hall and into an open doorway. With one liver-spotted hand upon his cane for balance, he used the other to motion toward the chair in front of his desk. "Have a seat, Miss O'Malley."

"Please call me Katie."

When she realized he continued to stand on wobbly feet, awaiting her compliance, she quickly pulled out a chair and sat down.

"What is it you have to say?" he asked, as he took his own seat.

"I have reason to believe your great-granddaughter is a little girl named Sarah Jane."

"Is that what Caroline named her? Sarah Jane?"

"Yes. I've grown to love her and would like your permission to adopt her."

Mr. Graves appeared to rally and gain both strength and control. "First of all, I haven't yet met this child. Secondly, I'm not sure she really is my great-granddaughter. And thirdly, I don't know you from Florinda Grimwood."

"Florinda Grimwood?" Katie arched a brow. "I'm afraid I'm not familiar with her."

"Neither am I." His smile began to loosen Katie's taut nerves.

At least Harrison Graves had a sense of humor.

"Let me explain, Mr. Graves. I've been offered a teaching position in the Wyoming Territory, where women have the right to vote."

"You're a suffragist?"

"Yes. I believe women are the intellectual equals to men. I also believe that Sarah Jane has great potential. I promise to love her and educate her and allow her the freedom to nurture her own strengths and dreams."

He seemed to think about that for a moment, although he didn't argue. That was a good sign, wasn't it?

"My solicitor worries that a charlatan might try to take advantage of my imminent death." Mr. Graves glanced out the study window and into the garden. "It's no secret that my holdings are vast and that the cattle industry is booming. My only heir, assuming it is the child in question, would be a very wealthy young lady—as would her guardian."

"I don't intend to live in Texas, nor do I want control of your estate. Perhaps you could place it in trust for Sarah Jane until she reaches adulthood."

Harrison leaned his head against the back of his chair and crossed his arms. "The money doesn't interest you?"

"Not at all. My father had a respectable law practice and holdings of his own, which I inherited. I'm not rich, but I'm quite comfortable. And although I have no intention of living in splendor, we won't live in squalor, either. I'll see to it that Sarah Jane will have plenty to keep her happy."

He studied her for a moment, then said, "Randolph Haney insists I'm losing my mind, but I assure you, Miss O'Malley, I'm in full control of my faculties."

"I don't doubt that for a moment, sir. Place everything you want Sarah Jane to have into a trust until she comes of age. I don't want a thing."

"Thank you for your confidence, but I'm not about to give a child I've never met a penny. I've asked McCain to bring her to me. If there's a resemblance, I'll see it for myself."

"And if you do see it?"

"I might allow you to live here and care for her."

"Mr. Graves, that's not at all what I had in mind."

"I'm sure it isn't."

Katie took a deep breath. "Then I'll just hope and pray that you don't see any resemblance to my little girl. I'm not going to give her up."

"Why do you call her your little girl?"

"Until today, I was the only one in the world who

could offer her a proper home and stability, along with love."

"You're a stubborn woman, Miss O'Malley."

"So I've been told."

A slow smile warmed his wrinkled face. "Then I suppose we'll continue this conversation when my alleged great-granddaughter arrives."

It wasn't quite what Katie had been hoping for—but it was certainly a start.

Chapter Ten

Katie hadn't been in the house long before Abel began to chuckle.

"What's so funny?" Tom asked.

"You are, *mijo.* Your fight isn't with *la señorita,* it's with yourself."

"What are you talking about?"

The old man merely smiled. "Feelings like anger and love can be very strong. Sometimes it's difficult to tell the two apart."

"You're *loco.* I have no feelings for her at all—other than pure exasperation."

Abel laughed again. "Maybe you should kiss her and see if that clears things up."

He *had* kissed her—twice. And each time it had only made things worse. In fact, last night, as she'd pulled him close, cloaking him in lilacs and lace, he'd nearly lost his head.

She'd certainly lost hers. Hadn't she realized the risk she'd taken in kissing him? Thank goodness, he'd come to his senses and sent her back to the house.

"Señor McCain?" Maria asked from the wrought-iron gate.

Tom turned to the sound of her voice. "Yes?"

"Señor Graves would like to see you. He was having breakfast in his room when I left him, but he asked me to find you and have you meet him in his study."

After asking Abel to excuse him, Tom followed Maria into the house. When she turned toward the kitchen, he made his way to the hall that led to Harrison's study.

The door was closed, so he knocked.

"I'll be with you in a minute," Harrison said from behind the closed door.

"Take your time." Tom shoved his hands in his pockets, then paced along the hall. His steps slowed near an oil painting of Robert Graves that hung over a small mahogany table.

Robert, who'd been fair-haired like Caroline, had been in his early twenties when that portrait had been painted. He'd been a good man, a kind soul. But he'd never stood up to his father. If he had, things might have been different.

He might have married Runs With Horses, the Indian woman he'd fallen in love with when he'd been nineteen. And if he had, Tom would have been legitimate—whether Harrison accepted him or not.

Several moments later, the door to the study opened and closed. Tom turned and watched Katie exit.

Well, what do you know? She'd wanted to talk to Harrison and had sought him out.

Their eyes met, but only for a moment. Unwilling to make a scene, Tom shook his head, then turned his back to her, refocusing his gaze on Robert's portrait. Yet he couldn't shake the urge to stomp after Katie and…

And what?

Give her another piece of his mind?

Kiss her into submission?

As her footsteps disappeared down the hall, Harrison's voice sounded from behind. "I wasn't a good father to him."

Tom turned and watched as the old man shuffled through the doorway and into the hall, his cane tapping along with his steps.

"Robert died before I ever told him I was proud of him." After a pause, Harrison added, "Or that I loved him."

"I'm sure he knew," Tom said, although he had no idea why he'd made such a claim. As far as Harrison Graves knew, Tom "Lone Wolf" McCain had never stepped foot on the Lazy G until he'd been summoned here just a couple months before.

Harrison shook his head. "No, I'm not sure that he did."

Tom figured the old man wanted to talk, not necessarily converse, which was just as well. He'd waited a long time to hear what the old man had to say, even if the words were only addressed to the bounty hunter he'd hired and not to the boy he'd run off the Lazy G years ago.

"Would you like to go back to your study?" Tom asked.

"That's probably a good idea. I'm not as strong these days, and I tire easily."

As Tom followed the old man through the open doorway, Harrison added, "Funny thing about life. You spend each day as though it's your last. Then one day you wake up and learn that it just might be. And you realize that you never got the chance to do half of the things you should have done."

"What would you have done differently?" Tom asked.

"I would have taken my son to the swimming hole, tied a rope on an oversize branch, watched him swing and drop into the cool water. I would have taken my lovely granddaughter to town, proudly displayed her on my arm for all the world to see what a delightful young lady she'd become, what a quick wit and bubbly laugh she had."

And now it was clearly too late to do any of that.

Harrison took a deep breath, then slowly let it out. "Do you believe in God, McCain?"

The question took Tom aback, but he answered, "Yes, I do."

Harrison eased himself into the leather chair behind his desk. "Glad to hear it. You'll find yourself standing in front of Him before you know it. And that's a frightening thought for a man like me."

"Why is that?"

"Every person God placed in my life, I either browbeat, took advantage of or abandoned."

Sadly, the old man probably didn't even know half of all the pain he'd caused, all the people he'd hurt—like Tom and his mother.

Harrison pointed to a shelf on the wall. "See that crude wood carving, next to the cigar box?"

Tom couldn't make out what it was. "Yes, I see it."

"Robert gave it to me for my birthday. He must have been about eight years old back then. Made it himself."

It was nice to think that Harrison had given the carving a place of honor.

"I found it in his bottom drawer after he died," Harrison added.

"But I thought you said it was a gift."

"Oh, he gave it to me. I tossed the creation into the fireplace—or so I thought. The boy must have retrieved it afterward and kept it."

Tom sat quietly, allowing the man to talk, to confess his guilt.

Harrison nodded toward a Saratoga trunk in the corner, a few feet from the bookshelf. "Do you see that?"

Tom nodded.

"I kept Caroline's photographs hidden in a drawer for nearly six years. Didn't want to see them. One evening after I drank myself into a senseless rage, I nearly burned them. Maria threw such a fit that I locked them up in that chest instead. But now I cherish her memory."

"You told me that you'd show those pictures to me," Tom said.

Harrison nodded. "So you could see if the child looks like Caroline."

Tom didn't need to see them, though. He'd never forget what Caroline had looked like as a child. And Sarah Jane favored her.

"You didn't tell me the girl's name was Sarah Jane," Harrison said.

"Didn't I?"

"No, your friend Katie O'Malley did."

Tom hadn't intentionally kept the news. "What does her name have to do with it?"

"My mother's name was Sarah Jane."

Tom hadn't known that, but then, how would he? He'd never been privy to any of the Graves family stories. At least, not very many of them.

"Tell me about the girl," Harrison said, his eyes hopeful yet leery.

Tom wasn't sure what to tell him, other than to offer a physical description. "She's six years old, blonde and has large, expressive eyes."

"What color are they?"

"Blue."

"Like Caroline's." Harrison faced him, his gaze searching Tom's. "Tell me about her heart, about her spirit. Did she get Caroline's zest for life—or my stubborn streak?"

"She's a beautiful child, inside and out."

"I want to see her for myself. And I don't have much time left. How long will it take for you to bring her back?"

"That's the problem, Mr. Graves. I'm not sure if she'll be safe in Stillwater."

Harrison lifted a white eyebrow. "Why not?"

"She witnessed an assault back in Pleasant Valley. And the man tried to silence her." He still didn't want to mention that he also thought Caroline's death was a little suspicious, especially when he didn't have anything to base it on except a feeling.

"Surely you don't think the girl would be less than safe here," Harrison said. "I can close this place up like a fortress. No one can get to her."

Tom was really stepping out on a limb, but he couldn't help saying, "I haven't ruled out the idea that it might actually be someone from Stillwater."

"Who? And why?" Harrison's brow knit, and he cocked his head. "You're not suggesting Caroline's death wasn't an accident, are you?"

"I think a fall down the stairs is a little suspicious. I also know that she moved to several different towns over the last six years. She might have been running from someone."

"I'll double your pay if you find whoever may have killed her."

"If her fall wasn't an accident, I'll find her killer—eventually."

Harrison, who'd seemed frail just moments ago, steeled himself. "I may not be around long enough to see the culprit come to justice, but my solicitor will see that you get paid."

"I'm not doing it for the money, so don't worry about paying me. And I'd rather you didn't mention anything to Mr. Haney."

"Why is that?"

Tom and Harrison might have struck the first chords of respect and friendship, but he wasn't ready to tell the man that his primary suspect was the man Harrison trusted most in this world.

"I'd like to keep my suspicions to myself for now," Tom said. "So please keep our conversation between the two of us. I'll notify Mr. Haney when the time is right."

"All right." Harrison pushed back his chair and got to his feet, signaling that their conversation had ended. "By the way, Randolph invited Miss O'Malley to the Cattleman's Ball tonight with him and Jeremiah. I think it's a good idea if you go along with them."

So did Tom.

Because the thought of Katie on the arm of either of those scoundrels was as welcome as a poke in the eye or a punch in the nose.

* * *

In the solitude of Caroline's bedroom, Katie stood before the full-length mirror and studied her reflection.

Earlier today, Maria had set out one of Caroline's gowns for Katie to wear to the ball, going so far as to alter it to fit. She'd also insisted upon fixing Katie's hair, painstakingly weaving the red tendrils into a fashionable coiffure while leaving soft wisps of curls to frame her face.

Katie tugged at the purple satin zinnias that trimmed the neckline of the gown, hoping to cover more of her cleavage. She felt uncomfortable with that much exposure.

Still, the lavender gown was lovely. Maria had done an exceptional job making it fit as though it had been made for Katie alone. Caroline had stood taller and had larger feet. The matching doeskin slippers Maria had set out nearly fit. Katie just hoped she could get through the evening without tripping or slipping out of them. She was nervous enough as it was. In a few minutes, she would be meeting Jeremiah Haney, Randolph's son and the man Tom intended to meet—the man he hadn't wanted Katie to speak to.

Tom should have realized Katie O'Malley didn't obey anyone unless she wanted to. Just because he didn't consider her especially competent on the trail didn't mean she wasn't bright enough to judge a man's character and do a bit of investigating on her own. If Sarah Jane wasn't safe in Stillwater, Katie would determine that for herself.

"Randolph and Jeremiah are here," Maria said from the doorway. When Katie turned, the woman's face broke into a radiant smile. She clasped her hands together and brought them to her heart. "How beautiful you are."

"I have you to thank. You're a talented seamstress."

Maria shook her head. "Oh, no. God blessed you with beauty. The gown only frames His handiwork."

Katie's cheeks warmed. Never having primped and preened over herself, the compliment unbalanced her. She stole a quick glance in the mirror to see whether her cheeks were flushed and she winced when she saw that they were. But there wasn't much she could do about it. She'd always blushed easily.

"I'd better go," she said. "I don't want to keep the gentlemen waiting."

"For you, they will wait." Maria winked. As she stepped aside, Katie lifted her hem and strode out the door.

In the sitting room, the men stood beside the settee speaking in low voices. When Katie entered, they paused and turned.

Surprise flooded Randolph's face. "Miss O'Malley, you look absolutely stunning. Allow me to introduce my son, Jeremiah."

Dignified, and dressed to perfection in a black suit and crisp white shirt, the younger Haney reached out his hand and greeted Katie with a warm, engaging smile.

He was older than her by close to twenty years, but the well-dressed gentleman was rather handsome, with a distinctive mole on a strong chin that made him quite memorable.

Jeremiah brought her hand to his lips. "It's a pleasure to meet you, Miss O'Malley."

"Thank you."

"My father says you're from Missouri."

"Yes, I am."

"I was in St. Louis last summer. It's a bustling city—and impressive."

Randolph placed his hand on Katie's arm. "Our carriage is ready, my dear. Shall we go?"

"Yes, of course."

Twenty minutes later, they arrived at the Cattleman's Ball, which was held in the well-lit and gaily decorated town hall.

With Jeremiah at his side, Randolph introduced Katie to several of the Stillwater residents. As far as she could tell, they all seemed to be decent people, friendly, welcoming and courteous.

"Katie, would you like a glass of punch?" Randolph asked.

"I'm sure she would," Jeremiah said. "Why don't you bring her one?"

When the elder Haney strode toward the refreshment table, Katie looked at the dignified escort at her side.

"Have you always live in Stillwater?" she asked.

"Yes, I have."

"Then you knew Caroline Graves."

"Our fathers were very close, so Caroline and I grew up together, so to speak. I was older than she. Ten years to be exact. I looked at her as a little sister and assumed the role of a big brother."

"I wish I could have met her," Katie said.

"I'm not sure you would have liked her. She had a wild side."

Katie wondered if people often said that about her.

"You may find this odd, Mr. Haney, but I might have admired that about Caroline."

Rather than quiz her about that, he asked, "So where did you meet McCain?"

"In Pleasant Valley."

"I see."

She wasn't sure what he thought he *saw* or why he was interested in how she knew Tom. But she had a few questions for him, too.

"I hear Harrison sent you in search of Caroline when she ran off," Katie said. "And that you weren't able to find her."

"Actually, I found her—several times."

Katie couldn't hide her amazement. For at least the past six months, and maybe even the past few years, Harrison had desperately wanted to find Caroline. And his friend's son had known of her whereabouts all along? "Then why didn't you tell Mr. Graves?"

"I couldn't. It would have crushed him."

"I'm not sure that I understand."

"If it would have actually helped Harrison to know the truth of her occupation, I would have told him." His brown eyes searched hers, as if he'd just given her some kind of cryptic message he hoped she'd understand.

Katie lowered her voice to a whisper, even though the music was so loud it really wasn't necessary. "Her *occupation?* You mean…she and Daisy were both…?"

"Oh. So you knew Miss Potts." Jeremiah lifted a single brow. "In Taylorsville she went by the name of Erin Kelly. And they were friends, weren't they?"

Katie didn't know what to say, what to think. She'd been told that Caroline and Erin had respectable jobs in Taylorsville.

"You thought Harrison would hold her…occupation against her?" she asked.

"I'd hoped that, in time, Caroline would have come to her senses and seen the error of her ways. And that I'd be able to talk her into coming home of her own accord."

"But that didn't happen?"

"Time ran out."

"I still think Harrison deserved to know," Katie said. "He might have been more forgiving than you thought."

"The real problem wasn't one of Caroline's sinful life. She hated her grandfather with a passion. I couldn't bring myself to tell the poor old man she wouldn't ever return. Knowing how she felt about him would have killed him faster than the disease that's eating away at him now. My father and I love Harrison. His death will be a cruel blow, even though we know it's coming. But I don't want to see it happen any sooner than need be."

Katie still believed that Harrison had deserved to know the truth. Perhaps if he had known sooner, he could have gone to see Caroline, spoken to her face-to-face, met Sarah Jane.

"Come, my dear." Jeremiah took her arm. "Let's drop this horrid subject before I embarrass myself with tears. Dance with me."

As the musicians played fiddles, banjos and a slightly off-key piano, Jeremiah swept Katie into his arms and onto the dance floor before she had a chance to object. And she soon found her steps matching his.

She had to admit that Jeremiah Haney was an exquisite dancer. And a kindhearted human being, it seemed.

Each time he spun her to the right, she spotted Tom McCain standing near the refreshment table.

He appeared rather dapper himself tonight, in a pair of dark slacks and a white shirt.

Yet a scowl on his face spoke volumes, all of it directed at her.

As Katie and Jeremiah graced the dance floor, Tom stood beside the refreshment table, a glass of punch in his hand and a knot in his gut.

Katie appeared utterly captivated by the scoundrel who held her in his arms. And right now Tom wanted to pry the starry-eyed redhead from his grip, then knock the arrogant Haney on his backside.

Anger flared, and Tom did his best to tamp it down. But he wasn't the only one in the room who resented what might be considered an uncivilized presence.

A few haughty glances and condescending looks told him half of the people in this room didn't appreciate a half-breed being here. And the only thing keeping the town fathers from asking him to leave was the fact that Tom had a business arrangement with Harrison Graves, which meant he had the cattleman's approval.

When Katie smiled up at Haney, Tom fought the need to protect her as well as give her a piece of his mind. She had no way of knowing why he despised and distrusted both Randolph and his son, but as far as Tom was concerned, Katie O'Malley had just entered the enemy camp—with a pretty smile and of her own accord.

Her soft auburn locks, swept up in a riot of curls, exposed that slender neck. The lavender gown she wore was more than becoming. It actually suited her. Tom could almost smell her lilac scent, and a sense of ownership flooded over him.

As he emptied his punch in one quick gulp, his eyes

followed her every move, and he wished he could hear the conversation she was having with Jeremiah Haney.

"Would you like some fresh air?" Jeremiah asked Katie. "There's a beautiful courtyard outside. The townspeople hired a custom craftsman to build it. The fountain alone took over six months to complete."

His brown eyes beseeched her to agree.

The privacy would give Katie a chance to question him further, get to know him better, to decide for herself whether he could be trusted or not.

"All right," she said.

As the fiddlers stepped forward, the Virginia reel was announced. Applause, laughter and gaiety broke out in the crowd. The other men scampered for a partner, while Jeremiah escorted Katie off the dance floor and out the side door.

The moon was no longer as big or silvery as it had been on the night she'd joined Tom outside, the night he'd kissed her, but the air was cool and calming.

Jeremiah tucked her hand in the warm crook of his arm. "You look lovely."

"Thank you." Compliments didn't often affect Katie, but she felt especially pretty tonight. It must have been the lavender gown. Or perhaps the atmosphere that made her feel special. Either way, his words touched her.

Jeremiah looked impressive, as well, but she didn't say so. Some women fussed over men, but Katie had never been one of them.

"Miss O'Malley, I've always appreciated a woman with a compassionate heart. However, I've never had the pleasure of meeting one that also looked like a goddess." Jeremiah patted the top of her hand as it rested on his forearm.

Katie laughed. "A goddess? Now I doubt your sincerity."

Jeremiah touched her chin with the tip of a long, tapered finger and drew her gaze to his. "You'll never find a man more sincere than I."

Katie's cheeks warmed, and she hoped the lack of lighting hid her flush. She wondered if anyone could see them but decided she and her escort had wandered a bit too far from the gathering. They probably should turn back, but she was enjoying the company and the night air.

"I'm thoroughly taken with you, Miss O'Malley. I enjoy your bright mind."

At that she broke into a warm smile. "Now, that's a compliment I'll thank you for."

Festive lanterns around the community hall cast a faint light, enabling Katie to catch the intensity in his gaze. She felt oddly flattered yet embarrassed at the same time.

She wiggled her toes inside the loose-fitting doeskin slippers.

He tilted her chin with his finger again, and when she looked up, his mouth lowered toward hers.

He was going to kiss her.

For a moment, she wondered if another man's kiss would be as moving as Tom's, if it would have the same effect on her. But there was something unsettling about kissing another man, especially this one, so she placed her hands on his chest to push him away.

Another man might have realized that she wasn't in

agreement, but Jeremiah pressed his lips against hers anyway.

She pushed against his chest, trying to free herself, but he didn't let go. So twisted her head, breaking the unbidden kiss and intending to slap him senseless.

That is, until a familiar voice cut in. "Good evening, folks."

Jeremiah released her, and Katie glanced over her shoulder, although she didn't need to see who'd joined them.

Tom glared at Jeremiah as though he wanted to throttle him with his bare hands.

And had she not been so embarrassed and guilt riddled for agreeing to go outside in the first place and to wander so far from the festivities, Katie might have helped him do just that.

Chapter Eleven

"What are you doing here?" Jeremiah asked, his tone crisp and cool.

Tom smiled, but not with his eyes. "I'm worried about the lady's safety. She's new around here."

"She's in good hands," Jeremiah said. "Go back inside."

The men stood eye to eye, and although they'd said very little, Katie sensed their hatred and distrust of each other. And for once, she found herself on Tom's side, although she didn't want to admit her foolishness—or the uneasiness she'd felt with the man she'd been warned about.

"If you don't mind," she told Jeremiah, "I'd like to speak to Mr. McCain."

"You don't need to address an Indian as *mister,*" Jeremiah said. "Not around here."

Katie's stomach knotted. "Then, if you don't mind, I'd like to speak to Tom."

"Now *I'm* the one who's worried." Jeremiah put an arm around her. "You shouldn't be alone with him, especially outside in the dark."

She placed her hand on Jeremiah's chest, felt his heart pound beneath his jacket and gave him a push toward the dance. "I'm perfectly all right. Please leave us alone. I'll be inside soon."

Jeremiah hesitated but turned to go. Pausing, he glared over his shoulder. "If you so much as treat her with an ounce of disrespect, you'll deal with me, boy."

Tom stood silent, his eyes boring into Jeremiah.

"I'll be *fine,*" Katie repeated. "Please go inside. *Now.*"

She waited for Jeremiah to leave. When he finally reached the lighted building, she turned to Tom.

He crossed his arms and scowled. "What are you doing out here?"

She wished he hadn't witnessed the brief but intimate exchange, but she didn't want him to know she had any regrets. Or that Jeremiah had actually frightened her, that he hadn't stopped when she'd tried to push him away. She'd felt so out of control that a sense of relief had surged through her when Tom had arrived, in spite of her embarrassment at being caught.

"I wasn't doing anything out here. Not really."

"You *kissed* him."

No, she hadn't, but telling Tom that Jeremiah had been so bold, so forceful, would only make things worse between the men. And a physical altercation at this point wouldn't help their investigation.

"You don't have any claims on me," she said.

"No, I don't. But I suspect Haney's wife wouldn't appreciate you kissing her husband."

"His *wife?*" Katie's jaw dropped, and she took a step back. "Jeremiah's married?"

"I take it he didn't tell you."

"Why, no." Katie hoped it wasn't true. She might not

intend to marry anyone, but that didn't mean she didn't value the institution of matrimony. Had she known, she wouldn't have allowed the man to walk her outside alone.

Maybe Tom was mistaken. "Why would Jeremiah come to the dance alone if he had a wife? Why isn't she here?"

"She's at home. From what I understand, she's sick and bedridden."

Katie dropped her hands from her hips, momentarily taken aback. Why hadn't Jeremiah mentioned something as important as that? And why on earth had he tried to kiss her?

"Would it have made a difference?" Tom asked.

"Of course, it would have." Katie's temper flared, and with Jeremiah out of range, she focused all of it on Tom. "What kind of woman do you think I am?"

"I'm not sure."

Katie raised her hand to slap him, and he caught her wrist in a hard grip. "I told you once before, don't ever strike me again."

Katie truly wasn't prone to violence, but Tom Mc-Cain seemed to bring out the worst in her. "You're the only man I've ever wanted to strike."

Of course, that wasn't true. Right now she wanted to pummel Jeremiah Haney.

With her arm still raised, Tom's hand holding hers at bay, Katie knew she'd never overpower him. But then, she really didn't want to. She'd had no business coming outside with Jeremiah in the first place. Tom had warned her about him, and she hadn't paid him any mind.

When she relaxed her pose, Tom released her wrist.

"Coming out here with him was a bad idea," she admitted.

"Then why did you do it?"

"To talk to him. And to see the fountain." Katie scanned the grounds, just now realizing there was no fountain in sight.

"If you're looking for the courtyard, it's on the other side of the building." Tom glared at her. "You came out here to kiss him."

Katie tapped his broad chest with a pointed finger. "Not intentionally. And to be honest, we didn't actually kiss, although he tried to force himself on me. However, you can be sure that I won't ever go off with him alone again."

Tom removed her tapping finger from his chest, his hand encompassing hers. *"Good."*

"Don't tell me you're jealous." Katie hoped her words might embarrass him, cause him to back down and leave her be.

Or maybe she wanted him to admit that he didn't like the thought of her kissing another man.

"I'm not jealous," he said, pulling her close.

She ought to fight the intimacy, but his touch and his scent caused her thoughts to jumble, her knees to weaken.

Yet no matter how badly she might be tempted to lose herself in Tom's embrace, they had no future together. After all, they were an ill-suited pair. Tom insisted upon obedience, and Katie wouldn't give up her independence for anyone.

"Go inside," he told her. "Tell Jeremiah that you have a headache or that you've suffered an attack of the vapors. Use whatever excuse you women make. I want you to return to the ranch."

Katie fought the urge to challenge him, but for the

first time in her life she actually wanted to retreat. And even more distressing and unusual, she felt foolish for not listening to Tom in the first place. He'd been right, and she'd been wrong.

Jeremiah Haney couldn't be trusted. He'd lied, first about the courtyard, but more importantly by omitting the fact that he had a wife.

Why had he escorted her to the one side of the building that would hold little interest to the others in attendance?

Had he wanted to speak to her privately, the kiss being entirely unexpected? Or had he wanted her away from the crowd for something more clandestine?

Something nagged at her in addition to the cloying scent of his tobacco-laced breath. Something that told her to respect the niggle of fear she'd felt when he'd disregarded her wishes and tried to force a kiss she hadn't wanted.

Eager to escape the accusations in Tom's eyes, she turned on her heel and strode toward the community hall in a most unladylike fashion, her temper barely in control.

In her haste to make her way back to the festivities, her foot lifted out of her shoe, leaving one foot bare and a lavender slipper along the pathway. She turned to retrieve the oversize dancing shoe, stepping on a stone in the process. "Ouch," she mumbled under her breath.

"Did you throw a shoe?" Tom asked.

Katie glanced up awkwardly, the wry grin on his handsome face only serving to escalate her humiliation and fuel her anger. How dare he tease her? Did he actually mean to refer to her as a horse?

Katie reached for the doeskin slipper, tempted to sling it at him.

He stood still, arms crossed. "Planning to throw it at me?"

"How did you know?"

"Lucky guess."

"I'd rather wait until I'm wearing a boot or something that's a lot heavier and would inflict more damage." She bent and hobbled while placing the slipper back onto her foot.

She could imagine him chuckling behind her back, but she ignored her annoyance as she returned to the community hall.

Once inside, she forced a smile, trying to appear unruffled, even though hiding her emotions had never been easy.

Moments later, Jeremiah was at her side, handsome, gallant and—*married*. If she'd worn sturdier shoes, she might have kicked *him* in the shins.

"Are you all right?" he asked.

"Yes, I'm fine. Please tell your father I'm ready to go." She didn't have a headache and had never had an attack of the vapors in her life. She wanted to leave, and that's all there was to it. No excuses or explanations needed.

"I'm ready to go, too," Jeremiah said. "But first, I want to tell you something."

"What's that?" Katie expected to hear a long overdue confession of his marital status. She crossed her arms and would have tapped her foot if the instep wasn't so tender.

"Please be careful what you say to McCain."

Katie stiffened. The man who'd taken her to see a nonexistent fountain and had neglected to tell her he had a wife at home was offering her a piece of "trusted" advice?

"What do you mean?" Katie asked.

"I think he intends to blackmail Harrison."

His words caught her off guard. "Why would he do that?"

"Since he followed Caroline's trail, he knows what she was up to the past six years. And some people have no conscience, especially where money is concerned." Jeremiah took her arm and led her toward the door. He motioned to Randolph, alerting the older man of their impending departure.

"Tom doesn't seem to be the type to be impressed with money," Katie said.

"My dear, *everyone* has a price."

Perhaps they did. Her mind whirled with facts that didn't quite add up.

Something told her there would come a day when she'd have to place her trust, maybe even her very life, in someone's hands.

She just hoped and prayed that when that day came, she would make the right choice.

The next morning, while Katie sat at Caroline's dressing table, brushing her hair, Maria pulled a dress from the closet.

"Did you have fun at the dance?" Maria asked, a wistful smile crossing her face.

Katie didn't have the heart to tell her no. "It was a pleasant evening. But I'm curious about something. What do you know about Jeremiah's wife?"

Maria clucked her tongue. "*Que lastima.* Such an unhappy woman."

"Why do you say that?"

"Martha Haney lost her mind. Her husband had to hire a nurse to look after her. *La medicina* helps. She does not rave and cry as much as before."

"What's wrong with her?"

"Jeremiah said it happened slowly over time, but I think it was sudden."

"Sudden? What do you mean?"

"She stopped by here about six months ago and spoke to Señor Graves alone in his study. She left with a paper in her hand. She mumbled something about hiring a detective. I thought that was odd." Maria shook her head. "That is the last I saw of her. She seemed *inojada,* angry. But she did not seem *loca.*"

"How long after that did she become ill?"

"Three weeks? Maybe more. Maybe less. The doctor confined her to bed."

"Has anyone gone to see her?"

"No. Señor Jeremiah does not allow visitors, but the woman who takes care of her is my friend."

"What does your friend have to say?"

"Only that Martha sleeps most of the time, which is a blessing because she cries without the medicine."

"And when she raves? What does she say?" Katie couldn't believe she was questioning the words of a crazy woman, but quite frankly, she found it all very odd.

"My friend speaks only Spanish, so she doesn't understand very much, but she told me Martha cries for her father and for Señor Graves."

"Where does Jeremiah live?" Katie asked. "I'd like to meet his wife."

"Oh, no. That is not possible. Señor Haney told my

friend that she would lose her job if she couldn't keep his wife quiet or if she ever let anyone into his house when he isn't home." Maria frowned, large brown eyes watering. "*Por favor, señorita.* My friend is a widow. She needs the money to feed her children."

Katie placed a hand on Maria's shoulder. "I won't do anything to put your friend's job at risk."

But thoughts of Martha Haney tugged at her heart.

Something didn't seem right, and she didn't mean Martha Haney's illness.

Jeremiah had told an entirely different story about Caroline than Tom had, and neither man trusted the other. Quite frankly, after last night, Katie didn't trust Jeremiah. And while Katie might have plenty of reason to resent Tom's attitude toward women—or, at least, his attitude toward her most of the time—he'd never lied to her.

"Maria," Katie said, "do you know where I can find Tom?"

"He rode off early this morning, but I saw him come back about an hour ago."

"Thank you. I need to speak to him. Will you excuse me?"

"Yes, of course."

Moments later, Katie found Tom at one of the corrals near the barn, cooling down his gelding.

"I'd like a word with you," she said.

He turned, his expression unreadable. "What's on your mind?"

"What do you know about Martha Haney?"

"Are you wondering if she's likely to pass on and leave the dashing Jeremiah Haney a widower?"

Katie blew out a ragged sigh. "That was uncalled-for."

"I'm sorry. Sometimes the uncivilized savage comes out in me."

Is that what had set him on edge? The fact that he felt he had to prove to her and everyone else that he wasn't tainted by his Indian blood? That he was just as worthy as any other person on the ranch or in town?

Did he think that she felt the same way as the Haneys? If so, he didn't know her very well.

"I learned the hard way that Jeremiah Haney can't be trusted," she admitted. "And I've come to believe that you and I need to join forces and work as a team if we're going to protect Sarah Jane."

When he didn't object, she uncrossed her arms and leaned against the corral. "I'm not sure what you know, but Maria told me that Martha Haney lost her mind."

"I'd heard that."

Katie lifted her hand, shielding her eyes from the glare of the morning sun. "I was told she's on medication to keep her quiet."

Tom stepped to the right, blocking the sun's glare for her, a thoughtful move that took her by surprise.

"I'm not sure about her condition or the treatment," he said.

She bit down on her lip, unsure how much she should share of the information she'd gathered. Finally, she opted to trust him with all of it. "Did you know that Martha came to see Harrison a few weeks before she became ill?"

"The families have been friends for a long time."

"I know that, but Maria said that Martha left with a piece of paper."

"I'm sure there wasn't anything unusual about Martha asking Harrison for advice or information."

"Aren't you curious?"

"Yes, and I'm glad you told me, but don't get any wild ideas about investigating."

"Why not?"

"I told you that I don't trust that man or his father."

"But you never told me why."

"I shouldn't have to."

"If you want me to follow your orders and instructions, you'll need to give me reason to."

He seemed to ponder her words for a moment, then said, "Years ago, Randolph Haney used to be a cruel man, and I have no reason to believe he's changed."

"You used to know him?"

"Yes, I spent a lot of time in Stillwater when I was a kid. But he knew me as Lone Wolf back then, and I've changed."

He'd grown up, of course. And he'd apparently taken Hannah McCain's name. "What makes you say that Randolph was cruel? What did he do?"

"A lot of it was hearsay. But I can tell you for a fact that he hated Indians. He threw my mother off the Lazy G twice, the last time when she was dying and begging for help."

"Why did he do that?"

"He said he was doing Harrison's bidding." Tom lifted his hand and fingered his forehead, where a scar marred his brow.

"Does Harrison know who you are?" she asked.

"No, he hired me to find Caroline because of my reputation as a bounty hunter."

"And you took the job in spite of the bad blood between you and Haney—and Harrison, as well?"

Tom tensed. "Yes, I took the job."

"I don't understand. Why would you do that? If someone hadn't shown my dying mother any kindness, I wouldn't have given them the time of day."

"I had my reasons, but I'd rather not talk about that now."

While curious and tempted to prod him, Jeremiah's words came to mind. *Everyone has a price.*

Had Tom hired on for more than the money he'd been promised in payment?

Had Katie been wrong about him?

They stood like that for a moment, lost in the silence, lost in their thoughts.

Did she dare tell Tom the other piece of information Jeremiah had told her?

Did she dare not?

"Jeremiah knew where Caroline was all along. He told me that she'd been living a sinful life, just as Erin had been in Pleasant Valley. And that she hated her grandfather and didn't ever want to go back to the ranch. He never told Harrison because the news would have broken his heart."

"He's lying. I had a feeling he'd been the one who'd been following her. Erin may have had a shady past, and I grant you that she wasn't living a respectable life at the Gardener's House. But that's not true about Caroline. She was never a prostitute. And while she might have been angry with Harrison, she would have come home if she'd known he was dying, especially if she knew he wanted to make amends."

"How do you know that?"

"I just do. Caroline might have been quick to anger, but she had a kind and loving nature."

"You knew her personally?"

"Only when we were children."

Again came the silence, the drifting thoughts. Katie suspected Tom was remembering Caroline, until he said, "Tell me something."

"What's that?"

"You kissed Jeremiah Haney last night. Why?"

Her cheeks flushed, and her heart thumped. Her first impulse was to lie or downplay what had actually happened when Jeremiah had taken her outside. After all, she wasn't sure if she could trust Tom with her heartfelt revelations—or her uneasiness.

But she knew without a doubt that Jeremiah Haney was a scoundrel. And that was something upon which they both could agree.

"I'll admit that I momentarily considered kissing him," she said.

"To see how it compared?"

Her cheeks burned with the shame of it, but she pressed on. "I was curious, yes. But only for the briefest of moments. I wouldn't have gone through with it. But when I told him no and tried to push him away, he persisted. I may have snapped at you last night after your arrival, but I was actually relieved to see you. Then, when I found out that he was married... Well, he's not an honorable man."

"Stay away from him, Katie."

That was one order she intended to keep, but she'd rather wrestle a pig in a mud puddle than admit it. "I'm going to return to the kitchen before my coffee gets cold," she said. "So if you'll excuse me?"

"Did you *hear* me?" he asked.

"I heard. And I think it was wise advice. I think

I'll probably heed it." Then she turned on her heel and headed for the house.

As she approached the kitchen, she heard the low mutters of whispered voices.

Her steps slowed, more to avoid interrupting than to eavesdrop. Still, she couldn't help hearing Maria speak, her words a mixture of English and Spanish.

"That boy and his mother came here years ago— that last time—asking to speak to Señor Graves. *Por que,* Abel?"

"I do not know."

"*Sí, tu sabes.* Tell me the truth."

"I cannot. I made a promise many years ago. I will not break my word unless Lone Wolf asks me to."

"I have known you for many years. *Somos como familia.* You can tell me. I can keep a secret."

"No," Abel said, determination in his voice. "If a man's word means nothing, he is worth nothing."

"Caroline spoke of him once."

"Que dijo, la señorita?" Abel asked.

"She said that she had met her Indian brother."

Katie's breath caught. Caroline had an Indian brother? Surely that wasn't possible. Even if she'd wanted to back away from the voices, she couldn't. Her feet wouldn't move.

"Caroline was just a child," Abel said, dismissing Maria's claim. "Who knows what she meant by that."

"*Sí.* You are right. She was only six years old at the time."

"Children have big imaginations," he added.

"Sometimes. *Pero quién sabe?*"

"Did you question her at the time?"

"No," Maria said, "I thought she was…*como se dice?*"

"Dreaming?"

"*Sí.*"

"*Es possible.* Why do you care now?"

"Because if she was talking about Lone Wolf, I believe he has come back. And I do not know why he would, not after he was sent away so cruelly, especially that last time." Maria sighed heavily. "Did she speak the truth, old man?"

"How would I know? You will have to ask the boy."

"He is a man now," Maria said, "but I will ask him."

Katie cleared her throat to announce her entrance as she stepped into the warm kitchen. The aroma of spicy beef and eggs sizzling on a cast-iron skillet filled the air.

"Something smells delicious," Katie said, her mind on anything but food.

There were more than a few secrets at the Lazy G, and Katie planned to uncover them all, beginning with Tom "Lone Wolf" McCain.

Chapter Twelve

Tom had planned to leave early in the morning to get Sarah Jane, but this new piece of information Katie had provided needed further investigation.

He wanted to know why Martha Haney had visited Harrison Graves and what she took with her when she left. And only one person could give him that answer.

So he knocked lightly on Harrison's study door, hoping the man was awake, alone and ready for an unexpected visitor.

"Come in," the cattleman called from within.

Tom turned the brass knob, stepped inside and closed the door behind him.

Harrison sat at his desk, shrunken—now just a temporary fixture in the office he once ruled. Sunlight streamed through the window behind him, giving him a heavenly glow and reminding Tom of how little time the man had left.

"I'm leaving for the girl," Tom said. "But I'd like to ask you a few questions before I go."

Harrison motioned toward the leather chair in front

of the large desk, then studied him momentarily. "Have a seat. What do you want to know?"

"I heard Martha Haney came by to visit you about six months ago." Tom pulled out the chair and sat. "Do you mind if I ask what she wanted?"

The question seemed to take Harrison by surprise, but he held a blank expression as he studied Tom warily. "She wanted the name of a detective I'd used in the past."

"And you gave it to her?"

Harrison nodded. "I probably would have been more inquisitive, but I felt faint and wanted to get rid of her before I keeled over and embarrassed myself."

"Did Mrs. Haney mention why she wanted an investigator?"

"No, but about that same time, someone had broken into the Haney house and stolen some heirloom jewelry. I assumed it had something to do with following an old employee."

"Why didn't Jeremiah approach you?" Tom asked.

"He was out of town at the time."

"It seems he's away from home a lot." Tom watched Harrison carefully, trying to gauge what the old man thought.

Harrison leaned back in his chair and placed his elbows on the armrest. "He has a lot of business to take care of."

"Maybe Martha was suspicious of her husband."

"Of Jeremiah?" Harrison snorted. "I wouldn't doubt it. The man played around more than most men would. I suppose he still does."

Tom bit back his opinion. He didn't trust a man who was unfaithful to his wife. Sure, some men thought it was part of their nature to exercise their prowess, but if a man couldn't hold himself to a marital vow, Tom found little to admire or to trust in him. People were either loyal and honest or they weren't.

"Did Martha mention anything about Jeremiah?" he asked.

"If she actually wanted to have him followed, I don't think she'd tell me. She would have been worried that I would have tried to talk her out of it. Or that I would have told Randolph. But like I said, I was in no mood to quiz her, and she didn't explain." Harrison crossed his arms. "For the most part, I tried to appease her. Jeremiah had confided in me that the woman was acting very strange."

"Was she?"

Harrison threw his hands up. "She's a woman. They all act a bit strange, if you ask me."

"I suppose they do," Tom said, thinking of Katie and cracking a slight smile. "Who did you suggest she contact?"

"Cord Rainville. I'd gotten his name from a friend of mine. I'd heard he was a good man—smart, trustworthy, discreet. He lost his wife and child in a fire a couple of years ago and took it hard. I was told that he tends to drink to forget, but that he's good at what he does and will get the job done."

That struck Tom as odd. "Why didn't you ask him to look for Caroline? Why did you hire me?"

"Actually, I tried. Cord had a job out of state, and my schedule didn't fit his. I hear he might be back now."

"Where can I find him?"

"Rio Seco."

That was a three-to-four-hour ride from Stillwater.

"Do you know whether Martha Haney ever contacted him?" Tom asked.

"No, I don't. What's on your mind?"

"Just a hunch." Tom didn't know if he dared to share his suspicions.

Harrison eyed him critically. "You don't think it had anything to do with Caroline, do you?"

"I have a bad feeling about all of this, sir."

"You said that before, but I'm sure you understand my reluctance to believe it."

Tom had meant to spare Harrison as much of the ugliness as possible, but the man had to face the truth. "Caroline's daughter witnessed an attack on the woman Caroline met at Casa de Los Angelitos. The trauma left the child mute."

"Just exactly where is the girl now?"

"She's safe. But it wasn't that difficult for me to find Caroline, even though she moved several times—once in the dead of night. I think she was running from someone. And Jeremiah Haney traveled a lot. I also have reason to believe that he's known where Caroline was all along."

Harrison's lips tightened. "Don't let your thoughts wander in that direction. Jeremiah loved Caroline. She was like a sister to him."

Tom could taste the bitterness that rose in his throat. "But he *wasn't* her brother."

"No, but as children, they—"

"No, sir." Tom shook his head. "Jeremiah was more than ten years older than Caroline. He never thought of her as a sister."

Harrison frowned. "How would you know how he felt about her?"

Because a brother would look out for his sister. He

would have done anything he could to help her, to find her, to bring her home.

"It's just a gut feeling," Tom said.

"You seem to have a lot of those."

"I haven't been wrong very often."

"You're wrong this time." Harrison slowly scooted his chair from the desk.

"I hope so." But as Tom stood, he knew his intuition was too strong to discredit any longer.

"When will you leave for Sarah Jane? I don't have to tell you how anxious I am to meet her. Your horse should be rested by now."

"Soon," Tom said, implying he would go immediately after Sarah Jane, but that wasn't his intent. First he would go to Rio Seco.

"Will you take Miss O'Malley?"

"No, I'll leave her here. I think it might be a good idea if you took the time to get to know her."

"She asked if she could raise the child." Harrison's tired blue eyes searched Tom's as though he wanted his opinion.

"She'd be a good mother," Tom said.

Now, if he could only convince himself the child would live to adulthood, everything would work out fine.

Just after breakfast, while Katie read a book in Caroline's room, a horse whinnied, drawing her attention. She might have ignored the sound, but curiosity got the better of her, and she padded to the window. After drawing the curtains aside, she peered out and spotted Tom leading one of the ranch horses from the stable, a saddlebag draped over his shoulder.

Where in the world was he going? And why wasn't he taking his own horse, Caballo?

If he thought he would sneak off without telling her what he was up to, he was horribly mistaken. She dashed out of the house and entered the yard, just as he was about to mount a dun gelding.

"Are *we* going somewhere?" Katie asked, while catching her breath. She batted a loose strand of hair from her eye.

He turned slowly, then looked her up and down. "*I'm* going somewhere for a while."

"Without telling me?"

His eyes swept over her again, this time granting her an appreciative smile. "I didn't think I needed to."

Katie stood tall and crossed her arms. "Under the circumstances, we're partners of a sort. And you at least owe me the courtesy of telling me where you're going. Or giving me the opportunity to go with you."

"I'm going to speak to a man named Cord Rainville. Martha Haney had asked Harrison to refer her to a private investigator, and I'd like to know why. And since I need to be back late tonight, I'll be riding fast and hard. So I'm going alone."

"What's wrong with Caballo?" she asked.

"Nothing's wrong with him. I'm leaving for Sarah Jane tomorrow before dawn, and I want my horse to be fresh."

Katie still didn't like the idea of being left behind.

"How do I know you'll be back tonight?" she asked.

"Because I told you I would." He touched her chin with the tip of a finger, the smile leaving his face. The intensity of his gaze took the fight from her. "Have I ever lied to you?"

"No," she answered again, realizing he hadn't. At least, not that she knew of.

He dropped his hand to his side, but his eyes remained on hers, unwavering. "May I suggest that you start considering the type of people you put your faith in? There are those who lie and those you don't. There are some who can be trusted, some who can't. Think long and hard about it, Katie. Your life, and the lives of those around you, could depend upon your ability to tell the difference."

"I will, but you have to admit, you don't say much to me at all. A person can lie by omitting the truth."

He shrugged, then turned toward the gelding.

Katie grabbed him by the arm, amazed at the swirl of goose bumps that fluttered over her whenever she and Tom touched. Did he feel it, too?

"Tom," she said softly, drawing his attention.

He turned warily, but his gaze fixed on hers.

"If there was something I should know, would you tell me?"

"Yes." His eyes grazed hers. "But the real question is, would you listen?"

Katie smiled. "I'd certainly give it a great deal of thought."

A grin brushed his lips as humor sparked in the depths of his eyes. Something else sparked, too. Something she didn't recognize.

Her stomach turned topsy-turvy. What was happening here? Had they reached a different level of familiarity? An intimacy?

Affection, maybe?

Katie almost preferred to get angry at the man rather than cope with this rush of uncomfortable and enigmatic emotions. She took a deep breath, wanting to broach another subject. "I overheard Maria talking to Abel earlier. I didn't mean to eavesdrop, but she asked him if you were Caroline's brother."

Tom stiffened, then scanned the empty yard. "What did Abel say?"

"He didn't answer."

Tom didn't respond, either.

"Is it true?" she prodded. "*Are* you Caroline's brother?"

"Let it go, Katie. Some things are better left alone."

She suspected, that if the answer had been no, he would have come out and said so. And her heart ached for the boy he'd been, for the hurt he must have suffered when he'd been cast out by the family who should have nurtured him.

Yet here he was, determined to protect Caroline's daughter, as well as her memory.

Katie reached out and touched his cheek, her fingers in plain contrast to his copper-colored skin. "What was your mother's name?"

"What does it matter?"

"It matters to me."

He studied her as if trying to decide if she was sincere or not. Apparently he decided she was. "Her name was Runs With Horses."

Katie smiled. "I wish I could have met her."

"Why?"

"So I could tell her that she had a brave and loyal son. And that she could be proud of the man he grew up to be."

Tom placed his callused hand over hers and brushed his thumb over her knuckles. "I don't like leaving you here, but knowing you'll stay on the ranch and keep away from the Haneys would make me feel a lot better about it."

Katie's heart fluttered like a swarm of honeybees soaring over a meadow of wildflowers.

Would he kiss her again?

He'd said he wouldn't, but suddenly she wanted his arms around her, his lips on hers. And while her pride begged her to pretend that she couldn't care less whether he did or didn't, her heart leaped when he dropped the saddlebag to the ground, then wrapped his arms around her waist and drew her lips to his.

Tom knew he'd be sorry for this later, but he couldn't help himself. His mouth came down on Katie's, as if making a claim on her, as if making some kind of promise.

Yet something deep within him called out for reason, and he sobered.

What was he doing? He was yearning for a woman that would never be his, dreaming of a life that he could never have.

This madness had to stop, and it certainly looked as though Katie wasn't going to do anything to help him. So he pulled his lips from hers, took a step back and dropped his arms to his sides.

"Is something wrong?" she asked.

Yes, something was terribly wrong. "This isn't a game. We can't keep doing things like this."

"Like kissing each other?" She cocked her head. "Why not? It's becoming rather enjoyable."

"In case you've forgotten, I'm a half-breed. We also fight like cats and dogs. We're like oil and water. We don't mix. Neither one of us wants marriage, at least, not to each other. It would never work out between the two of us. We're too different."

"Who said anything about marriage?" she asked.

"You can't keep kissing me like that and not expect things to progress in a serious direction."

"When you put it that way…"

"We can talk about this later. Right now, I need to go. The sooner I leave, the sooner I'll get back."

"If it makes you feel better," she said, her voice husky, "I promise not to be with Jeremiah alone."

He ran his knuckles along her cheek. "That does make me feel better, but I don't think Jeremiah will be around here very long."

"Where's he going?"

"He's going to follow me."

She placed her hand on his arm, and worry filled her eyes. "Be careful, Tom."

He could tell that she meant it, that the games and contests of wits and wills they each had been trying to win had ended, at least for the time being. And that touched him.

"Don't worry about me. Jeremiah Haney couldn't track a fat old cow in a snowdrift." Then he picked up his saddlebag, slung it over the back of the saddle and mounted the gelding.

Considering the fact that she always had an opinion or a comment to make, her silence surprised him. And it pleased him.

He glanced down at her. In the morning breeze, loose strands of auburn hair whipped across her face, and she brushed them aside from her pensive eyes.

"Be careful," she said again, this time in a near whisper.

Her concern sent a warm rush through his chest. "I'm always careful."

Then he urged the gelding onward, prepared to bring Jeremiah Haney to his knees.

Katie's heart tightened as she watched Tom ride away, handsome, solemn and gallant.

She still didn't know nearly as much about Tom "Lone Wolf" McCain as she wanted to, but as sure as the sun rose in the east and set in the west, the brooding loner had found a place in her heart. She cared for him deeply.

Could it be love?

Perhaps, but if that were the case, what was she willing to do about it?

Dreams and plans, once carefully structured, tumbled in her mind. Questions, too.

She could pray about it and ask for divine guidance. But ever since her very first run-in with Reverend Codwell back in Pleasant Valley, she'd found herself uneasy in church.

The pompous and self-righteous minister had called her a rebellious woman so often that she'd found more and more reasons not to attend.

And ultimately, she'd turned away from God, too. Not that she didn't believe in Him. But He'd… Well, He'd come to seem so distant and not at all like the benevolent Father or the comforting friend she'd once considered Him to be.

A sense of loneliness cloaked her shoulders as she watched Tom ride away, and for the first time since meeting him, she feared for his safety.

Please, Dear God, watch over him, protect him.

And bring him back to me....

She continued to watch Tom ride until she could no longer see him. Then she slowly made her way back to the house.

She entered the vast kitchen, breathing in the scents of beans simmering on the stove and yeast and cinnamon baking in the oven.

Maria stood over the table, skillfully patting balls of dough into round, flat pancakelike circles and humming a tune Katie had never heard before.

The older woman smiled, a smudge of flour on her cheek. *"Buenos días."*

"Good morning." How could she resort to tact and grace when she had only one thought on her mind?

"I have a question, Maria. I'm not sure if you remember this, but years ago, a young Indian woman named Runs With Horses came by here with her son, Lone Wolf. Do you know why she came and why she was sent away?"

Maria sighed and shook her head. "That was a long time ago. She and her boy were hungry. She wanted work and asked if there was anything she could do. The old caretaker, the man who worked in the yard and garden before Abel, felt sorry for them. So did I, but we knew how Señor Graves felt about Indians. His parents had been killed by renegades when he was a child."

"How long did the woman and boy stay?"

"Señor Graves was not home, so were going to feed them and let them spend the night. But Señor Haney arrived. When he saw them here, he chased them off. He had a walking stick, and he struck the woman with it. She fell down, and that little boy ran at him, swinging his fists. Señor Haney pushed the boy down, then kicked him." Maria lifted her hand and touched her brow. "His boot cut that boy's head, and all Señor Haney worried about was the blood on his pants."

"Did they leave?"

"Yes, but I went in the house and got some clean rags and warm water. Then I snuck it out the back door and took it to the woman. I helped her clean the boy's wound. It was very deep. But he did not cry. He was very brave."

"What did Mr. Haney do?"

"He went into the house and fixed himself a glass of whiskey. The caretaker felt so bad about it, he didn't eat or sleep for days."

"Which Haney did that?" Katie asked, not sure Jeremiah would have been old enough. Of course, how much brute strength and courage did it take to run off a woman and her small child?

"Señor Randolph." Maria itched the tip of her nose with the back of a flour-covered hand. "He dresses in fine clothes and acts like a gentleman, but he is not a kind man."

Katie didn't doubt it. She wondered just how cruel he and his son could be, especially if Jeremiah found out what she intended to do while he was gone.

"I want to talk to Martha Haney," Katie said.

"Oh, no, you must not do that." Maria continued her rhythmic hand motions. "Jeremiah will not allow it."

"Then I'll wait until he leaves town."

"You cannot go alone. My friend does not speak English."

"Are you willing to go with me?"

Maria sighed, her face grim. "Only if Jeremiah is far away."

"We'll wait until he's gone," Katie said. "I think he intends to follow Tom."

"Why would he follow Senor McCain?"

"I'm really not sure. It's just a hunch."

After a four-hour ride, Tom arrived in Rio Seco. As was his habit, he stopped first at the sheriff's office and asked where he could find Cord Rainville.

"Look in the Silver Buckle," Tom was told. "The man hasn't left the saloon in days."

Tom strode through the swinging doors and scanned the nearly empty room. Hazy sunlight filtered through dirty windows, and specks of dust floated in the stale air. In the far corner, a grizzled older man sat hunched over a table.

"Cord Rainville?" Tom asked.

The man looked up, steel-gray eyes drilling into his. A pink, ragged scar ran down the length of a bristled cheek. He had a hardness about him and a haunting pain in his eyes that whiskey apparently hadn't stilled.

"Yeah," he said, his voice raspy from either lack of use, too much tobacco or drink. "What do you want?"

A Colt .45 sat on the table beside a half bottle of whiskey. Tom didn't see a glass.

"Can I buy you a cup of coffee?" Tom asked.

Rainville began to chuckle, then broke into a booming laugh. "You gonna try and sober me up?"

"I thought it might be a good idea before hiring you." Tom didn't smile. "Otherwise, I'll try my luck and see how loose your tongue is."

Rainville studied him like a man facing a growling dog, sizing him up quickly. Apparently he chose to wait it out instead of drawing a gun or retreating.

Those cold eyes held a wariness, but Tom figured the man might talk—some.

"What's your name?" Rainville asked.

"Tom McCain."

"I don't know you."

"No, but you've probably heard of my employer, Harrison Graves." Tom hadn't meant to drop the old man's name so quickly, but he hadn't anticipated the suspicion behind those reddened eyes.

"Well, order that coffee and sit down. I don't like talking up to a man."

Tom called to the apron-clad Mexican bartender sweeping the floor. *"Dos cafés, señor."* Then he pulled out a chair and took a seat.

Rainville had that fermented smell of dust, sweat and stale liquor. Still, he didn't appear to be too inebriated to talk.

Of course, Tom had a feeling Rainville wouldn't disclose anything he didn't want to say in the light of day or in the dark of night—drunk, sober or with a noose around his neck and a gun to his head.

Tom liked that in a man.

The bartender brought two cups of steaming hot coffee. His hands trembled slightly as he set them down.

"Gracias," Tom said.

The man nodded and quickly returned to his broom.

Tom focused on Rainville. "I'd like to hire you to complete the job you started for Martha Haney."

"I finished that job."

"Then I'll pay you to extend the work."

Rainville leaned back in his chair and pushed the bottle away. "All right. You got yourself a deal. Tell me what you want me to do."

Chapter Thirteen

The Haney house loomed before them, dark and vacant like a forgotten crypt. Katie shivered as she helped Maria climb from the buckboard.

"I think it is best if we go to the back door," Maria whispered. She pulled a rusty lantern from the wagon. "Come this way."

The flame cast an eerie glow as the two women made their way around to the rear entrance of the two-story house. Maria opened a side gate and waddled past a large oleander bush.

A branch whipped back and scratched Katie's arm, but she didn't cry out.

When a coyote howled in the distance, Katie envisioned a vicious wolf bounding at them, teeth bared. "They don't have a dog, do they?"

"Not that I remember. Watch your step."

After making their way to the back porch, Katie rapped lightly at the door. "Should I knock louder?"

"No, Olivia sleeps in the bedroom just off the kitchen. She should hear us, even if we are quiet."

"*Quién es?*" a voice asked.

"Olivia, soy Maria."

The door creaked open, revealing a woman wearing a pale blue robe and holding a flickering candle.

When Maria explained in Spanish why they'd come, the woman's dark eyes widened. She clutched at her robe and stepped back. *"No, el señor dice nadie puede vistar."*

Maria turned to Katie. "Olivia says that Señora Haney is not allowed visitors."

"Tell her we won't stay long, and that we won't tell anyone she let us inside."

Maria nodded, then interpreted for Katie.

As Olivia stepped aside, Katie and Maria entered the house. Maria introduced the women, and Katie attempted a sincere smile. Still, the hired nurse didn't appear to appreciate their presence.

They followed Olivia up the stairs. A loose step creaked under Katie's foot, causing her to jump and her heart to beat wildly. She reached for the banister and continued to climb.

At the landing, Olivia paused, whispering a few words in Spanish to Maria, who then turned to Katie. "She is worried she will lose her job."

"Tell her I have money. I'll hire her myself." The words rolled out of Katie's mouth without any forethought, but she wasn't lying. She had some money put aside for unexpected emergencies, and if need be, she could assist the family until other employment was found.

Maria addressed her friend, and a look of relief crossed Olivia's matronly face before she opened the door.

Without warning, a musty, medicinal smell assaulted

Katie, making her gag. She wanted to open every single upstairs window to air out the room at once but held her tongue.

Light from the hallway illuminated their way until Olivia could strike a match and build a flame in the small hurricane lamp on the bedside table.

Katie stepped closer, watching Martha Haney's chest rise and fall. The woman was stout, with dark hair, her coloring pale and ghostlike.

Taking a chair beside the bed, Katie reached for the woman's hand. "Martha, wake up."

"Dios mío," Maria uttered, crossing herself.

Heavy lids blinked once, then opened. "Who are you?" the woman asked in a soft, gravelly voice.

She might be as crazy as a loon, or perhaps wildly dangerous, but Katie believed everyone was entitled to courtesy, so she stroked the top of her hand. "I'm a friend of Harrison Graves. My name is Katie."

The woman sighed then closed her eyes.

"Martha, please wake up. I'm here to help you."

The eyelids lifted again, and she blinked several times. Finally, she whispered, "Need…help."

"I'll do whatever I can. Can you answer a few questions for me?"

Martha Haney shook her head slowly. "Sleepy."

"I know. You're taking strong medication."

Martha didn't respond.

"Are you in pain? Do you need the medicine?"

Martha's eyes flickered open momentarily. "No. Yes. I…don't know."

"I'm going to ask your nurse not to medicate you. Can you hear me, Martha?"

The woman nodded, but her eyes didn't reopen.

"When you cry out, it frightens Olivia. She doesn't speak English." Katie placed a hand on Martha Haney's brow. "I'll return tomorrow. Try to be patient. I need to talk to you. I want to hear what you have to say. It's very important that you not take the medicine."

"Uh-huh," the woman mumbled, as her head rolled to the side.

Katie realized that would be her last chance to speak to Martha Haney tonight.

"Maria, tell Olivia to soothe Martha if she cries, but not to give her the medication as long as she stays calm." Katie pulled a gold coin from her purse and handed it to Olivia. "I'll bring her more money tomorrow."

Maria smiled and nodded, then directed her words to her Spanish-speaking friend.

Olivia responded.

"What did she say?" Katie asked.

"She will try."

"I can't ask for more than that." Katie made her way to the door. "Let's go. It's late, and there's not much more we can do here. Tell Olivia to call on us if Martha gets wild and out of hand. I have a feeling she'll be as eager to speak to me as I am to speak to her."

"She did *what?*" Tom slammed down his fist on the scarred oak table near Abel's bed.

"She went to speak to Martha Haney." Abel, who'd been sound asleep in the adobe bunkhouse when Tom had returned to the Lazy G late that night, scratched his head and yawned. "She took Maria with her."

Tom rolled his eyes. "Why in the world did she do that?"

Abel shrugged. "The nurse does not speak English."

"I mean, why did she go at all?" Tom raked his fingers through his hair.

All he'd wanted Katie to do was to stay out of trouble, but apparently, the only thing she knew how to do was to chase after it.

"Why didn't you try to talk her out of a fool notion like that?" he asked Abel.

"For one thing, I told Randolph Haney that you'd gone to Pleasant Valley after the little girl, just like you asked me to. And you were right, Jeremiah suddenly had business to attend to and left town right after that. So when Katie heard he was gone, she went to his house."

"Didn't you try to talk her out of that?"

"Yes, but her mind was set. Did you ever try to talk a woman out of something she was determined to do?"

Not *that* woman. Tom shook his head and scowled. There was no telling what mischief Katie would manage to get into if he left her on the ranch for a couple of days.

"I'm sorry," Abel said.

"I can't leave her here when I go after Caroline's daughter. It's too risky—there's no telling what she might do. Now I have no other choice but to take her with me."

"What did Señor Rainville have to say?" Abel asked.

"Among other things, Jeremiah had been visiting Caroline for years, yet he always told people in Stillwater he hadn't found her. When Martha had him followed, she found out about Sarah Jane. She was absolutely convinced that Jeremiah had fathered Caroline's baby and was furious with him."

Abel blew out a long, slow whistle. "Did she get crazy mad?"

"I don't think so. Maybe she just got angry enough

to need quieting, because Jeremiah clearly didn't want anyone to know where Caroline was—or that she'd kept her daughter."

"Is Jeremiah the girl's father?" Abel asked.

"I don't think so, but he had some reason for wanting to keep Caroline and Sarah Jane away." Tom patted the old man on the back. "I'll fill you in on the rest of what Rainville told me after I inform Katie that she's going with me."

Abel nodded, and Tom strode to the house. When he reached the bedroom in which Katie was sleeping, he opened the door without knocking. He intended to wake her and didn't care how polite he was in the process.

"Get up," he told her sleeping form.

Clearly startled, she bolted upright in bed, clutching the blanket to her chest, her eyes open wide. "What are you doing here?"

"I came to take you with me. Get out of bed."

"Where are we going?"

"To get Sarah Jane. But let's get something straight. I don't like the idea of taking you, but you've left me no choice. I can't trust you to keep your nose out of things that don't concern you."

"As a matter of fact, Martha Haney does concern me."

Tom slapped his hands on his hips and sighed. "You don't even *know* the woman."

"She asked for my help."

"She'll have to wait for your help. Abel's saddling Gully Washer as we speak. So get dressed. I suggest you wear those old clothes of mine, if they're clean. It'll be easier to keep a faster pace that way. And be outside in ten minutes."

"That's not enough time."

"Nevertheless, that's all the time you'll get."

Katie crossed her arms, the blanket dropping to her lap. "We'll have to stop at the Haney place. I told Martha I'd be back. I don't want her to think I don't keep my word."

"You're not in charge—no matter what you might think."

"I *promised*," Katie stated simply. "And I *never* break a promise."

Tom wanted to plow his fist through the wall. Instead, he turned and strode toward the door. "If you want to make a quick stop by the Haney's house, you'll need to be outside in *five* minutes."

"I'll do my best."

"Don't lollygag. If you're not outside and ready to go by the time the horses are saddled, I'll…"

"You'll what?"

Instead of an answer, he pulled out his gold pocket watch and made a note of the time. Then he spun around and closed the bedroom door.

Katie surprised Tom by coming outside—and wearing his old clothes—just as he was about to go in looking for her.

So after they mounted the horses, he kept up his part of the bargain.

Twenty minutes later, they reached the Haney residence, just as the sun peeked above the horizon.

The white two-story house stood alone, far from town. Weeds had overtaken a struggling garden, hinting that Jeremiah Haney hadn't concerned himself with day-to-day chores since his wife had taken ill.

A thin wisp of smoke rose from the chimney, snaking up into the dawn sky.

Someone was awake.

Tom didn't expect Jeremiah to be home, but he figured he'd better have an excuse for coming here without an invitation. Yet, other than the truth, he couldn't think of anything else a reasonable man would believe.

Katie swung down from the mare, the denim fabric stretching to accommodate her movements and revealing each feminine curve. Tom heaved a frustrated sigh, wondering if it might have been wiser if he hadn't insisted she wear his old clothes.

She tucked a loose tendril behind her ear. "Let's go around to the back. I'll show you the way."

"I knock at a man's front door," Tom said.

She gave an exasperated sigh. "But Olivia's room is in the back. She may not hear us if we're in the front."

Tom strode up the front steps, leaving Katie standing in the yard with her hands on her hips.

Shortly after he knocked, a Mexican woman answered the door, her eyes leery. When Tom introduced himself in Spanish, she nodded, then smiled shyly.

Katie, who'd relented and climbed the porch steps, reached into the front pocket of her pants and handed Olivia a ten-dollar gold coin piece.

"What are you doing?" Tom asked.

"I'm her new employer."

"It looks like a bribe to me," he said, somewhat surprised at her resourcefulness.

"Oh, no. It's not a bribe. Maria told me she has to support three young children, and she's afraid she'll lose her job. So I guaranteed her employment."

While her compassionate foresight surprised him—pleasantly so—he still resented her insistence upon making this stop, so he merely shook his head. "Come on. Let's make this quick."

Tom and Katie followed Olivia into the house and up the stairs.

When they reached the darkened bedroom, Katie strode inside as if she were a delegate of the Ladies' Aid Society and took a seat next to the bed. "I'm back, Martha."

As she stroked Mrs. Haney's arm, the woman's eyes shot open. "Daddy? Where's my daddy?"

"It's me, Katie. I came back, just as I said I would. How are you feeling this morning?"

Mrs. Haney's eyes were glassy, but when her gaze caught Tom's, she paled. A look of fear crossed her face.

"I'm Tom McCain," he told her. "I've just come from talking to Cord Rainville."

She swallowed hard and made an attempt to lift her head.

"Don't try to talk, Mrs. Haney. I want to help you. Jeremiah is more cunning than you think."

She nodded weakly, then covered her eyes and began to weep until she cried out with long, sobbing breaths.

"Dele la medicina," Tom told Olivia.

The nurse rushed to the bureau, grabbed a spoon and uncorked an amber bottle.

"No," Katie said. "Don't give her medicine. She needs to be lucid if she's going to talk to us."

"You can't just take her off the laudanum. She's been on it for close to four months, as far as I can figure." Tom turned to Olivia. *"Es importante que tome la medicina, pero reduzca la dosis."*

The woman nodded, then questioned him in Spanish, and he responded.

"What did you tell her?"

"To decrease the dosage slowly."

"Why? She seems to be taking too much. She doesn't make much sense."

"Laudanum is a form of opium," Tom said. "If she suddenly stops taking it, she'll get very sick."

"Do you think the medication is making her ill?"

"I'd bet on it. Jeremiah is no fool. He had to know what laudanum would do to his wife. The question is, why did he give it to her? And why did he instruct Maria to continue giving it to her?"

"To keep her quiet?" Katie asked.

"That's one way to ensure her silence and coopera-tion."

Fortunately, Katie held her tongue while Martha Haney took her medicine. He hoped that meant she un-derstood what he'd been talking about, which he found surprising. Up until now, she'd fought him every step of the way.

They both watched as Martha closed her eyes and slowly relaxed into a state of slumber.

"She asked for her daddy," Katie whispered. "I hope that's not a sign of her mental state. I'd feel horrible if she was being drugged for good reason."

"I think she's mentally sound, if that makes you feel better. And I think she'd be happy to have her fa-ther come take her home. I'll tell Olivia to have Maria send word to him. In the meantime, let's get out of here. There's a storm brewing in the wind, and I want to be well on our way when it hits."

Katie took him at his word, and moments later they were mounted and on their way.

They rode for an hour, yet the sky never lost the gray of dawn, and coal-colored clouds enveloped the sun.

"You said you wouldn't bring Sarah Jane to the Lazy G unless you were sure she'd be safe." Katie tucked a strand of hair behind her ear. "Will she? Be safe?"

"I have a gun, and I'll use it if necessary." He slowed his horse to let Katie ride up beside him, and looked her in the eye. "I won't let anything happen to her. She's Caroline's child, and I'll protect her with my life if I have to."

She had no doubt that he would, and the thought of his loyalty, his vow to protect Sarah Jane, warmed her heart. Yet it struck fear in her, too. She'd just begun to see an unexpected side to Tom McCain, and she didn't want anything to happen to him.

A flash of lightning cracked across the Texas sky, followed by a rumble of thunder.

Katie shivered, but more from the intensity in Tom's gaze than from the chill in the air.

He urged his mount forward before she could respond, and she followed his lead.

Within minutes, the rain began to fall, first in sprinkles, then in sheets. Lightning cracked and ripped across the sky in jagged streaks. Thunder, deep and ominous, rumbled and roared, causing the horses to become fretful and agitated. Still, Tom seemed to ride harder, faster.

"Where are we going?" she asked, her voice straining to be heard over the sound of pelting rain, creaking leather and her pounding heart.

"To find cover," he called over his shoulder. "Can you keep up?"

"I'll try." Katie hoped he knew where he was going,

because the horses weren't the only ones uncomfortable and skittish.

"There's a cave not far from here."

Katie envisioned a long, narrow tunnel—cold, dank and dark, with bats clinging upside down from a craggy ceiling. "I think I'd rather get wet than go into a cave."

"We'll be fine. It's more of a hollowed-out spot under a rock ledge."

"How do you know about it?"

"My mother and I once stayed there for a few days." He urged his horse forward, and Katie did the same.

With the wind and the rain in her face, Katie tried to keep her eyes on his back. She certainly hated to lose sight of him now. When Tom pulled up, she stopped beside him.

He nodded toward a dark space in the rocky hillside. "That's it. We'll wait out the storm in there."

Katie nodded, only too happy to dismount and escape the drenching rain. When they reached the small shelter, she climbed from the mare. "What will we do with the horses?"

"I'll take care of them." He handed her his bedroll and saddlebag. "Take these, then go inside and change into some dry clothes."

Shivering, Katie nodded and surveyed her newfound shelter. They might stay dry in here, but they certainly wouldn't have any privacy.

She called to Tom's back. "There's no door. How will you knock before coming in?"

"Make it quick and you won't have to worry about me interrupting you."

Katie ducked her head as she stepped under the ledge, her arms laden with her bag, as well as his bedroll that

was protected by an oiled-canvas cover and the wet saddlebag. She set them just inside the opening. Peeking
over her shoulder, she saw Tom tethering the horses outside, his back to the open entrance. She doubted he'd
stay out in the rain any longer than necessary and decided to hurry.

Her fingers fumbled with the metal buttons. She
struggled to peel away the wet denim clinging to her
skin and change into something dry. She wouldn't bother
with underclothes, or with tucking in the tails of a red
flannel shirt.

Once in dry clothing, she scanned the three-sided
shelter protected by rock walls and tried to imagine
a mother making a home here for her son. Had they
camped here to hide? Or had they stayed here after
they'd been told to leave the Lazy G?

Sighing, Katie opened a bedroll and made a place to
sit and wait out the storm.

"Will you hand me my bag?" Tom asked from the
entrance.

Katie tossed him the saddlebag and watched him
withdraw a change of clothing.

"Turn around," he said.

Katie did as she was told. She listened to the sound
of the rain pelting the ground and ignored the sounds of
him changing his clothing.

When it was clear that he'd finished, she asked, "Now
what do we do?"

"Wait."

"Then sit by me." Katie patted a spot beside her on
the blanket. "There's no need to stand for the next few
hours."

He ambled toward her, although she sensed reluctance in his steps. Still, he took a seat beside her.

"Tell me about your mother," she said, hoping to learn more about him.

He furrowed his brow. "Why?"

"Just curiosity. I'd like to know more about her."

He glanced outside, watching the rain splash off the gray ledge. "She was a pretty woman who worked long and hard. Sometimes she sang in the Comanche dialect, but usually she spoke Spanish. It was the language my parents had in common."

"Tell me about your father." Katie wondered if he would mention him by name. Would he admit to being Harrison's grandson, and Caroline's brother?

"We didn't see him often. My mother and I lived in a small cabin near the Lazy G. My father would visit us at times, but for the most part, we only had each other."

Katie couldn't imagine having no one to talk to as a child. "It sounds like a lonely life."

"Sometimes it was. It was also tough. Yet, as mean as some people could be to her when she'd go into town for supplies, she never complained about the life she was forced to lead."

His answer brought only more questions to mind, but Katie didn't want to ask too many at once. She preferred to quiz him gently. "How old were you when she died?"

"Ten."

"Losing both parents while you were so young must have been difficult," she said.

"It was." His jaw tensed. "I think it was hardest on her, though. She knew she was leaving me alone, with no one to look after me."

"So she knew that she was dying?"

"I think so. When she took me to the Lazy G and they ran us off, she tried to take me to her people. On the way, we camped here."

"Did she suffer?" Katie hoped that she hadn't.

"Some, but I think she suffered more from the rejection of my father's people than from her illness. They hated her for being an Indian and blamed her for loving a white man and having his illegitimate child."

Katie saw the pain in his eyes as he continued to stare out into the rain. It gripped her heart. "Were you with her when she died?"

"Yes, and I did my best to bury her deep enough so the wild animals wouldn't disturb her bones." He grew quiet, pensive.

Katie grieved for the small boy who had lost his mother. Longing to take Tom into her arms and console him, she reached for his hand.

At her touch, he turned to face her. When she looked into his eyes, she saw his pain, felt his need for love and affection. And maybe even more than that, his need for acceptance.

She couldn't think of anything to say that would sufficiently convey her sympathy or her desire to make things right.

"I'm sorry," she said again, knowing it wasn't nearly enough.

"It was a long time ago."

Tom turned his head, facing the gray wall of the cave, shutting her out of the memories he'd only begun to share. Out of his life, so it seemed.

Well, Katie wouldn't let it be that easy. Even though they fought like a stray hound and a wayward tabby, there were things she respected him for, things she admired.

And whether either of them liked it or not, she'd fallen in love with Tom McCain.

Chapter Fourteen

Katie and Tom remained in the cave until the rain let up, then they proceeded to ride until they reached Hannah's house.

Lobo heard their approach first and ran out of the barn. When he spotted Tom, he barked then raced toward him like a long-lost friend—or maybe a brother.

Next came Trapper, who limped out of the barn much slower. When he realized Tom and Katie were back, he called out, "Hannah! Come on outside. Tom's home."

The old man tried to pick up his pace, then reached for his right knee, his efforts to hurry clearly causing him pain.

The front door swung open as Hannah came out of the house. She wiped her hands on the dish towel she carried. Then she tossed it over her left shoulder and cupped her hands around her mouth. "Sarah Jane! Look who's here!"

Lobo stopped about six feet short of Tom's horse, turned his woolly head back to Sarah Jane, who'd just ventured out from the barn, as well, then he looked at Tom and barked several times.

"It's okay," Tom said. "I understand."

Lobo then trotted back to the child.

It was amazing, Katie thought. She wouldn't have believed it if she hadn't seen it for herself. Tom and the dog seemed to have communicated, just as Hannah had said they could.

Tom had told Lobo to look after Sarah Jane, and the dog had understood the order. Even now, he seemed to be questioning whether that order still stood.

When Katie and Tom reached the yard, they dismounted. Katie had no more than turned around when Hannah greeted her with a warm hug. "It's good to have you back."

"It's nice to be back. How's Erin doing?"

"Better," Hannah said. "The bruises are fading, and she's getting up a little more each day. I had Dr. Crandall come out to check on her yesterday, and he said that her larynx was injured when the man tried to strangle her, so it's difficult for her to talk. He says it will heal, but he wants her to rest her voice."

"I'm glad to hear that. I'd like to talk to her when she's able."

"The doctor seemed to think that would be in a week or so."

"How about Sarah Jane?" Katie asked. "Is she talking yet?"

"Not a single word. Dr. Crandall said to give her time—and plenty of love, which is easy to do. She's a real sweetheart."

As Sarah Jane approached the adults, the wolf-dog at her side, Katie offered her a smile. "I hope you had fun with Lobo, Hannah and Trapper while I was gone."

Sarah Jane nodded.

"Did you miss me?" Katie asked the girl.

Sarah Jane smiled and, again, she nodded.

"I'm glad, honey. I missed you something fierce. Do you have a hug for me?" Katie dropped to her knees and held out her arms. When Sarah Jane stepped into her embrace and squeezed her back, Katie's heart soared, and she offered a prayer of thanksgiving.

"How'd it go?" Trapper asked Tom.

"Not bad."

For a moment Katie's eyes sought Tom's. She saw a flash of sentiment, but for the life of her, she couldn't quite peg what it was—pain? Regret? Tenderness?

"We can talk while you help me cool down the horses," Tom told Trapper.

"Come on inside," Hannah said to Katie. "You, too, Sarah Jane. I'll fix us all something to eat."

As hungry as she was, Katie would have preferred to stay with the men and listen to what Tom had to say, but she followed Hannah into the house.

Once inside the kitchen she washed her hands in the tub of water in the sink. Then she watched the older woman move effortlessly about, removing plates, slicing bread and meat.

"Can I help?" Katie asked.

"Absolutely not. You sit down and rest."

When Katie complied, Hannah turned to Sarah Jane. "I have some cookies I'd like you to take to Erin."

"I'd be happy to take them to her," Katie said.

"Are you sure?"

"Yes, of course." Maybe Katie would get a chance to ask her a couple of questions. Erin might not be able to talk, but there were other ways to give a yes or no response—like nodding her head or squeezing her hand.

After Hannah filled a plate, Katie carried the cookies into the bedroom that had been assigned to Erin. Although the door was open, Katie remained in the hallway and said, "Good afternoon. How are you feeling?"

The brunette turned to the doorway and gave a little shrug.

"You certainly look better than you did when we first brought you here."

Again, Erin gave a slight shrug of the shoulder.

Katie carried the cookies into the room and set them on the table near the bed, where a piece of paper and a pencil sat next to a Bible. Apparently, Hannah had found a way for Erin to communicate, which was good.

"Would you like a cookie?" Katie asked.

Erin shook her head no.

"I'm not sure if Hannah told you, but Tom and I went to Stillwater to meet with Harrison Graves. Did Caroline ever mention her grandfather?"

Erin nodded.

"Did she like him?"

Erin reached for the paper and pencil. After a few minutes, she handed it back to Katie.

He was stubborn and hateful. They fought a lot. He sent her away and cut her out of his will.

"That's not true," Katie said. "I mean, he didn't cut her out of his will."

Erin bit down on her bottom lip, then reached for the paper and wrote again.

A man used to visit Caroline sometimes. He said her grandfather hated her for disobeying him and never wanted to see her again.

"Her grandfather had been looking for her. I'm not

sure for how long. Maybe not for six years. But recently he hired Tom McCain to find her."

Erin's brow furrowed as if she was trying to make sense of that information.

"Who told Caroline about the will?" Katie asked.

Again, Erin wrote out her answer. *Jeremiah Haney.*

Just as she suspected. Katie blew out a sigh. What would provoke Jeremiah to tell Caroline that her grandfather hated her and that he'd disinherited her? Had Harrison really threatened to cut her out of the will? Or had Jeremiah wanted to keep her away from the Lazy G?

And if he'd wanted to keep her away, how far would he have gone to keep her away permanently?

"Okay, now you can tell me how things went in Stillwater," Trapper said, as he and Tom led the horses to the barn. "What did Harrison Graves have to say?"

"He believes that I was able to find Caroline's trail—and that she's dead." Tom removed the saddle and blanket from Caballo and draped them over the top rung of the corral. "But he stopped short of believing me when I told him not to trust Jeremiah Haney."

"Who's that? Randolph's son?"

"Yes. And I think he's somehow responsible for Caroline's death. If I can prove it, I'm going to make sure justice is served."

"They got a sheriff in Stillwater. That's what he's paid to do. I don't know why you have to make it your business."

"You know why."

Trapper sighed. "So in the meantime, what are you going to do with Sarah Jane? She's a pretty little thing.

And she don't make no trouble. Hannah would love to keep her here."

"I'd feel good about her staying here, too," Tom said, "but that would deprive her of the ranch and estate that are rightfully hers."

Trapper kicked at the ground with the toe of a scuffed boot. "I suppose you figured out a way to take her to Stillwater and to keep her safe."

"Yes. I just hope my plan works."

Trapper crossed his arms and eyed Tom carefully. "And if it doesn't work?"

"Then I'll bring Sarah Jane back here."

Trapper began to brush Gully Washer. "I really like that little moppet. And Hannah near glows when she's fussin' over her. That wolf-dog likes her, too."

That was good because Tom planned to take Lobo back to Stillwater with them. Sarah Jane needed the extra protection the dog would provide.

Trapper grinned, his eyes crinkling. "Did you know that little girl snuck Lobo into her room last night after she thought Hannah went to sleep?"

"Does Hannah know?" Tom didn't think so. Hannah had always been pretty fussy about animals sleeping in the house. It had taken him a long time and a lot of coaxing to talk her into just letting Lobo come inside on occasion.

Trapper chuckled. "Yep, only a blind woman would miss seein' the dog hair on the sheets. But Hannah didn't say nothing about it at all for fear Sarah Jane would run off and sleep in the barn with him and me."

Tom couldn't help but smile. "It sounds like Sarah Jane is starting to feel at home here."

"I think so, too. And I gotta tell you, I hope your plan don't work out and she comes back with you."

"Don't hope too hard, old man. If my plan doesn't work, there's a good chance none of us will come back."

Bright and early the next morning, with a knife in his boot, a gun on his hip and a Winchester rifle attached to his saddle, Tom got ready to return to the Lazy G.

Hannah had tried to hide her tears while fussing over Sarah Jane. It tore at Tom to see her fretful and sad. He would have given anything to let Sarah Jane stay, but there was no other way.

Besides, he'd promised Harrison he'd bring her back. And the Lazy G belonged to Sarah Jane—not to Randolph Haney.

As he adjusted the saddle on Gully Washer, he heard footsteps and glanced up. Katie, again dressed in denim and flannel, approached. She appeared comfortable in his outgrown clothing, filling it out in a way that made him struggle not to gawk at her.

She tucked her thumbs in the back pocket of her jeans. "Can I talk to you before we leave?"

"Sure," he said.

"There's something I have to tell you, something I think you should know."

"What's that?"

She paused, as if she'd come to confess something that was sure to ruin his entire day, maybe something that would ruin his entire life.

And knowing Katie O'Malley as he'd come to know her, he didn't doubt it for a moment. She was as unpredictable as she was lovely.

"Spit it out."

She stood tall, and as was her habit, she lifted her chin. "I'm not sure what will happen when we return to the Lazy G, but I want you to know…"

He'd never seen her at a loss for words, which ought to worry him. "What did you do?"

The question seemed to take her aback. "I didn't *do* anything. It's just that I… Well, I've come to admire and respect you."

Was there a "But" coming from her?

"I care for you, Tom McCain."

The muscles in his cheeks tightened, and the proverbial cat not only caught his tongue but ran off with it.

Of all the things she could have told him, of all the things she could have said to put his life on edge, to set him off balance, he'd never expected that. She admired and respected him? And she cared about him?

Where had a confession like that come from? And why had she felt the need to tell him now?

And what in the world did she expect him to do with it? Admit that he was feeling something for her, too?

Well, maybe he was, but nothing could come of it. Loving Katie O'Malley would be the death of him.

What did she expect him to do now? Weaken and say something soft and sentimental?

He thought back to the first kiss they'd shared. She'd wanted it as badly as he had. And just like *that,* she'd slapped him.

"Don't say things like that, Katie."

She crossed her arms. "Don't you care for me at all?"

Care for her? Yes, but did he dare admit that kind of vulnerability to a woman like her, a woman who had the power to break his heart when she came to her senses?

"I care for you," he admitted. "But if you're suggesting anything more than friendship, you're overlooking the obvious."

"What's that?"

"The difference in our skin color."

"I don't give a fig about that."

Knowing Katie, she probably didn't. But that's not where the problem lay, and she ought to be bright enough to figure that out.

"Not all people are as broad-minded as you are," he said.

She sighed, then offered him an impish grin. "You do have a point, I suppose. I've been cursed with skin that sunburns easily and freckles beyond compare. I've learned to live with it, in spite of all the taunts I had in the schoolyard. I'm just surprised that you're allowing it to bother you."

"Don't make light of this, Katie. Do you have any idea how difficult life would be if you and I were to start courting?"

"I couldn't care less."

"Well, I care a great deal. I've seen how cruel some people can be. And I won't allow them to hurt you the way they've hurt me."

"People have said a lot of cruel things to me over the years, and I've learned to overlook them."

That might be true, but she brought on a lot of her trouble just by speaking her mind. A little common sense and tact would make her life much easier. She had no idea how difficult things would be if the two of them even considered something romantic—no matter how appealing the thought might be to either of them.

But if they were to succumb to temptation and marry,

what about a child they might conceive? Would their son or daughter grow up to have a happy, charmed life?

That was highly unlikely. Besides, Tom had given up the thought of fathering a child a long time ago. He wouldn't risk putting a kid through something like that.

So he decided to diffuse her romantic thoughts, even if it set her off again.

"The last thing either of us needs to do is to act on any feelings we might have for each other," he said.

"Why?"

"When I fall in love, it'll be for keeps. My wife will have to promise to love me—and to *obey* me. And you'd be hard-pressed to make a vow like that, let alone keep it."

"If I ever marry anyone, he would have to agree upon our marriage being a partnership."

"Something tells me that a partnership with a woman like you wouldn't be good enough. You'd want to wear the pants in the family." He glanced down at the outfit she wore, the britches that had once been his.

He hadn't been trying to make a point, it just seemed to…jump out at him.

"*You* told me to wear your pants to make traveling easier," she said. "Tom McCain, you are the most exasperating…" She lifted her hand as if she were going to shake her finger at him—or maybe even let him have it. Then she lowered it almost as quickly, turned on her heel and marched away.

As Tom watched her stride from the barn, he told himself how much better off they both were now that she'd gotten any foolish romantic notions out of her head.

Of course, they might be better off, but the ride to

Stillwater was going to be one of the longest trips he'd ever had to make—even if it was only ten hours.

As they prepared to leave, Katie berated her foolishness. Why had she thought telling Tom how she'd come to feel about him would make things better, easier?

Thank goodness she'd never mentioned love, because just admitting that she'd come to care about him hadn't gone over as she'd hoped it would.

She'd hoped it would make them a better team, a stronger team. And she'd hoped that he would have...

What? Told her he was falling in love with her, too?

She grabbed the reins and placed a foot in the stirrup, the leather groaning as she swung herself up on Gully Washer. She'd almost bared her soul to Tom, revealing feelings too new and too vulnerable to be exposed. Instead she'd only tiptoed around it.

Tom placed Sarah Jane behind the saddle of his gelding, then mounted. And without a backward glance, they were off.

Every once in a while, Katie ventured a surreptitious glance at him, hoping to catch a glimpse of emotion, an indication that he struggled with his feelings, too. Instead, she saw a stoic profile.

So be it. She'd just have to put it all behind her, too. She cleared her throat and spoke to Sarah Jane. "How are you doing, honey?"

The little girl smiled and pointed to the big dog trotting alongside the gelding.

"You're happy Lobo gets to come along?"

Sarah Jane nodded, eyes glimmering. It was good to see a spark of life returning to her. Katie had worried

more than she let on that Sarah Jane might not fully recover. Maybe the child's voice would return soon.

Tom turned in the saddle, giving Sarah Jane a warm
smile. "Let me know if you need to stop, sweetheart."

Katie adjusted the old gray felt hat she wore, tilt-
ing the floppy brim to block the sun, as well as Tom's
profile.

She wished she could block out her disappointment
and the ache in her heart just as easily.

Chapter Fifteen

When Jeremiah heard McCain had gone to Pleasant Valley to get Caroline's daughter, he'd tried his best to pick up the half-breed's trail, but he hadn't had any luck at all. Fearing that he might lose track of McCain altogether, he'd chosen another tactic and had gone back to the Lazy G, hoping to catch him on the way back.

If McCain planned to bring the kid to the ranch, they'd have to ride through the pass, so Jeremiah would wait on the bluff, with the sun on his back, and pick them off like tin cans on a fence post.

Then, finally, the killing could stop.

Every now and again he had a pang of conscience, but he wasn't a real murderer. If he was, he wouldn't have spared Martha's life when she accused him of fathering Caroline's baby and threatened to tell Harrison the wild story she'd dreamed up.

Jeremiah wasn't the father of Caroline's brat, but he had gone to great lengths to make sure Harrison didn't know the kid even existed.

And what about Caroline? Her death had been an accident, really. Her own fault, not his.

If she'd only kept her mouth shut, if she hadn't tried to run, she'd be alive today. But no, she had to threaten to tell the Taylorsville sheriff that Jeremiah had taken advantage of her. And he'd done no such thing. He'd offered to pay her for her favors.

Sure, she'd sniffled and cried after, but the tears had been for effect, to make him feel guilty. But Caroline had wanted him as badly as he'd wanted her. Women just didn't find it easy to come out and admit it. It was a game they all played.

Besides, she'd been born a harlot. Oh, she'd looked pure, even as a child, but she wasn't. She might have fooled Harrison, but she'd never fooled Jeremiah.

That's why she'd always avoided being alone with him whenever he'd visited the ranch.

Overhead, a flock of sparrows took flight. No use dawdling. He may as well get himself ready and in place.

Jeremiah stroked the butt of the rifle strapped to the side of his horse. Then he placed a booted toe in the stirrup and swung a leg over the saddle. He clicked his tongue. "Come on, boy. We're going to wait them out in the perfect spot."

But three hours later, in that prime location, as the sun burned high overhead, Jeremiah lowered the spyglass and cursed.

He could have sworn they'd come this way. Getting rid of them would be easier away from the ranch. He reached into his saddlebag, pulled an apple from his dwindling supplies and buffed it against the sleeve of his shirt before taking a bite.

It was hot today, and he was getting anxious to sleep in his feather bed instead of on the hard ground. He seated himself on the flat side of a big gray rock, drew up a knee and tilted his hat. He'd wait one more day before going back, but not with his tail between his legs. Of course, he had a secondary plan. A wise man always did. But he preferred to do it this way. Fewer questions asked, fewer answers needed.

When he bit into the apple, a burst of sweetness filled his mouth. A dribble of juice spilled between his lips and ran down his chin. He caught it with a shirtsleeve.

He liked apples. Fresh off the tree, stewed or baked in a pie. Martha used to make the best apple cobbler. That was one of the things he missed most. That and the lively tunes she played on the fancy piano he'd bought her.

He shook his head. He could live without cobbler and music. And had Martha carried out her threat to tell Harrison Graves what that private investigator had told her, he stood to give up a lot more than that. All Jeremiah had to do was to keep Martha quiet until after Harrison died. With Caroline gone—and no kid in sight—the estate would pass to Jeremiah's father and ultimately to him.

Martha's father might be angry if she ran home to him in tears, but her daddy's ranch paled in comparison to the Lazy G. Besides, Martha would come to her senses in time.

Jeremiah reached for the spyglass and placed it to his eye. "Well, what do you know? McCain chose this route after all."

And Katie O'Malley rode with them.

Jeremiah had thought she was just a nosy do-gooder, but he'd underestimated her. Apparently, she had plans of her own to lay claim to the Lazy G. What a pity. He'd hoped she might prove to be a willing lover during her brief visit. Now her visit would have to be cut short.

He slipped the rifle from the pouch, raised the weapon, adjusted the scope and aimed carefully.

Just a little bit closer. Then it would all be over.

The killing would stop.

It was nearing the end of the trail. As much as Katie would have willed it otherwise, she and Tom had yet to strike up a friendly conversation since she'd opened her heart to him in Hannah's barn.

Instead, he'd pushed hard for them to return to the Lazy G by nightfall.

Katie rode Gully Washer, Hannah's mare, while Sarah Jane rode with Tom on Caballo and Lobo trotted along beside them.

The blazing sun had finally lowered into the west, but the air was still too warm for comfort. What little breeze came their way only served to chap her lips and parch her throat.

Katie wiped the perspiration from her brow. She figured they must be getting close to the ranch. The land looked vaguely familiar.

"How much longer will it take to get there?" she asked.

"About an hour's ride once we enter the pass. It's just up ahead." Tom scanned the rocky horizon.

She'd noticed that his vigilance had increased the longer they rode and the closer they got to the Lazy G. If there was something she'd learned in the past few days, it was to trust his instincts.

But she didn't want Sarah Jane to sense her apprehension, so she said, "I'm looking forward to arriving back in civilization."

Tom stopped abruptly, the gelding sidestepping, snorting and throwing its head. "Hold up."

Katie pulled back on the reins. "What is it?"

"Up there. Near the top of the ledge." He didn't point. He merely nodded to the west. "Do you see the glare of sunlight reflecting off something?"

She placed a hand over her brow and searched, her eyes catching a glimmer of light. "Yes. What is it?"

"My guess is a gun barrel. Come on, we've got to make sure we're out of range. Then we'll take an alternate route."

He reached for Sarah Jane's hands, making sure they were snug around his waist. "You'll need to hold on really tight, sweetheart. We're going to ride hard and fast."

The child nodded, her eyes bright and trusting.

"Good girl," he told her.

As they turned, a shot ricocheted off a rock near the horses' hooves.

Tom cursed under his breath. "Hang on, Sarah Jane. Let's go."

Another shot rang out, this one grazing Katie's head. Afraid to take time to assess the damage, she ignored the sting of her brow and urged the mare to follow Tom and Sarah Jane. Several more shots followed, but she doubted they remained within the rifleman's range.

Something warm eased onto her eyelid, and she quickly swiped a hand across her face to clear her vision. Her fingers felt damp and sticky, yet she didn't dare look at them. She didn't have to. She'd been shot.

Afraid to do anything but follow Tom's lead, ride fast and hold on for her life, Katie looped the excess rein around the saddle horn and gripped it tightly. At first, she worried that Lobo had taken a bullet, or that he wouldn't keep up, but he ran to the side of them, his strides even, his tongue hanging from his mouth.

Then, as the thundering hooves plowed on, she worried about her own ability to keep up. Tom had slowed the pace, but still they all rode hard. Her head hurt and a wave of dizziness made it difficult to focus, but she didn't dare complain.

When Tom glanced over his shoulder, perhaps to see if she still followed behind, his expression grew solemn and he halted the ride.

"You've been shot," he said. "Why didn't you say something?"

Katie tried to read his expression, but his features all blurred together.

"You didn't ask," she said, her words ringing and spinning and echoing in her ears.

She clutched at the pommel with clammy, tingling hands. She probably looked a fright, and she hoped the sight of blood wouldn't upset Sarah Jane.

"I'm all right," she told the child. "Don't worry about me, honey."

But as she tried to manage a smile to reinforce the assurance, the world began to spin all around, and darkness enveloped her.

She was going to collapse, and there wasn't a single thing she could do about it except hope and pray Tom wouldn't leave her in the dirt.

Katie awoke in one of the guest rooms at the Lazy G Ranch, but she wasn't alone.

Tom sat beside the bed, watching over her, his eyes darting across her face, his hand holding hers.

"How are you feeling?" he asked.

"My head hurts, but I'm...all right."

He gave her hand a gentle squeeze, and when she gazed into his whiskey-brown eyes, when she saw the compassion brewing deep inside, the worry and vulnerability etched upon his handsome face, she realized she was seeing a different man than the one she'd thought she'd known before.

"Where's Sarah Jane?" she asked. "Is she all right?"

"She's taking a bath in Caroline's room, and she's in awe. Maria is filling her head with stories about her mother as a little girl."

"Good. Does Mr. Graves know she's here?"

"Not yet. Maria said he had a severe spell early this afternoon. He hadn't wanted to take the medicine the doctor left for him, but she finally insisted he do so. He'll have to wait until tomorrow morning to meet Sarah Jane."

"He'll be disappointed."

"That's why he resisted taking the medication—until he couldn't stand the pain any longer."

"I suppose that's just as well." Katie had wanted to be present when the introductions were made. "Is Sarah Jane nervous about meeting him?"

"She's still not talking, but you should have seen her brighten at the sight of Caroline's bedroom. She stood before the large portrait, then studied each small photograph for the longest time. The only way Maria could talk her into taking a bath was to promise to brush and curl her hair the same way she used to fix her mother's."

Katie smiled wistfully. She knew Sarah Jane would find comfort in these surroundings. And Maria would appreciate telling Sarah Jane stories of Caroline as a child. Katie almost wished she could be there with them, that she could listen to those memories unfold, too. But even if she were physically able, she didn't want to intrude upon a special moment she had no right to witness.

"And what about Lobo?" she asked. "Where is he? Vanquished to the barn?"

"Actually, he's overseeing Sarah Jane's bath. It took some convincing on my part, but Maria finally agreed to let him remain with her."

Katie smiled, then began to sit up, but Tom gently placed a hand on her shoulder and pushed her back onto the white cotton sheets of the feather bed. "The bullet only grazed your scalp, but you lost a lot of blood. I don't want you passing out again."

"I'm all right." She touched her forehead and fingered the gauze bandage.

"I believe you, but I'd feel better if you took it easy."

He'd feel better? Something hadn't just changed about him. Something had changed about...them.

"Why would you feel better?" she asked.

"I should have been more careful. I didn't figure he could reach us that far away, but he had a scope."

Katie had been prying and prodding Tom into revealing his feelings, but when he reminded her of the danger, of the man who'd tried to ambush them, her focus changed to one that was more immediate. "Who shot at us?"

He didn't answer, but she assumed he had a suspect. She had one in mind, too. "Do you think it was Jeremiah?"

Tom's eyes, once compassionate and loving, grew hard. "I'm going after him before he hurts either of you."

His resolve surprised her—not so much because he meant to protect Sarah Jane, but because he included

her in his vow. She chuckled softly while searching his
face, hoping to see a revelation of his feelings. Did she
dare hope to see love in his eyes?

"What's so funny?" he asked.

"I would have thought that you might have been relieved to be rid of me."

"Katie," he said, his voice soft and husky. "I'm beginning to think that I'm going to be burdened with you
for the rest of my life."

"Burdened?" she asked. "And maybe just a wee bit
blessed?"

He smiled. "That's left to be seen."

She glanced down at their hands, which were still
clasped together. He might be fighting what he was feeling, just as she had fought it since the first time she laid
eyes on him on the street in Pleasant Valley, but it was
there—plain as day. She wasn't sure how she knew what
he was feeling—or why. She just did.

"Don't you think you could care for me?" she asked,
hoping he'd admit it. "Just a little?"

He sighed, closed his eyes momentarily then opened
them again. "I do, Katie. But love isn't enough for what
we'd have to face."

Katie's heart fluttered. "Your love would be enough
for me."

He shook his head. "Maybe right now, but not as the
days passed."

She squeezed his hand. "God seems to have brought
us this far. Let's see where He leads us next."

"Fair enough." Tom lifted their hands to his lips, his
breath warm, vibrant and promising. Then he placed a
kiss on her fingers.

She opened her heart again, hoping this time he would

accept her gift and not toss it back at her feet. "I love you, Tom McCain."

"Don't say that." His voice came out soft and gruff at the same time.

"I'll say it as often as it comes to mind, so you'd better get used to hearing it."

He glanced away, as though struggling with himself somewhere deep inside.

"You said that you cared for me," she continued. "Did you mean it?"

"Yes. And I care for you enough to walk away rather than ruin your life." He ran his knuckles lightly along her cheek, setting off a rush of warmth to her very core.

"I won't let you walk away," she said.

He reached for a strand of her hair, letting it curl around his finger. "I can't see this working out between us."

"It will work, Tom. And someday you'll thank me for being so insistent."

"We'll see about that. But just so you know, I do love you, Katie O'Malley. More than I should."

"No, never more than you should. Kiss me, Tom."

Good man that he was, he did just as she asked.

The morning sunlight danced upon the west wall of Harrison's study as Tom paced the tiled floor and awaited the old cattleman's entrance.

Katie, her skirts fanned upon the brocade divan near the bookshelf, fiddled with a crocheted handkerchief. She looked every bit the lady as she faced the unknown.

Tom knew relinquishing Sarah Jane to Harrison's custody would be difficult for her, but it had to be done. Caroline's daughter belonged to the land, and so did her

descendants, who would live in the adobe-walled hacienda, ride the vast range and raise strong, healthy sons
and daughters.

Dwarfed by the tufted leather chair on which she sat,
Sarah Jane swung her feet and tapped her fingers on the
hand-carved mahogany armrests.

Tom thought of her mother. Like Harrison, there were
things he wished he could say to her, too. *I brought
your little girl home, Caroline. I only wish I could have
brought you, as well.*

As the door opened, everyone turned and watched
Harrison enter the room.

The old man shuffled inside, but as he spotted Sarah
Jane, he stopped to study her. After a moment, a slow
smile crossed his face. "You do, indeed, favor your
mother, young lady."

Sarah Jane perused the old man just as intently as he
studied her, then returned his smile.

That said and done, Harrison slowly took a seat behind the large, mahogany desk. He'd no more than set
his cane aside when the little girl got to her feet, crossed
the room and approached his desk. Then she reached
behind her neck and removed the leather medicine bag
Tom had given her.

The silence of the room was palpable as Sarah Jane
loosened the leather drawstrings and pulled out a small,
gold locket.

"What do you have there?" Harrison asked, leaning
forward and arching a gray brow.

Katie opened her mouth as if she intended to answer
for the child but, appearing to have second thoughts,
remained silent.

Tom sat beside her and took her hand in his. She

smiled at him, her bottom lip quivering, then gave his fingers a gentle squeeze. They both watched intently as Sarah Jane offered the locket to her great-grandfather.

Harrison fingered it before springing the tiny clasp. When he peered inside, his mouth dropped open.

"This is me," he said, as tears filled his eyes. "Where did you get it, child?"

Sarah Jane pointed to the portrait of Caroline hanging on the wall.

"Was that woman your mother?" he asked gently.

She nodded.

He took a deep breath and sighed. "About eight years ago, I took your mother to Dallas. She insisted I have my photograph taken. We argued about it for two days, but I gave in—that time. I should have given in more often, but I was a stubborn old man. I can't tell her how very sorry I am, but I'll tell you now. Will you forgive me for not being a better grandfather to your mother, and for not being a part of your life until now?"

Sarah Jane nodded, then reached out small, thin arms to hug him. Harrison embraced her, and his shoulders shook as he wept.

Moisture filled Tom's eyes. Unwilling to let anyone see it, he turned and glanced out the window.

He'd wanted to meet his father's people. To learn what kind of blood he carried in his veins. And he'd wanted the satisfaction of seeing Harrison Graves apologize for not helping him and his mother years ago.

Never had he entertained even a brief hope that Harrison would accept him as the grandson he never knew he had, nor had he thought to find peace with the stubborn old man. He still didn't. But this poignant display of love and acceptance for Sarah Jane would be enough. And it would last a lifetime.

Harrison Graves had redeemed himself in Tom's eyes.

"Sarah Jane," Harrison said, "I'll have Maria get your mother's dollhouse out of storage. She used to play with it for hours. I think you'll like it."

"I'd like to see it, too," Katie said. "Perhaps we can play together later. I never had a dollhouse of my own."

Sarah Jane broke into the liveliest smile Tom had seen since Erin's assault, and it seemed as if her healing might truly take place on the Lazy G.

"You'll both enjoy playing with this dollhouse," Harrison said. "It cost me a small fortune to have it made years ago. Perhaps you ladies can make new curtains— or whatever else you think it might need."

Katie smiled. "We'll have to ask Maria for help. I'm not much of a seamstress."

"I'm sure she'd be delighted to be included." Harrison patted the top of Sarah Jane's head, his fingers lighting upon the long strands as though they were spun gold. "Katie, would you mind taking Sarah Jane to find Maria and asking her to get the dollhouse?"

Tom expected an objection of one kind or another, but Katie surprised him by getting to her feet, striding toward Harrison's desk and reaching out her hand to Sarah Jane. "Certainly. Let's go, honey."

When they'd left the room, Harrison turned to Tom. "Now that we're alone, I'd like to have a word with you."

"What's on your mind?"

Harrison took a deep breath, as though unsure of whether he should share his thoughts. "I saw Jeremiah Haney early this morning."

"Where?"

"In my kitchen. He said he was coming to check on me, but I found him rummaging in a drawer. He had a candle beside him because the sun had yet to rise."

Tom clenched his fists, and fought off a curse word. "Do you really think he came to check on you?"

"I'd like to think so." Harrison leaned back in his chair and closed his eyes, but Tom wasn't fooled. The old man, his complexion pale, was in pain. And the meeting with Sarah Jane had weakened him. "But to tell you the truth, I didn't like the uneasiness I felt when I looked into his eyes."

"Then maybe you're ready for the truth."

Harrison gazed steadily at Tom. "I'm always ready for the truth. What's on your mind?"

"A couple of days ago, I rode to Rio Seco."

Harrison arched a gray brow. "Why?"

"To find Cord Rainville and ask why Martha Haney hired him to follow Jeremiah."

"And?"

"He followed Haney to Taylorsville, where Caroline and Sarah Jane lived. Rainville told Martha that Jeremiah had been visiting Caroline off and on for years."

Harrison paled, and his jaw tensed. "He'd better have a good reason for not telling me he knew where to find her."

"I'm sure he had a good reason, but one that only suited him."

"What do you mean by that?"

"It wasn't long after Rainville reported back to Mrs. Haney that word got out in the community that poor Martha Haney had lost her mind. Jeremiah hired a Spanish-speaking nurse to continue to medicate her with laudanum."

"What are you speculating?"

"My guess is that he wanted to insure her silence and cooperation."

Harrison leaned his head back in the seat. "Suspecting my friend's son of wrongdoing doesn't sit well with me."

"I don't suppose it does. Murder is a very serious charge."

Harrison shook his head. "I can't believe he'd go to that extreme."

"Then I suggest you speak to Rainville yourself. I asked him to meet me here."

Harrison studied Tom intently. "I'm not admitting I agree with you, but tell me something. Why have you gone to the trouble of trying to solve the mystery of this crime?"

Because Caroline had meant more to him than Harrison would ever know, but Tom didn't think the old man would care to know why.

Then again, maybe he feared that none of it would even matter. So instead, he said, "Caroline was a loving, goodhearted woman. And I don't believe she stayed away from you because she was angry. I think she would have come home years ago if she hadn't been convinced that you'd disowned her."

"I threatened to disown her," Harrison said, voice rising. "But I never followed through. I never would have. I had a terrible temper, and so did she. Our arguments were loud and furious, but they rarely lasted more than a day or two. Until that last one."

"Someone, other than you or Caroline, created the estrangement, Harrison."

"How do you know?"

"Caroline suggested as much to a friend." Tom sauntered toward the door, his steps slow and methodical. He paused at the doorway and looked over his shoulder. "I also think Sarah Jane's life is in danger. Someone tried to ambush us when we rode to the Lazy G. So I asked Cord Rainville to hire on for a few days. I want that little girl watched at all times."

"I told you before that I could lock this place up tighter than a fortress. I'll have guards posted. No one will get to her except by our invitation."

"Good. Why don't you invite Jeremiah and Randolph to come for dinner this evening. I think it's time to confront them both."

Harrison cocked his head. "What are you planning?"

"Let's watch Sarah Jane's reaction when she meets him."

"You expect her to recognize him?" Harrison asked.

"I think she'll expose him as the one who assaulted her mother's friend, and possibly as the man who shoved her mother down the stairs."

"I hope you're wrong."

"I'm sure you do."

As Tom opened the door, Harrison spoke to his back. "Were you in love with my granddaughter?"

Tom turned his head, his response slow and deliberate. "No, sir. I thought of her as a sister."

Harrison nodded, then locked his eyes on Tom's. "She would have been lucky to have a brother like you. I only wish you would have found her sooner."

"So do I." Tom stepped from the room and closed the door.

He hadn't been able to save Caroline. But, God willing, he'd lay down his own life to save her daughter.

Chapter Sixteen

Katie sat with Maria, watching Sarah Jane arrange small furniture inside a little, open-sided, blue-and-white house.

While growing up, Katie didn't have dolls or toys like other little girls had. She really hadn't known what she'd been missing since her love of reading had provided her and her father with so many hours of conversation and debate.

Yet living in a world of adults or literary characters had put her at a disadvantage when it came to conversing with the other children at school, most of whom struggled to comprehend the stories in their McGuffey Readers.

Looking back, she supposed that was one reason the other girls excluded her so often. She hadn't minded being left alone to read under the shade of a tree, but it would have been nice to have been included in games of tag sometimes. Or to have been defended when one of the boys had pulled her braids or called her names.

"I remember one Christmas," Maria said, drawing on yet another memory to share with Sarah Jane. "Your mother decorated that little dollhouse with sprigs of pine needles and red ribbon. Then the following spring, she went out into the meadow beyond the adobe walls and picked the colorful wildflowers that grew near the cottonwood trees. Then she made tiny bouquets and placed them in each of the rooms."

Sarah Jane looked up from her play and smiled, her eyes brighter than Katie had ever seen them before. She really was thriving at the Lazy G. The memories of her mother were helping to make her whole again.

Harrison had been right. The child would undoubtedly enjoy playing with her mother's dollhouse for hours.

Boot steps sounded, and Katie glanced up to see Tom enter the sitting room. Lobo, who was lying contentedly upon a gray-and-black woven rug in front of the fireplace, wagged his tail and whimpered a greeting.

"Katie," he said, "will you come out into the courtyard with me?"

"Yes, of course."

After asking Maria to excuse them, Katie followed Tom outside.

He lifted his hat and adjusted it on his head. "I'm going to ride into Stillwater to see the sheriff."

"What about?"

"I'd like to set up a meeting between Jeremiah and Sarah Jane. I think she'll be able to identify him as the man who assaulted Erin in Pleasant Valley. And after those shots were fired at us when we arrived today, we should have enough evidence for an attempted murder investigation—on you, as well as Caroline, especially if Erin has anything to add."

Katie reached for Tom's arm. "Please be careful. He might have been gunning for you."

"I'll be all right. If everything goes according to plan, I'll be back in an hour or two. But before I leave, Harrison wants me to have a couple of his men guard the house and yard."

"Do you think Jeremiah will come looking for Sarah Jane here?"

"I doubt that he'd be that daring. But just to be on the safe side, keep Sarah Jane in the house until I return with the sheriff."

"I'll look after her," Katie said. "And we'll both stay in the house. I promise."

Tom stroked her cheek, his gaze locking on to hers. "Watch yourself, too."

"I will. And just so you know, I may not follow orders, but I always keep my promises."

"So you told me."

She thought he might kiss her before he left, but he merely smiled then walked away.

Still, they were a team. And she'd never been more committed, more determined to follow one of his orders, than she was today. She would stay inside the house. And she'd guard that child with her life.

After Katie returned to the sitting room, Maria rose from the chair on which she'd been seated. "I'm going to find some old toys and some scraps of cloth and ribbons for Sarah Jane to use to decorate the little house. Do you want to help me?"

Katie glanced at the child and saw her playing happily, the dog resting beside her. Knowing that guards were being placed outside the house, she felt comfortable leaving the room.

"Sure." Katie followed the housekeeper down the hall,

around the corner and into one of the guest rooms at the back side of the hacienda.

"We do not use this room much anymore," Maria said, as she opened the door of an ornate mahogany wardrobe. "Just for storage."

She pushed aside a stack of blankets on one of the bottom shelves, then pulled out a basket filled with small pieces of fabric and doodads.

"I thought these scraps would come in handy one day," Maria said.

After she set the basket on the table, they began to sort through the ribbons, lace and pieces of cotton and flannel. Next they searched the wardrobe for other odds and ends Sarah Jane might find useful.

When Katie and Maria finally returned to the sitting room, carrying a doll, a wooden horse, a stuffed dog, the basket of fabric scraps and a box of buttons, they spotted the dollhouse in the middle of the floor but no little girl playing beside it.

"Sarah Jane?" Katie called. "Where are you, honey?"

She placed the basket on the settee. Where had she gone?

"Perhaps she went to the kitchen," Maria suggested.

Katie hoped so, but an uneasiness settled around her. She'd promised Tom that she would look after the girl, but now she didn't have any idea where she was. At least the dog was with her.

"She has not been gone long," Maria said. "Maybe she wanted another cookie. Or some milk."

"Maybe, but I'm not going to be happy until I know where she is. I'd better look for her."

"I will start in the kitchen," Maria said. "Then I will check the rest of the house."

"I'll go outside." Again, Katie reminded herself that Lobo was with the child, and that Tom had instructed the dog to protect her.

Fortunately, two cowboys now stood at the edge of the courtyard. She assumed they were the men Tom had asked to guard the house, and she felt instant relief.

"Excuse me," she said. "I'm looking for Sarah Jane. She was supposed to be in the sitting room, but she's not there."

"We just took up our post," the taller man said. "But we haven't seen her. Maybe she's in the outhouse."

"I'll check."

But Sarah Jane wasn't there, either. She hadn't been gone long enough to go very far. Still, Katie couldn't shake a growing sense of dread.

When she returned to the courtyard, she checked inside the house. Maria hadn't found her yet.

Back outside, one of the guards in front said he'd check the barn and the gardens while the other had to remain at his post. "If I don't find her, I'll gather up some of the men to go in search of her."

"Yes, please have the men look for her," Katie said. "In the meantime, I'll check outside the perimeter of the courtyard."

There was still no sign of the dog or the child.

Katie searched the horizon. To the east lay a grassy meadow, and farther ahead, a thick copse of cotton-woods.

Oh, dear. Had the girl gone in search of flowers to decorate her dollhouse, just as her mother had?

Had she left before Tom had sent the men to guard the courtyard entrance?

She spotted Abel heading for the barn, obviously

searching for her there. And several men were striding toward the outbuildings.

Katie cupped her hands to her lips and called out as loud as she could. "Sarah Jane!"

No answer.

Well, for goodness' sake. What did she expect? The poor child couldn't speak.

Again, Katie looked ahead, hoping to see the black-haired dog or the blue color of the gingham dress Sarah Jane wore. But she feared Sarah Jane's blond head would blend with the high, wheat-colored grasses swaying in the breeze.

Where in the world could she be?

When Katie had been that same age, she'd wandered off at least five times and had been brought home by the sheriff on one occasion. But then, Katie had always been a rebellious and adventurous child. On the other hand, Sarah Jane seemed quieter, more eager to please.

Picking up her skirts, Katie rushed forward, scanning the grassy areas while keeping her eyes on the trees ahead. Surely, her imagination had begun to play tricks on her, frightening her and goading her into over-reacting.

Why, Sarah Jane might be at home this very moment, sitting safely in the kitchen, munching on oatmeal cookies and drinking a large glass of frothy milk. And here Katie was, gathering thistles and foxtails in her stockings and along the hem of her skirt. Perhaps they would all laugh about it later, about how Katie had come back looking like a frazzled wild woman.

Still, Katie couldn't settle the knot in her stomach, the ache in her heart. Nor could she fight back the sting of tears in her eyes. After all, Maria would have called her back to the house if she'd found her, wouldn't she?

Unseen insects, buzzing and chirping along the way, reminded Katie of the nasty rattlesnake she'd frightened nearly a week ago, with its ugly head raised, rattles shaking, eyes staring her down.

She blinked back the memory, fought the bone-chilling fear and took care in watching her steps while looking for the child.

Dear Lord, she prayed, *I know it's been a while since You and I have talked. And that's my fault. I've drawn away from You—out of pride, stubbornness and just plain foolishness. I'm sorry for that. It's just that I've always tried to do things on my own before, but I'm finally beginning to realize how much I need You. And how much I need others—like Tom and Sarah Jane. So please forgive me. I need You, Lord. Especially now.*

"Help me find Sarah Jane," she said aloud, raising her eyes heavenward. *"You know where she is. Be with her and protect her. Be with me, too. And guide my steps."*

Well, would you look at that? Jeremiah was in luck.

About a hundred yards from the hacienda, just inside the copse of trees where he hid, Sarah Jane peered to her right and then her left, as if she was searching for something.

"Lobo?" she whispered. "Come back, Lobo. Where did you go?"

When she turned her back, Jeremiah stole away from his hiding spot and grabbed her from behind. Then he clamped his hand around her mouth before she could scream.

"So we meet again," he told her.

His arm circled her tightly. He could feel her little heart pounding like a runaway locomotive.

"I told you I'd be back. Remember what I said I'd do if I caught you talking about me? And what I'd do if you told anyone you'd seen me?"

Her head nodded.

"I ought to strangle you here and now, then leave your body for the wild animals to find."

Her heart beat all the faster, as if she knew the danger she was in. But he continued to hold her mouth shut, keeping her quiet until he could insure her silence for once and for all. "There's a ravine not far from here. It would be a shame if you wandered off that way and fell to the rocks below. What a terrible accident. It would be even more tragic than your mother's unexpected tumble down a flight of stairs, don't you think?"

As he started across the grassy meadow toward the ravine, his grip loosened on her mouth. He started to adjust his hand, but before he could do so, she bit down on his finger as hard as she could.

Jeremiah swore, then struck her face, jarring her silly. The brat was as feisty as her mother, but he'd deal with them both in the same way.

He'd no more than taken two steps when he heard a bark. He looked to the sound and spotted a wolf racing toward him, eyes blazing, teeth bared.

Again he swore, then he drew his gun and shot the animal, dropping it in its tracks.

The kid let out a bloodcurdling scream. "No!"

"Shut up," he said. "I've got another bullet just for you."

"I hate you," she cried. "You killed my mother, and you killed my dog."

"Well, now. That surely hurts my feelings. Yes, it does." Then he slapped his hand across her mouth again, quieting her, and headed for the ravine, where he would rid himself of her for good.

As Katie continued through the meadow, following what appeared to be bent and broken blades and stems of grass, she spotted a mashed spot up ahead that had been trampled down.

Was it fresh? Could Sarah Jane and Lobo have passed this way and stopped to play here?

She wished Tom was here to read the tracks, to relieve her fears, to hold her hand.

But he wasn't, and Katie was all Sarah Jane had.

A gunshot sounded from where the cottonwoods grew in a thick cluster. Before Katie could consider her next move, she gathered her skirts and darted toward the trees.

"Sarah Jane," she called, realizing the foolishness of charging head-on into gunfire.

She slowed her steps as she reached the trees, all the while looking for a sign of Sarah Jane—a footstep, a hair ribbon, something that would convince her to continue into the shadows.

A whimper sounded to her left. When she turned toward the noise, her heart turned inside out. For there, in the grass, lay Lobo, his head and shoulders bloodied.

"Oh, dear God," Katie muttered. All her fear came rushing forth. If she had a gun, she would put the poor animal out of its misery, but she didn't have a weapon.

No weapon....

What was she to do now?

She'd been so intent upon finding Sarah Jane that she'd marched forward without forethought and had fallen into a trap.

Lobo raised his head and slowly hobbled to his feet. The poor dog. Katie wished she could take the time to help him, comfort him, but as it was, she feared she might not find Sarah Jane in time.

She hadn't gone far when a twig snapped under her foot, and she nearly jumped out of her skin. "Well, now," a male voice drawled. "You have someone to keep you company, kid."

Katie turned slowly, her eyes lighting upon the narrowed brown eyes belonging to Jeremiah Haney.

"Let her go," Katie said, hoping her voice didn't betray her fear.

Jeremiah cocked the hammer of his pistol. "Put your hands in the air."

Katie lifted her arms slowly, her mind reeling at how to save Sarah Jane. She'd worry about her own life later. "Take me and do as you will, but let Sarah Jane go. She can't talk, so she can't possibly hurt you."

He laughed, the tone hollow. "Oh, no? She didn't have a problem telling me she hated me just minutes ago." He glanced at the child he still held, his hand pressed against her mouth. "Isn't that right, kid?"

Sarah Jane didn't respond, but she didn't have to. Her face, which had lost all color, and her eyes, as wide as those of a cornered wild animal, said it all.

Katie didn't challenge the comment, either. She just watched Jeremiah warily, her heart pounding to beat the band.

Jeremiah chuckled. "The kid used to jabber all the

time, just like a mockingbird. How Caroline could stand it, I'll never know."

"What are you going to do with us?" Katie asked, ignoring the issue of Sarah Jane's speech and hoping to gain some time, time for someone to come to their aid.

"I can't let you go. Start walking," he said, nodding his head deeper into the grove. "I've got to get out of here before someone figures out where that gunshot came from."

Katie had no alternative but to advance in the direction he indicated, hoping and praying someone found them in time.

With each step through the trees, Katie's fears intensified. She had to think of something to distract Jeremiah, to slow him down. If she could buy some time, someone might find them before he killed her and Sarah Jane. For she had no doubt that was exactly what he intended to do.

"Why did you murder Caroline?" she asked.

Her question seemed to take Jeremiah aback. He slowed his steps but continued to point the gun at Sarah Jane's head. "I didn't. She fell down the stairs."

Katie decided to take another line of questioning. "Why are you keeping Martha medicated?"

At that he stopped. "What are you talking about?"

"I was at your house. I saw your wife, and I spoke to Olivia."

She had his attention now, because he stopped walking altogether. And her only hope was to stall for time until someone found them.

"Martha isn't sick," Katie said. "And she isn't crazy. Why did you imprison her in the house like that?"

"Because she accused me of marital infidelity. She would have gone to her father, who's been holding her inheritance over my head, even though he had his own share of indiscretions. And I need to keep her quiet, at least for a while longer."

Apparently, Jeremiah hadn't gone home yet. So he didn't know that his wife had left with her father. Either way, Katie had to keep him talking. "Martha accused you of having an affair with Caroline?"

"Oh, I was willing. I'd always had my eye on her, but she went out of her way to avoid being alone with me. I'm not really sure what kind of game she was playing."

"Perhaps she wasn't interested in you."

Jeremiah's eyes narrowed as though he could see something Katie couldn't. "She was a natural-born harlot. She wore those britches by day and low-cut gowns at night. So one day, when I caught her in the hayloft with one of the cowboys, I ran the guy off. Then, when she and I were alone, I had my chance. She struggled some and pretended she didn't want it. But I knew that she did. And when it was over, I wiped her tears and told her it would be better next time."

"You forced yourself upon her," Katie said, her fists clenching at her sides.

"Like I said, she only pretended not to want it. Besides, I wasn't her first. When Harrison had caught her and that no-account cowboy kissing, he'd threatened to kill the kid if he ever caught them together again. So I told Caroline that I would tell her grandfather I found them both in the hayloft."

"That kept Caroline quiet?" Katie asked, not sure why the young woman wouldn't have approached her grandfather first and simply told him what Jeremiah had done to her.

"Before that preacher started coming around here,

talking about love and forgiveness, Harrison had a fierce temper. He would have shot that kid before Caroline could blink an eye and she knew it. And she would have done anything to protect him."

"How old was Caroline when all of this happened?"

"Old enough to bear a child." Jeremiah glared at Sarah Jane, then chuffed.

"So when Martha hired that investigator and found out about Caroline's baby, she thought the child was mine. But look at her. Anyone can tell she's not. She's too pale and scrawny. She doesn't look at all like me."

Katie swallowed back the bile that had risen in her throat, trying hard not to imagine the painful thoughts going through Sarah Jane's mind. But before she could speak, the little girl turned her head, freeing her mouth from Jeremiah's grip.

"My daddy's name was Davie. And he was strong and brave. Mama never would have loved a man like you. My daddy was good and kind."

Jeremiah glared at her, "Oh, yeah? Well, your good 'daddy' left her when he found out about you."

"That's not true," Sarah Jane said, lip quivering slightly.

"What would you know? You're just a couple years out of a diaper."

"I know a lot," Sarah Jane said, small chin lifting. "I know my mama hated you, and I know why she fell down the stairs. She was trying to get away from you, and you pushed her."

"Yeah, I pushed her all right," Jeremiah said, all signs of humor leaving him. "And I'm going to give you and your pretty friend a push, too."

* * *

Tom hadn't ridden as far from the ranch as he'd hoped when he'd heard a gunshot and a child's scream. He didn't know how or why—just that the unthinkable had happened.

The thought that Katie hadn't kept her word hadn't crossed his mind. She'd promised not to leave the house, and he believed her. It was as simple as that.

He rode as fast as he could, following the sound toward a field of wildflowers before reaching a thick grove of cottonwoods.

As his eyes landed upon a patch of dried leaves soaked in blood, Tom stopped abruptly, his heart pounding.

No body, but a trail of crimson drops led deeper into the trees. If Jeremiah had hurt either Katie or Sarah Jane, Tom would make sure justice was served if he had to join the posse that went after him.

Walking lightly, he followed the blood trail. At first he thought he might only have imagined Katie's voice, but as he moved closer, she spoke again. His movements stilled as his senses keened.

"What do you think you're going to do after you've killed us? Tom will come looking for you."

Jeremiah gave Sarah Jane a push, then stepped closer to Katie and nudged her with the barrel of his gun. "I'd just as soon shoot that Indian as look at him. And nobody will care about the death of a half-breed. That's the way of it in these parts."

"Then I suggest you watch your back," Tom said, his gun already drawn.

Jeremiah grabbed Katie, jerked her close and pointed his own gun to her temple. "Drop it, McCain, or I'll shoot."

If he'd held another hostage, anyone except Katie, Tom might have refused to lower his gun, might have tried to call his bluff. But he couldn't risk the life of the woman he loved more than he dared to admit.

As Tom lowered his gun, he spotted Lobo, creeping along on his haunches, bloodied and battered, his dark eyes on Haney. As the Colt .45 dropped to the ground, Lobo jumped toward Jeremiah's leg, grabbing his thigh.

"Aah!" Jeremiah loosened his hold on Katie, but before he could aim the gun at Lobo, Tom lunged forward, knocking both the dog and the man off balance.

With one hand gripping the wrist that held the six-shooter, Tom landed on top of Jeremiah. He swung his fist, striking the man squarely in the jaw.

"Back off, Lobo," Tom called.

The wolf-dog growled and snapped one last time before obeying the command.

A crack sounded as Tom's fist connected with Jeremiah's nose. Slamming the hand that gripped the weapon to the ground, Tom managed to jar the pistol free. Then he snatched the gun and aimed the barrel at Haney.

His finger strained against the trigger. So intense was his anger at the man who'd surely murdered Caroline and would have killed Katie and Sarah Jane that, for a moment, Tom didn't know whether he'd fire or not.

"They'll hang you for shooting me, half-breed," Jeremiah said, his eyes wild with fear. "That's the way it is around here."

Haney was right. And nothing would ever change that. Tom could rid the world of a cruel, evil man, and then he would be punished for the deed—all because of the blood that ran in his veins.

But more than that, there was God's law to worry about. And it wasn't up to Tom to judge the man.

Letting Haney live would be more of a punishment because Jeremiah Haney, a pillar of the Stillwater community, would be tried, convicted and executed for what he'd done to Caroline.

At that point, several of Harrison's men arrived, with guns drawn.

"Can one of you get a wagon?" Tom asked. "I'd like to haul my dog back to the house. He was injured trying to protect Harrison's great-granddaughter."

Katie, who'd knelt to comfort Sarah Jane, slowly rose, lifting the whimpering child, who clutched her with a grip not likely to loosen anytime soon. "It's over, sweetheart. You don't have to be afraid any longer. Tom will see to it that you and I are safe—now and forever." Then she turned to Tom and smiled. "I knew, if I kept him talking long enough, you would come to find us."

"I'd hoped your clever wit would come in handy. It looks like we've both found some things we admire about each other."

"I agree."

"We can talk about this later, but maybe we ought to consider forming a permanent partnership."

"I'd like that." Katie tossed him a smile, then gently placed Sarah Jane onto the ground, took her by the hand, and led her back to the house.

Chapter Seventeen

Back at the Lazy G, Sarah Jane stood watch as Katie and Maria tended Lobo's wounds and refused to leave her heroic friend's side until she was sure he would live. The bullet had cut a deep gash across the dog's head, nearly taking off his ear before striking his shoulder.

Katie worried that someone might suggest putting him out of his misery, especially in front of Sarah Jane, but she hadn't needed to be concerned about that. Tom had insisted they treat the animal as if he were human, and she had no objections whatsoever.

A couple of Harrison's men had summoned the sheriff, and when he arrived, he found Jeremiah under armed guard, his hands and feet bound. Before taking him into custody, the sheriff took statements from both Tom and Katie.

"If you don't mind," Sheriff Tipton said, "I'd like to question the little girl."

"She's been traumatized," Katie said. "Please don't press her too hard."

"I'll go easy on her, ma'am. I have a couple of little

ones of my own. But she's a witness to more than just this incident."

Katie nodded, then followed him into the hacienda and to the sitting room, where Sarah Jane sat beside a sleeping Lobo, stroking his fur. The dollhouse, now forgotten, rested just a few feet away.

"That's a fine family of dolls you have," Sheriff Tipton said.

Sarah Jane nodded. "They belonged to my mama."

"Did they now." The sheriff took a seat in the chair closest to her, removed his hat and learned forward, resting his forearms on his knees. "Miss O'Malley tells me you were playing with these dolls earlier today, before all the trouble began."

Sarah Jane nodded. "I wanted to find some wildflowers to decorate the rooms, just like my mama used to do. So me and Lobo went outside for a walk in the meadow where they grow. And that's when Mr. Haney came and got us. Lobo tried to help me, and Mr. Haney shot him."

"You have a very brave dog."

She nodded. "He's the *best* dog in the *whole* world."

"That he is."

Sarah Jane gave Lobo a soft and gentle hug.

"Is this the first time you saw Mr. Haney?" the sheriff asked.

Sarah Jane slowly shook her head. "He's the man who hurt Erin when we were going to the mercantile. He wanted us to go with him that day, and she told him no because she didn't like him. Mama didn't like him, either. But he kept telling me and Erin that we had to go with him or else."

"Or else what?" the sheriff asked.

"I don't know. Something bad would happen, I think.

She told him to turn her loose, and then he hit her really hard. And he kept hitting her. I cried for help, and when Blossom came running, he grabbed my arm really hard and pulled me with him. I thought he was going to take me away, but I kicked him and bit him, and he let go. Then I ran as fast as I could."

"You're a smart girl. And very brave. Did you tell the sheriff who hurt you and Erin?"

"I was *afraid* to tell. Because when we were in Taylorsville, Mr. Haney told me that if I ever told anyone about him, he'd push me down the stairs, too."

At that, Tom eased closer to the child. "He'd push you down the stairs, *too?*"

Sarah Jane nodded, the tears welling in her eyes. "Just like Mama."

"I knew it," Tom said. "That fall wasn't an accident."

"Tell me about the day your mama fell down the stairs," the sheriff asked. "Who was at home?"

"It was almost dinnertime, and Erin went to see Mrs. Phillips about a job because they didn't need her to work at the restaurant anymore. Mama was in the kitchen."

"Was Mr. Haney there?"

"Yes. Mama never liked it when he came. When he left, she always cried. But this time, it was different. Their voices were loud. I heard them go upstairs. She told him to leave, but he wouldn't."

"Where were you?" the sheriff asked.

"Downstairs, in Erin's room playing with my doll. But I opened the door and came out."

"What were your mother and Mr. Haney doing?"

"He was all red in the face and angry. And Mama was crying. She told me to go back into the room, so I did. But then I heard her scream. I thought someone really big ran down the stairs really fast. When I came to see what happened, Mama was lying on the floor. And there was blood."

"Where was Mr. Haney?"

"Upstairs. He came down and looked at Mama. Her neck was crooked. And she wasn't moving or talking. She just laid there with her eyes open. Then he looked at me and said, 'I'm leaving now. But if you tell anyone you saw me here, I'll come back and push you down the stairs, too.' Then he left, but not out the front door. He went back upstairs to Mama's bedroom. I think he must have climbed out a window."

"Then what happened?"

"I knelt down by Mama, but she just laid there for the longest time, making funny noises. When Erin came home, she called the doctor. But Mama never woke up again."

Tom cleared his throat and said, "They told me in Taylorsville that Caroline broke her neck. She lived for a few hours, but never regained consciousness."

"Sarah Jane," the sheriff asked, "did you tell the sheriff what you saw and heard?"

She shook her head no. "I was scared. I thought he would come back and hurt me."

"And you didn't tell Erin, either?"

"No. Am I in trouble?"

"Of course not. Jeremiah Haney is the one who's in trouble. He's a bad man. And he'll be punished for what he did."

"Sarah Jane," Tom said, "I have a question you might not be able to answer. But I'm going to ask it anyway. Why did you and Erin move from Taylorsville? I thought you might have left because you were both afraid of Jeremiah."

"We left because someone took all the money Mama had been saving. And Erin couldn't pay the rent. After Mama died, Erin looked for it in Mama's bedroom, but it wasn't there."

Had Jeremiah stolen it? Is that what they'd fought about?

Either way, the child's account of her mother's death was enough evidence to charge him with murder.

After the sheriff and his deputy took Jeremiah back to town, Sarah Jane finally collapsed into tears.

Nearly an hour later, Katie still held her while she wept. The poor little girl's grief tore at Katie's heart until she wondered if the tears would ever stop. She glanced around the sitting room at Tom, Harrison, Abel and Maria, noting her concern was mirrored by them all.

Finally, Tom got to his feet and strode across the tiled floor. "Can't you do something? It's killing me to see her cry like that."

Katie continued to hold the girl, rocking her gently and stroking her back as she sobbed. "I think it's best if we allow her to grieve."

Maria nodded in agreement. "*Sí,* she has kept too much inside for too long."

She was right. The self-imposed silence had surely taken a toll on the child. Tom sighed and looked to Harrison as if hoping for a suggestion.

The old cattleman sat stoically in a chair next to Abel, his face pale, his jaw taut. Finally, he got to his feet, too. Then he shuffled forward, placing a frail hand upon Sarah Jane's head. "Sweetheart, I swear to you, Jeremiah Haney will pay for what he did to your mother."

Sarah Jane continued to cry as though her great-grandfather's words held no comfort whatsoever.

Katie knew she had to soothe the child for the sake of the adults who suffered along with her, all of them wanting to help but unable to ease her pain. "I know you miss your mother something awful. But I want you to know something. She's in Heaven with the angels now," Katie said.

Sarah Jane's cries began to abate just a bit, and Katie knew she was listening.

"You can't see her, but I know she was there with you today. She watched over you until we found you."

The little girl took a deep breath, shuddering as the racking cries began to subside little by little.

"Now that your mama has angel wings, she'll continue to be with you, even though you can't see her. She'll watch out for you always."

"But," Sarah Jane began, lip quivering and words coming slowly. "I can't…ever hug…her again. I…can't… tell her…that I love her."

"No," Katie said. "You can't hug her here on earth, but I think there will be times she'll be so close that you'll feel warm and loved and safe. And you'll be able to hug her again someday in Heaven."

"I miss her."

"I know you do, honey." Katie brushed a strand of hair from her wet cheek. "But there's something important she wants you to do."

Sarah Jane sniffled. "What's that?"

"Your mama wants you to enjoy all the earthly things she can no longer experience."

"How can I do that?"

Katie smiled warmly. "Well, you can take an extra

sniff of a lilac. You can enjoy the warmth of the sun on your face for just a moment longer. And you can walk barefoot in the wet sand along a creek bed a few more steps."

"How do you know that?"

"Because that's what I've done since my mother went to Heaven."

Sarah Jane looked at Katie, eyes red rimmed and puffy, nose runny. She sniffled again. "Do you think our mamas have met?"

"Absolutely," Katie told her. "And they're both smiling right now, knowing that we have each other. I can feel it. Can't you? Just a little?"

Sarah Jane wiped her nose on her sleeve. "Maybe. Does that mean you'll stay with me and take care of me, just like a mother?"

"Yes," Katie answered, her heart nearly ready to burst.

How she would have liked to have had a loving woman hold her, just like a mother. Someone who smelled of lilac and who always had time for a hug or a kiss.

A daddy might be special in his own right, but he wasn't a mama.

"What about Wyoming?" Sarah Jane asked. "Will you take me with you?"

"No, honey," Katie said, her decision already made. Sarah Jane belonged in Texas, at least while Harrison was still alive, and Katie wouldn't leave the child, not now, not ever. "I'm afraid the people of Granville will have to find another teacher."

Katie doubted Harrison would turn down her offer to raise Sarah Jane, especially after today, but she would just have to trust God that the details would work themselves out.

Sarah Jane turned to Harrison. "Can we live here?"

Relief flooded the old man's face and he broke into a broad grin, eyes twinkling. "Until long after your children have great-grandchildren."

For the first time in hours, Sarah Jane began to smile. She glanced at Tom. "And will you live with us, too? You and Lobo?"

A hard smile formed on Tom's face. "I can't live here, but Lobo can. I'll come by every once in a while to visit, though."

Katie's heart sank. She glanced first at Harrison, then to Tom and back to Harrison. Surely Tom understood she couldn't leave Sarah Jane. Not now, and probably not ever. The grief-filled little girl needed her.

Maria stepped forward. "I have prepared a bath for you, *mija*. Come with me to your mother's room."

When Sarah Jane and Maria left the room, Katie turned to face Tom. "Surely, you can stay for a while."

His features were cool and unreadable. "Just for a few days."

"But what about Sarah Jane?" Katie asked hopefully. "She needs to feel some stability right now."

And what about me? she wondered.

Tom scanned the faces in the room. "She'll have everything she needs right here. This is her home. It's where she belongs."

Katie's heart ached, torn between a man and a child. She doubted she was the first woman to feel that way, but it hurt. And right this moment, life seemed anything but fair.

At that point, Abel got to his feet, faced Tom and

lifted a gnarled finger. "Tell Señor Harrison who you are."

Tom didn't answer.

"If you don't want to admit it, then why don't you tell him what time it is. Pull out that pocket watch you carry, the one your father gave you."

Harrison cocked his head and looked at Tom. "What's he talking about?"

Tom still didn't respond.

Katie wanted to throttle him for not speaking up.

Harrison stepped closer to Tom. "Let me see the watch."

Slowly, Tom reached into his pocket. He withdrew the round, gold timepiece and handed it to Harrison.

The old man's jaw dropped and his eyes widened. "This is Robert's watch. I gave it to him. It was meant to be an heirloom. Where did you get it?"

Tom took a deep breath then averted his eyes. "My father gave it to me."

"Your father?" Harrison asked, his demeanor ramrod straight, focused.

"My father told me to bring it to you if I ever needed anything, if I ever wanted to convince you of my parentage."

Harrison stepped closer, taking in every feature of Tom's face. "You're Robert's son? My grandson?"

Tom appeared to lean back. "I don't need anything from you, and I won't be staying."

Harrison opened his arms, reaching out to embrace Tom. At first Katie thought Tom might pull away from the old man, refuse his offer of love. But as Harrison wrapped his arms around the younger man, he seemed to pull Tom right into his heart and family.

Katie could only hope the man she loved would find peace for the rejected little boy he had once been.

Quietly, she turned and left the room. Abel followed her out, granting grandfather and grandson a moment of privacy, such a precious gift in the short time they had left.

Katie sat upon the settee in the sitting room, staring in her lap at an unopened book. She almost wished for Sarah Jane's company, but the poor child had nearly collapsed in exhaustion after her bath. Even Maria had retired early, completely drained from the emotional turmoil following Jeremiah's arrest.

Fingering the gold lettering of the title on the dark blue cover, she glanced at the closed doorway to Harrison's study. Tom and Harrison had slipped in there an hour ago and had yet to emerge.

An ornate clock upon the mantel slowly ticked away the time. Reading was out of the question. Whenever Katie tried to focus on a passage, her mind raged with curiosity about the conversation taking place on the other side of the closed double doors.

She hoped the words that passed between the men would change Tom's mind about leaving. Sarah Jane wasn't the only one who belonged at the Lazy G. As Harrison's grandson, Tom was an heir, also.

Could the two of them work things out? She said a prayer, leaving it in God's hands.

Footsteps clicked upon the tile floor, and Katie turned toward the kitchen.

Abel walked into the room with a linen-covered tray. "I brought you some cookies and milk."

"Why, thank you." Katie hoped his company would divert her thoughts.

When a sharp rap sounded at the front door, Katie nearly jumped from her seat, jostling the book on her lap. She snatched one side of the cover to keep it from falling to the floor. The frightening ordeal with Jeremiah certainly had set her nerves on end.

After placing the tray upon a small, hand-carved table, Abel answered the door.

An older gentleman of medium height and build entered the room. He removed his hat.

"Come in, Señor Wellman," Abel said. "I will let Señor Graves know you are here."

The man wasn't at all handsome, but a fine linen suit and a crisp white shirt gave him a distinguished look. Katie didn't remember meeting him at the Cattleman's Ball. She wondered if he might be a neighbor.

"Thank you." Mr. Wellman's eyes met Abel's. "I'm actually looking for Jeremiah. Have you seen him?"

"Yes, but he is no longer here," Abel said.

The man narrowed his eyes. "Where did he go?"

"To jail," Abel answered.

The man scowled. "What's the charge? I have a few of my own to add."

"Murder," Abel said. "He killed Caroline Graves."

The man paled then mumbled something under his breath. He glanced at Katie. "I'm Martin Wellman. My daughter is married to Jeremiah, although she won't be much longer."

Katie set the book aside and stood. Walking toward Martha Haney's father, she extended a hand. "I'm Katie O'Malley. I met your daughter a couple of days ago."

Mr. Wellman's expression softened. "Martha told me about you. You saved her life."

Katie shrugged her shoulders. "I'm not sure if that's the case, but I believe Jeremiah had been drugging her for months."

Mr. Wellman snorted. "Drugged? According to the doctor, he nearly killed her. It's going to be a long and difficult recovery for her, but Martha is determined to regain her health."

Katie sighed in relief. "I'm so glad. He kept her a prisoner in that darkened upstairs bedroom."

Wellman shook his head. "A prisoner usually has his wits about him. Haney nearly drove my little girl mad. I'd ring his neck if he were here right now. As it is, I'll see she gets an immediate divorce."

"Let me get you a cup of coffee," Katie said. "I'm sure Harrison will want to speak to you."

Katie was right. After Abel left to announce Mr. Wellman's arrival, the study door opened and Tom and Harrison entered the sitting room. Her heart filled with expectation, but she held her questions.

Tom appeared relaxed, yet he didn't smile or offer a clue to his mood or whether he'd made a change of plans.

"Martin," Harrison said, his voice warm, his expression sober. "What brings you all the way out here at this hour?"

"I came looking for Jeremiah. I hear he's in jail."

Harrison nodded slowly. "He is. And my only regret is that I may not live to see him hang."

"I never did trust him," Mr. Wellman began.

"How is your daughter?" Tom asked the man.

The older gentleman looked at Tom, his eyebrows furrowed. "Who are you?"

Tom stiffened, but before he could answer, Harrison spoke up. "This is Tom McCain, Robert's son and my grandson. He'll be running the Lazy G from now on. Everything I own will be his. I expect you'll help me introduce him to the community, especially since he was instrumental in freeing Martha."

Wellman reached for Tom's hand. "It's a pleasure meeting you. I've got a spread about forty miles from here. It's not as big as yours, but it's a nice size."

Katie held her breath, waiting for Tom to take the man's hand, hoping he would confirm Harrison's statement—not just about his relationship with the cattleman, but his agreement to stay in Stillwater.

Tom shook Wellman's hand and thanked him. Then, turning to Katie, he smiled. "I assume you've met Miss O'Malley. If she'll agree to be my wife, we'll be inviting you to a wedding soon."

Katie nearly collapsed in a dead faint. "You're going to stay?" she asked Tom.

Harrison interrupted. "Of course, he's going to stay. He's a Graves, and this is his land."

Tom winked at Katie, and a slow smile stretched across his face. "You will marry me, won't you, Katie?"

She was in his arms before she could answer. She had no idea what problems life might present them, but their love would see them through. Of that she was certain.

Tom caressed her back. "I take it this means you've agreed."

"Yes, I'll marry you," Katie said. Then she cocked her head, staring into his warm, bright eyes, and grinned. "That is, under one condition."

"What's that?"

"About the vows…you really don't expect me to promise to obey, do you?"

He laughed, and the rich, baritone sound filled her heart. "I doubt you have an obedient bone in your body, but I love you, and I'll do my best to make you happy."

"Just promise to love me," Katie said, lifting her lips to his.

"Forever," he whispered softly, sealing his vow with a kiss.

Epilogue

The wedding day dawned bright and clear, not a cloud marring the Texas sky. The courtyard, festively decorated with flowers and lace, had an aura of happiness in the floral-scented air.

Tom would have married Katie the day he asked her to be his wife, but Harrison had insisted it would take at least a week to plan a proper marriage ceremony. The dying cattleman wanted to present his heirs to the community in grand style.

It was just as well. Hannah would have been hurt if she hadn't been included with the planning of the festivities. She and Trapper, along with a much-improved Erin, had arrived two days ago, Hannah and Trapper both grinning from ear to ear and proud as prize peacocks.

The trip had been difficult on Erin, so she'd been relegated to rest until the ceremony, but Hannah had been treated as a queen from the moment she stepped into the hacienda. Katie and Maria included her in every decision, both large and small. It warmed Tom's heart to see her so happy.

Erin had been included, too, although she stood on

the outside looking in most of the time. In some ways, Tom understood how she felt. Long after he'd moved in with Hannah, he'd felt out of place, too.

Being warmly accepted into a family had seemed too good to be true, but slowly and surely, Hannah's love had chipped away at Tom's hardened heart, finding the frightened boy inside. And he had no doubt that the same would happen with Erin, who'd already agreed to stay with Hannah indefinitely, helping her with the house and gardening.

Tom fingered the starched collar of the white shirt he wore under a new store-bought suit. He stood with Harrison, greeting each of the wedding guests as they arrived at the hacienda. Harrison introduced him as his grandson and made a point of telling everyone Tom was now the owner of the Lazy G.

As the chairs slowly filled with smiling friends and neighbors, Tom's thoughts turned to Katie. He hadn't seen her since the day before yesterday, thanks to Hannah and some silly old custom. Denying himself the sight of his bride-to-be, the lilt of her voice and the warmth of her embrace had begun to fray his nerves. But Tom only had a few more minutes to wait, then she would be his wife. He couldn't believe his good fortune, and, as Harrison had said, God had surely blessed them all.

With Harrison's overwhelming approval and the legal paperwork filed by an attorney in Rio Seco, Tom's acceptance in the community was all but set in stone. Katie would soon be his wife, and Sarah Jane would have both a mother and father to love and care for her the rest of her life.

Harrison nodded toward a distinguished, gray-haired

man who arrived in the back of a black carriage. "I believe Ian Connor is here. He's the only one I don't know."

Katie had sent a telegram, hoping Ian could make it in time. He'd responded, saying he would hire a coach, but that his sister was ill and unable to attend.

Tom strode out to greet the man who'd been like family to Katie. "Mr. Connor?"

"Yes," Ian said, as the driver helped him from the carriage and handed him his cane.

"I'm Tom McCain."

Ian extended his weak hand, a smile breaking out on his face. "I'm pleased to meet you, son."

"Thank you, sir."

"Call me Ian."

"I may not be the man you expected Katie to marry," Tom said, "but I want you to know that I love her, and I'll do my best to make her happy."

Ian straightened his tie. "I must confess that I never took the time to imagine who Katie might marry or what he might look like."

"Why is that?"

Ian laughed. "Quite frankly, I didn't expect to live long enough to see Katie's wedding day. She has a stubborn spirit, and not many men can handle her."

Tom grinned. "I think it would be best if another man didn't try."

Ian patted Tom on the back and laughed. "Son, I wish you a lifetime of happiness along with all the challenges Katie will undoubtedly present."

"I'll admit we've encountered a few disagreements along the way," Tom said with a chuckle, "but I'm looking forward to living the rest of my life with her."

Ian laughed. "You have no idea how glad I am to see you take on that responsibility."

"It's my pleasure," Tom said as he spotted Harrison making his way toward them.

Harrison sported a broad smile on his pale and wrinkled face. The event had undoubtedly placed a strain on him, but the tough old cattleman was determined to remain as strong as his frail body would allow.

"I hope I'm not interrupting anything," Harrison said.

"Not at all."

When Tom introduced the men, Ian stretched out a hand in greeting. "I'll be giving away the bride."

"And a beautiful bride she is," Harrison said. "I can assure you, she's getting a fine man in my grandson."

"Katie may have a stubborn streak and a quick temper, but her heart has always been warm and true. If she tells me she loves him, and that he's a good man, that's all the impressing I need."

In the far corner of the courtyard, a lone cowboy dressed in his Sunday finest began to pluck a melody on his guitar.

"It's time to take our places," Harrison said. "Come along, Ian. I'll show you where to find Katie."

Tom watched the men go, feeling a warmth like no other he'd ever known. His eyes sought Trapper, the man who'd become both a father and friend to an orphaned boy. It was time for the groom and his best man to stand before the minister.

Within minutes the murmurs of the wedding guests had stilled and everyone had taken their places. As Tom waited for his bride to walk down the aisle, he thought about the changes that were about to take place. He would become a husband, father and cattleman all in one fell swoop. And he vowed not to fail any of the people depending on him.

He scanned the guests seated on benches and chairs throughout the courtyard. Martin Wellman and Martha Haney sat near the front. Tom gave a slight nod to the gentleman and his daughter, acknowledging their support and presence.

Not everyone in Stillwater had come to the wedding, but then again, not everyone had been invited. Randolph Haney for one.

Shocked and embarrassed by his son's arrest, Randolph had apologized before packing his belongings and heading for parts unknown. All that remained of his law practice was a for-sale sign hanging on the front door.

The women in the crowd oohed and aahed as a happy Sarah Jane walked down the aisle, blushing and beaming.

Tom winked at her as she approached. No longer just his niece, but now his daughter, she took her position at the side of the table that served as an altar.

Next came Erin, her cheeks flushed, her eyes darting to the right and left, as if not sure she deserved to be a guest at the wedding, let alone Katie's maid of honor. There might be some in the community who wouldn't approve—if they'd known of Erin's past. But Katie believed Erin should continue to be a part of Sarah Jane's life, and Tom agreed.

As Erin stood beside the minister, the cowboy changed chords on his guitar, indicating that the bride would soon enter the courtyard.

Tom's heart nearly burst with love and pride when he saw Katie upon Ian's arm. Beautiful Katie, soon to be his wife.

Dressed in white organza, she'd never looked lovelier—or happier. God had truly blessed them this day.

Ian placed Katie's hand in the crook of Tom's arm, handing the bride over to her husband's keeping. He quickly swiped at an eye before taking his seat.

"I love you," Katie whispered to Tom.

"I love you, too."

Then they both turned to the minister, ready to vow before God and man to love, to honor and to cherish each other from this day on.

Tom had figured they may as well leave *obey* off the list, since Katie told him she'd promise to try, but he'd need to exercise patience with her.

And that was all right with him. Where there was love and respect, everything else would all fall nicely into place—now and forever.

* * * * *

COMING NEXT MONTH FROM
Love Inspired® Historical

Available February 4, 2014

HEARTLAND COURTSHIP
Wilderness Brides
Lyn Cote

Former soldier Brennan Merriday will help Rachel Woosley with her homestead—but only until he has enough money to leave town. Can Rachel convince him that he has a home—and family—in the heartland?

THE MARSHAL'S READY-MADE FAMILY
Sherri Shackelford

Discovering he's the sole guardian of his orphaned niece has thrown Marshal Garrett Cain's world out of balance. Luckily feisty JoBeth McCoy has the perfect solution: marriage.

HEARTS REKINDLED
Patty Smith Hall

Army air corps informant Merrilee Davenport will do anything to ensure her daughter's safety—even spy on her former husband. When a crisis forces them to work together, will secrets drive them apart again?

HER ROMAN PROTECTOR
Milinda Jay

To rescue her baby, noblewoman Annia will search the treacherous back alleys of Rome. A fierce Roman legionary holds the key, but she must trust him with her life—and her heart.

LOOK FOR THESE AND OTHER LOVE INSPIRED BOOKS WHEREVER BOOKS ARE SOLD, INCLUDING MOST BOOKSTORES, SUPERMARKETS, DISCOUNT STORES AND DRUGSTORES.

LIHCNM0114

REQUEST YOUR FREE BOOKS!

2 FREE INSPIRATIONAL NOVELS
PLUS 2
FREE
MYSTERY GIFTS

Love Inspired
HISTORICAL
INSPIRATIONAL HISTORICAL ROMANCE

YES! Please send me 2 FREE Love Inspired® Historical novels and my 2 FREE mystery gifts (gifts are worth about $10). After receiving them, if I don't wish to receive any more books, I can return the shipping statement marked "cancel." If I don't cancel, I will receive 4 brand-new novels every month and be billed just $4.74 per book in the U.S. or $5.24 per book in Canada. That's a saving of at least 21% off the cover price. It's quite a bargain! Shipping and handling is just 50¢ per book in the U.S. and 75¢ per book in Canada.* I understand that accepting the 2 free books and gifts places me under no obligation to buy anything. I can always return a shipment and cancel at any time. Even if I never buy another book, the two free books and gifts are mine to keep forever.

102/302 IDN F5CN

Name	(PLEASE PRINT)	
Address		Apt. #
City	State/Prov.	Zip/Postal Code

Signature (if under 18, a parent or guardian must sign)

Mail to the **Harlequin® Reader Service:**
IN U.S.A.: P.O. Box 1867, Buffalo, NY 14240-1867
IN CANADA: P.O. Box 609, Fort Erie, Ontario L2A 5X3

Want to try two free books from another series?
Call 1-800-873-8635 or visit www.ReaderService.com.

* Terms and prices subject to change without notice. Prices do not include applicable taxes. Sales tax applicable in N.Y. Canadian residents will be charged applicable taxes. Offer not valid in Quebec. This offer is limited to one order per household. Not valid for current subscribers to Love Inspired Historical books. All orders subject to credit approval. Credit or debit balances in a customer's account(s) may be offset by any other outstanding balance owed by or to the customer. Please allow 4 to 6 weeks for delivery. Offer available while quantities last.

Your Privacy—The Harlequin® Reader Service is committed to protecting your privacy. Our Privacy Policy is available online at www.ReaderService.com or upon request from the Harlequin Reader Service.

We make a portion of our mailing list available to reputable third parties that offer products we believe may interest you. If you prefer that we not exchange your name with third parties, or if you wish to clarify or modify your communication preferences, please visit us at www.ReaderService.com/consumerschoice or write to us at Harlequin Reader Service Preference Service, P.O. Box 9062, Buffalo, NY 14269. Include your complete name and address.

LIH13R

SPECIAL EXCERPT FROM

Love Inspired

*When the family he's been searching for finally returns,
Blake Cooper's not sure if he can ever forgive or forget.*

Read on for a preview of
THE COWBOY'S REUNITED FAMILY
by Brenda Minton, Book #7 in the
COOPER CREEK *series.*

"I can't undo what I did." She leaned back against the wall and with her fingers pinched the bridge of her nose. Soft blond hair framed her face.

"No, you can't." He guessed he didn't need to tell her what an understatement that was. She'd robbed him. She'd robbed Lindsey. Come to think of it, she'd robbed his entire family. Lindsey's family.

Jana's shoulder started to shake. Her body sagged against the wall and her knees buckled. He grabbed her, holding her close as she sobbed into his shoulder. She still fit perfectly and he didn't want that. He didn't want to remember how it had been when they were young. He didn't want her scent to be familiar or her touch to be the touch he missed.

It all came back to him, holding her. He pushed it away by remembering coming home to an empty house and a note.

He held her until her sobs became quieter, her body ceased shaking. He held her and he tried hard not to think about the years he'd spent searching, wishing things could have been different for them, wishing she'd come back.

"Mrs. Cooper?"

He realized he was still holding Jana, his hands stroking her hair, comforting her. His hands dropped to his sides and she stepped back, visibly trying to regain her composure. She managed a shaky smile.

"She'll be fine," he assured the woman in the white lab coat, who was walking toward them, her gaze lingering on Jana.

"I'm Nurse Bonnie Palmer. If you could join me in the conference room, we'll discuss what needs to happen next for your daughter."

Jana shook her head. "I'm going to stay with Lindsey."

Blake gave her a strong look and pushed back a truckload of suspicion. She wasn't going anywhere with Lindsey. Not now. He knew that and he'd fight through the doubts about Jana and her motives. He'd do what he had to do to make sure Lindsey got the care she needed.

He'd deal with his ex-wife later.

He's committed to helping his daughter, but can Blake Cooper ever trust the wife who broke his heart?

Pick up THE COWBOY'S REUNITED FAMILY *to find out. Available February 2014 wherever Love Inspired® Books are sold.*

Copyright © 2014 by Brenda Minton

LIEXP0114

Love Inspired **HISTORICAL**

An unexpected arrival

Former soldier Brennan Merriday will help Rachel Woosley with her homestead—but only until he has enough money to leave town. Still haunted by a dark past, Brennan recognizes his feelings for Rachel, but isn't quite ready to embrace love back into his life. A drifter since the war, Brennan needs a lot of convincing to stay in a town where only one woman is welcoming. Can Rachel persuade him that he has a home—and family—in heartland, before it's too late?

Wilderness Brides

Heartland Courtship

by

LYN COTE

is available February 2014 wherever Love Inspired books are sold.

Find us on Facebook at
www.Facebook.com/LoveInspiredBooks

www.Harlequin.com

LIH28250